FRASER VALLEY REGIONAL LIBRARY

?5

MW01016400

WRITTEN
in STONE

ALSO BY PETER UNWIN

FICTION

The Rock Farmers (short stories)

Nine Bells for a Man (novel)

Life Without Death (short stories)

Searching for Petronius Totem (novel)

NON-FICTION

The Wolf's Head: Writing Lake Superior

Hard Surface: In Search of the Canadian Road

Canadian Folk: Portraits of Remarkable Lives

POETRY

When We Were Old

WRITTEN
in STONE

a novel by

PETER UNWIN

Cormorant Books

Copyright © 2020 Peter Unwin
This edition copyright © 2020 Cormorant Books Inc.
This is a first edition.

No part of this publication may be reproduced, stored in a retrieval system or
transmitted, in any form or by any means, without the prior written consent
of the publisher or a licence from The Canadian Copyright Licensing Agency
(Access Copyright). For an Access Copyright licence,
visit www.accesscopyright.ca or call toll free 1.800.893.5777.

 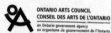

The publisher gratefully acknowledges the support of the Canada Council
for the Arts and the Ontario Arts Council for its publishing program.
We acknowledge the financial support of the Government of Canada
through the Canada Book Fund (CBF) for our publishing activities, and the
Government of Ontario through Ontario Creates, an agency of the
Ontario Ministry of Culture, and the Ontario Book Publishing Tax Credit Program.

LIBRARY AND ARCHIVES CANADA CATALOGUING IN PUBLICATION

Title: Written in stone / a novel by Peter Unwin.
Names: Unwin, Peter, 1956– author.
Identifiers: Canadiana (print) 20200238221 | Canadiana (ebook) 2020023823X |
ISBN 9781770866003 (softcover) | ISBN 9781770866010 (HTML)
Classification: LCC PS8591.N94 W75 2020 | DDC C813/.54—dc23

Cover art and design: Angel Guerra, Archetype
Interior text design: Tannice Goddard, tannicegdesigns.ca
Printer: Friesens

Printed and bound in Canada.

CORMORANT BOOKS INC.
260 SPADINA AVENUE, SUITE 502, TORONTO, ON M5T 2E4
www.cormorantbooks.com

To my family,
Deborah, Dorothea and Alicia,
for their crucial patience, love and support.

WRITTEN
in STONE

Everything must be made anew,
and to your hands I commit this great work.

AS TOLD TO SHAW-SHAW-WA-BE-NA-SE,
JOHN TANNER, 1799

POSTSCRIPT I: FOREVER

HER HUSBAND'S VAN STOOD IN the driveway waiting for her. She'd always thought of it that way, his van, *Paul's* van, a crepuscular Volkswagen Westfalia of hippy pedigree like him. Of late, it was listing to the passenger side rather like *her* she thought and now it shipped water when it rained hard. The vehicle had always been entirely faithful to her. It took the metal key at once, even aggressively, the way a snapping turtle had taken a stick out of her hand years ago on a trail with Paul, demanding it, claiming it as its own. That's my stick, she'd said, but she knew better than to fool with a snapper and gave it up.

Turning over the ignition she backed away from the house, out from under the church, with its shining new roof vaulting toward heaven, finally re-built now after the fire. Up the street onto the bridge above the Canadian Pacific train lines, turning off by the old industrial section where the Cadbury factory made the chocolate, past the baseball diamond and the high fencing where the multiple train lines ran off into a flickering haze of green and red signal lights, and beyond them to the Arctic, or so it felt like. From the factory the smell of melted chocolate poured in the windows. She steered down a close residential street glossy with recent rain, up Caledonia Avenue, forever it seemed, until the malls were reached, and coffee places, squat brutal buildings, warehouses the size of prisons, empty lots where trucks waited sulking in the dark shadows like bulls steaming from their dark and open nostrils.

Eventually she was out of the city and into an intermediate zone without men or women, no children at all, or even animals. Not even the darkest of birds tore the sky. Only vehicles and lights. By the time she reached the rock cuts and the pines, the rain had left a black skin on the highway and the odour of earthworms permeated the van. She glanced down at the dash and the Blaupunkt radio that had not worked in several years. Without thinking, she turned it on and was greeted at once by the cough of static and white hysteria. After several moments of that peculiar song she snapped it off, only to have the black knob come away in her fingers. Marvelous, she thought. Absently she reattached it to the metal spar while the incoming road filled the windshield, the road signs flying past her, as she read every one: a long habit established as a girl during the terse car rides of her childhood, her parents forever disputatious and fighting in the front seat, her in the back, alone, barricaded by books.

Dokis First Nation . . .

Waubaushene . . .

Soon came the waters of the Magnetawan River, the once-great sturgeon waters, the sloppy shore banks where swooped the mighty kingfisher, places that existed without corruption if only for the sound of their names, Wiikwemikoong and Shining Tree. The French River, black and quiet, trundling forever west, briefly underneath her like a sullen crouching beast, then gone. So many had come and passed and returned on that river. Champlain, the old bird watcher. Brébeuf, who could make it rain, and other schoolroom names. Brûlé who was eaten. She knew so much of it, had read so much of it. It was her father's fault. Him and his *Dictionary of Canadian Biography*. The man had given her an additional volume each year, sometimes two, with its yellow creamy covers and the red foxing on the pages like clusters of tiny veins. He had given her history. "It's history," he said, and handed it to her. He told her that. "History. You can't live without it," he said smiling. She had them still. Every one. Her father, however, was gone. Everything real happened in those books. Only there. Nowhere else. Brûlé was boiled and eaten there. What a little prick he was. She imagined a hunk of his obscene body held to the lips like side dishes in a Greek restaurant on the Danforth. Maybe it tasted like chicken? Everything tasted like chicken, they said. Perhaps Paul. She wondered if her husband tasted like that. She wondered, not for the first time, what sort of a sick woman she was.

The river was gone, far behind her, and had been replaced by another, also gone. And another. Now every few miles the railway intersected the highway and the long trains slanted against the green land, rolling with dignity through the vast swamps from which rose a primal fog. Their black sooty sides showed graffiti brought back from the city blazing with purple swashes, weirdly angular, festooned with coloured and unfathomable tags. The painted language of urban tribes.

Wabagishik, White Cedar ...

The sign bolted by her ...

Land Of Whispering Pines, another insisted soothingly. But she didn't believe it.

On her right side a donut place shone with neon signage, the parking lot crowded with cars like cows jostling at a salt lick. She spotted more than a few white surgical masks on the people getting into the cars or getting out. Fewer than before, she thought. People were taking their masks off. A few of them.

For the first time, she allowed herself to glance at the oblong tablet that vibrated on the passenger seat beside her; the dented, gold-coloured tin that once held a bottle of Aberlour twelve-year-old single malt scotch. She turned her eyes away from it immediately. Then the great rocks were directly on top of her, their veined and scarred faces painted with declarations of love. *Eddie loves Liz always/99*. Brand new, she realized, the paint still fresh and red. So many declarations of love had been written on those stone faces that flashed by the windows of a million cars. She didn't want to see them. She didn't want to look upon the passionate pictographs of the very young. She wasn't passionate any longer. She wasn't particularly young anymore, not in any way that mattered. She had no idea what she was, except that she was someone who didn't want to be exposed to a foolish love that had no awareness of anything except its own selfish certainty. Jen and Dave, their union circled in a red woozy heart. Where were they now? Jen and Dave with their woozy red hearts? High up on a remote rock face she saw that someone had ungraciously painted *I love Phat Chicks*.

Five minutes later, the writing that she knew was coming — the writing she had no desire to see — appeared in front of her. The words, the characters, that Paul had painted years ago with a can of red lacquer and a barbecue sauce applicator employed as a paintbrush. The rock was four billion years old. He had insisted on that. Four billion. As many years as there were loves. *Paul loves Linda* he'd written in red and, then, appraising his work and her, he said, "Paul loves Linda. Forever? Or for a while? You decide."

"For fifty bucks?" she'd answered saucily.

He frowned at her and wrote *forever*.

1

THE CANOEIST

They are a small race of people who talk fast.
CHIEF NORMA FOX, COCKBURN ISLAND, CIRCA 1985

SHE MET THE MAN A million years ago at a time when she was sleeping with men who practised yoga and wore beards that were not convincing. She had just finished a tetchy major research paper, "The Function of the Interior Vocabulary in the Works of Malcolm Lowry," and, as a master, or rather a mistress of the arts, she slipped easily into a bohemian half-world of theatre, ritual, and drinking too much. At the time she was living the unregulated life of her body, the El Mocambo on a Friday night, lines of cocaine vanishing off the sink in the bathroom, wearing black tights, ankle bracelets, and heels. There were nights she arrived with Pete, danced with Tony, got felt up by Leonard, smoked a joint with Perry, and finally went home with Phil. It was easy. Men were easy.

She had taken to the stage as if to a sanctuary and performed in a small, unpaid, and unauthorized production of Beckett's *Happy Days* at the Poor Alex Theatre. She was appeasing the burden of her mother, she told herself, a highly theatrical woman who had died in a blaze of alcoholic anger, and who sang old show tunes when she ironed, or when she did anything around the house.

The theatre stank of scorched curtains, and during the most dramatic moment of any production the heating pipes would bang loudly and without fail. In the afternoon, when the stage manager switched on the house lights for rehearsal, the same large rat exited stage right. For six nights a week, two weeks in a row, she was buried up to her breasts inside a papier mâché sand dune that she'd constructed with the help of the director and a lighting technician, who brokered bags of marijuana to a succession of budding artistic youngsters, all of them showing up on bicycles and leaving quickly. During the performance, she stuffed cotton batten under her lips to make her look older. "I used to think," she intoned, "I used to think I would learn to talk alone."

She met him at a cast party, a nearly nightly romp where the cast and delinquents from the street hovered about a table crammed with liquor, goat cheese, and whole-wheat crackers. He was a sullen older man who cast an atmosphere of sullen disapproval. She knew him to be the murky ex-lover of the stage manager, still hanging about for obscure and sullen reasons. There were rumours about him, or at least a rumour of rumours; he'd been drummed out of a university appointment due to some indelicacy with a grad student. Or something more sinister, something never spoken. He was a murderer. A mass murderer. Or he had written books. More than one. He was tolerated but not embraced. He knew the scene rather well and was decidedly unimpressed by it; these wearers of attractive clothes who made attractive comments to one another, who said scathing and clever things in their pursuit of being epically themselves. They were of the age when they turned heads, took lovers, got rid of them in restaurants, took in stray cats that they christened with ornate literary names and treated with great tenderness. None of them had exactly starved, he knew that, but they had suffered tragedies, often at the hands of older men who betrayed them and turned out to be married with kids. Soon, one by one, he understood they would vanish into advertising. He'd seen it before. Eventually, they all turned their backs on the big truth and began to cozy up to the great big lie.

He did not approve of Beckett, either. He made this known to her. He did not approve of the death rattle of the modern world with its modern art and sickening devotion to comfort, to status, to greed. He approved of her, though. Approved of the pleasure she gave his eyes. Her hair that swung from red to brown, the heavy chest, the figure, the jeans. He approved of these matters.

The man was at least a decade and a half older than any of them, he did not practice yoga, and, for the time being at least, boasted no beard. His face was the weather-beaten texture of the bark of the ironwood tree. (He had told her that, later: "My skin is the texture of the bark of the ironwood trees" he said proudly.) His eyes grey, the skin surrounding them lined and articulated like something from the Pleistocene Age. Also grey. A tangible inner disquiet radiated from him. If this disquiet had a smell, it was the odour of basements where things had been stored and forgotten, old fencing gear from twenty-five years before, ice skates that had rusted. He was in the habit of forgetting that he was staring at the front of her shirt, or unaware he was doing it. He found no shame in this. He told her that. He found his shame elsewhere. There was no shortage of it, he said. Linda had not heard a man make this particular admission before. She was not impressed by it. There was so much she was not impressed by when it came out of the mouths of men. So much had fallen crapulously out of that place, for so long.

In this posture, him holding a glass of beer tilted so that the lamplight flayed into it, his face stuck substantially close to her, he first addressed her.

"Are you any good in a canoe?" He spoke with a sort of muffled weariness that seemed to require some effort on his part to keep it to mere weariness. In fact, he was extremely nervous she would reject him on the spot.

"Excuse me?" she said.

"Canoe. From the Portuguese *canoa*, into the French *canot*, and into the English, if we can call it that. Canoe. Are you any good in one?"

"Are you making a joke?" She sounded appalled by this line of questioning. As if somehow it was beneath her.

"It's a simple question," he said, cringing inside. She was preparing to destroy him, he knew it.

It was a simple question. Linda was young enough to presume herself to be skilled at just about everything, thank you, even though her most recent experience in a canoe was an August afternoon a number of years ago, shortly after her mother's funeral, when she had ventured out in her father's antique sixteen-foot Peterborough with the bronze-coloured ribs made of maple, and immediately cracked it on the wharf at the cottage they rented. It struck her suddenly what a handful she'd been for that man. He had died in a hospital, quietly. His body stiffened oddly, like the root of an ancient tree.

"Pretty good," she offered. "Good enough."

"Great," he said. "Let us go canoeing then, you and I, when the night sky is spread out like a something something on a table. Do you know what I'm talking about?"

"Yes. I do. More than you do. Etherized. The word is etherized." He had mixed his metaphor, and not successfully either. She would learn that he did that.

"Good," he said. "Good. Let us go canoeing then, you and I."

That's how it happened. Rather than let a somewhat tedious burly man try to best her in a match of literary trivia, she went on a canoe trip with him.

2

THE GRAND RIVER

I was at a large dinner party and wore a very fine gown and was taken to dinner by
Mr. Somebody. I forget his name. I talked politics and told them there was
no government existing save the confederated government of the Iroquois.

PAULINE JOHNSON, 1894

SHE DIDN'T KNOW THIS AT the time, but there on either side of her on
the soft brown shoulders of the Grand River stood the finest and
the most dense tracts of Carolinian forest remaining in the country.
Nor did she know the difference between an eastern box turtle and
a painted red ear. If she knew turtles at all it was in the collective
sense as harmless ugly creatures not much good on their backs,
and given to long and rather morose lives.

As they feathered their way through the slow brown water, she
saw the turtles perched at steep angles on every log. They looked
rather comical to her, like elderly matrons at the opera, or what
she presumed elderly opera-going matrons looked like — Linda had
denounced opera as a ten-year-old, after a furious fight with her
mother, and had never looked back. Show tunes were different.
She loved show tunes. Her mother had loved them too. Show

tunes had kept them from killing each other. *It's May, it's May, a libelous display* ... She thought the man up front might be paddling them to Camelot. She had no interest in going there.

The domed creatures craned their necks forward and slipped into the river with a distinct *plink*; one by one they dropped in, like birds releasing themselves from a high branch.

"Their blood freezes," said Paul. "In winter, their blood freezes solid. Actually becomes ice. Amazing isn't it?"

Linda felt no reverence toward the turtle, eastern box or otherwise, nor for the blood of the turtle, frozen or not, but for diplomatic reasons she conceded to him that it was amazing. It was, really, when she thought about it. She was disturbed by other things, in particular her shoulders now ached painfully and a muscle in her neck had begun to pulsate. She considered that maybe she wasn't ideally suited to paddle a canoe. Her bare shoulders showed the proud Richardson "breeding," as her father had put it, contemptuously. He would be referring to the band of ex-criminals and hard-drinking future criminals who had poled a barge up the Ottawa River to approximately Pembroke, where they quickly drank themselves to death or died of hatchet wounds. Her lineage.

She was ready to accept that her shoulders were not the sort of shoulders designed to paddle canoes down sluggish brown rivers. They served better as a platform to uphold and reveal her neck; an extraordinary neck in her opinion, and in the opinion of others. A neck Modigliani would have painted were he not preoccupied painting the necks of those young women who were pregnant by him and seemed to always throw themselves off tenement rooftops. "Your neck, Linda dear, has been stretched out too far by your mother's straining to see into the higher echelons of higher society. Bless her sodden soul." Her father's voice came to her, remote and ironic as ever. She missed him.

After several miles, Linda put her paddle into the water for purely cosmetic reasons alone. The man occupying the stern did not seem to mind or notice. He was in his element, she thought; outdoors, on water, in a small craft, in the company of — her. He appeared to be fully enraptured in his role as the River Man; his one duty in life was to squire the fair lady through the lurking mysteries of the new world, to inform her and protect her. From the stern, he boomed his stentorian enthusiasms in her direction. He seemed entirely filled with them. Linda had begun already to suspect that the man's skin was meant not so much to contain his flesh as to collect and hold random enthusiasms, capturing them the way a sail captures wind. Did she know the Algonqui language possessed nine conjugations and that each of those had both a positive and dubitative form? No, in fact Linda didn't know that. It seemed the man was on a first-name basis with every county, district, and acre of the province, every tree that grew in it, every bush and thistle. Did she know the Vikings believed the world was held together by the ash tree? That according to De Quincey the trembling aspen trembles because Christ was crucified on a cross made of it? Did she know that? The way that trees communicated with each other through the centuries? The stories they told one another? "I don't know anything," she laughed. She was forced to admit she'd never divined water with a forked branch from the witch hazel. It suddenly seemed there was so much she didn't know. So much she had not divined. "I really don't know anything," she said again, with some alarm.

"Don't worry," he said. "No one does. Not me. Especially me."

They slid with a musical slapping of water down the storied brown river, him pointing the paddle to indicate to her the landmarks of his wonderment. On either shore showed the rich jungle foliage, the vines and the knotted ropes that hung from stout willow branches, the farmed pastures and farmed interiors that crept to the ragged shoreline of willows and twisted cedars. It was from those branches that she spied the boys and girls of the Six Nations swinging themselves with alarming agility into the sun and out again. Children on ropes, their loose easy bodies swung over the river and swung back like superior little Tarzans, crying out from the belly as they released themselves to the sky, cannonballing into the river, crashing like osprey, sending frothing white spumes up from the surface. Their heads reappeared moments later, little dark dots, as the divers kicked their way to the green shore to do it again.

"Kids've been swinging on those ropes since the Battle of Stoney Creek," Paul said. He seemed greatly proud of this. "And before."

She would learn that he was enthusiastic about first people and first ways. He was enthusiastic about anything that offered another way into the world, or another way out of it; about the craft of polishing river stones with sturgeon oil, imprinting birch bark with human teeth. Or dreaming in trees. He was one of those men who searched for a way to live, and had not found it at home, or in the crass achievements of the world. He was enthusiastic about all things that were not him; all the entities that belonged to the world he had grown up in; the fish and otter, the smell of books, old books that no one cared for. He was enthusiastic about obscure writers of forgotten books and even more obscure travelogues. British and Canadian texts, beefy orators of dead patriotism often expressed in strict rhyming couplets and soul-crushing sincerity. Pauline Johnson was one of his favourites. "The Mohawk Poetess," he called her. Linda cringed.

Silently they shored the canoe on the west bank and he led her brazenly by the hand through a thicket of swishing green grasses and prehistoric fern. Monarchs and sizeable blue dragonflies filled the air. They exited through a towering chamber of black oaks to the front of a house planted unexpectedly on the river side of an old wagon road, now paved. She found herself standing in front of a square white pile of a Georgian mansion from which the stucco was beginning to go.

"She was born in this house, Pauline Johnson," he said. She saw that the man was filled with childish and almost idiotic enthrall-ment. "She had a nickname for her canoe. 'Wildcat,' she called it. What else can a girl raised on the side of a river call her canoe? Wildcat. Perfect."

Paul examined her face for some acknowledgment of this per-fection, but didn't find it. "She believed that 'the Indian and the Paleface were one race,' that's how she put it, and they would come together, right here beneath the oaks and the walnuts, and together they'd become the greatest people in all of history. The greatest people in all of history, that's what she thought. She wrote that. You're not part Native are you? I would take part native over *pure laine* any time."

"Sorry."

He looked at her suspiciously, "What are exactly are you?"

"I'm in transition."

He did not seem sure this was the right answer.

"Her father was very special," he said, and stopped. It seemed he would let the story die there on the crest of all this specialness.

Linda laughed. "Are you going to tell me?"

"All right," he conceded, as if she was forcing him. "The man's name was Smoke Johnson. John Smoke Johnson. His wife's mother was ethnic Dutch captured as a girl by the Mohawks. Smoke Johnson refused to wear gloves because he believed he breathed through his hands. He was maybe the only man on the planet who could still translate the Iroquois Book of Rites, and he had a tough job with a beautiful title. Warden of the Trees and Forest. Has a ring to it doesn't it? Would you want to be that? Warden of the Trees and the Forest?"

"Sure." She sounded insolent and knew it. They were starting to fray against each other. She didn't care.

"What exactly are you again?" he asked. "You're not one of those precious young people with a job in event planning or something like that? You're not a consultant, are you?"

"I'm just another dysfunctional paleface with a Masters degree in modern English lit. What are you, mister?"

"It so happens that I'm the world's greatest authority on aboriginal rock art."

"Is that right?"

"East of the Rockies of course. I wouldn't go so far as to take credit for the work of a bunch of tenured west coast academic potheads whose work for the most part is bullshit. Her father was murdered here, right here."

She followed his finger into the sun-scattered glade where the grasses danced and the stout black oaks towered. She couldn't see death there, only sun and the silver-blue circles of the dragonflies that caught the sun's rays and shone like mother-of-pearl in the air.

"The timber companies did it. He was the world's first tree hugger. He was good at it. They hired assassins, four extremely foul fellows who shot him twice, broke his ribs, broke his teeth, and heaved him in the swamp. That swamp right there. He dragged himself out and, somehow, he managed to get into the house. He died up there in that room. Right there."

She discerned the delicate lace curtains greying in the shadow of the window frame. The establishment was closed, semi-permanently it seemed, and they turned from it and walked back toward the river. On the path between the oaks and the walnuts and the ferns that waved the heat at them, they had their first spat. He ventured that a certain poem by Pauline Johnston was the finest poem in the English language. She laughed in his face and ventured that he was full of shit. Really. She'd spent five years studying the dense black pages of Beckett, Joyce, Wolfe, Lowry, and to listen to him go on about some uptight virginal poetess who'clanked rhymes like chains was more than she could tolerate. She quoted Santayana. He surprised her by throwing Lawrence back in her face, and gave her his "death rattle of modern art" speech. He marched ahead of her down the path with the cicadas clinging to the high branches, screaming at both of them.

"Recite it for me," he turned suddenly on her.

"Recite what?"

"The Song My Bloody Paddle Sings."

"I've never read it."

"And you have a postgraduate degree in English literature?"

He insisted once again the world was going down the toilet.

She agreed, but for entirely different reasons.

They fit themselves into the canoe and paddled five miles beneath the whispering willows without speaking a word. Turtles watched their passage with an intense and unknowable gaze. Over their heads, swallows hunted, veering in dizzy course changes, righting themselves and flitting without effort to perch next to one another on a fence near the shore.

Eventually, the village of Caledonia made an appearance above the trees, a white feed mill and a few listing antennae scouring the sky. With the keel scratching on the river bottom, they shored in the shadows of a creosote-soaked train trestle off which another gang of boys were tossing their half-bare huckleberry bodies, falling a great distance straight down, entering the river with a mushroom-shaped spout opening and closing over top of them. She envied them. She envied their beauty.

WRITTEN IN STONE | 19

The van waited, his brown Westfalia. She noticed with some concern that it was embossed with indecipherable Celtic hippy designs.

"They were there when I bought it," he said defensively.

"I didn't say a word."

She realized with some alarm that a strange intimacy had sprung up between them, whether she wanted it or not. Together they secured the canoe to the top of the van with a homemade octopus of stretch chords, bicycle inner tubes and nylon rope. Then he drove to an empty turnout and picnic spot with a vandalized bench on which *I fucked Tanya* had been ungallantly carved in deep proud letters on the surface. The bank of the river showed the Styrofoam detritus of budget fishermen: crushed worm tubs, heaps of cigarette butts, and thick webs of nylon line; an obligatory condom like a white slug, hung in the bushes.

He slid shut the cloth curtains on a retractable cot and pushed his body on top of hers. She didn't fight him, she fought instead with a troubling image of skinny boys on the train bridge, ribs showing, their shorts hanging low on skinny hips. She had little notion of resolving a fight with a man without going to bed with him.

They were done quickly, first her shouting, him following, breathing wildly. Then he sat next to her, attempting to find words that were fitting to sudden romance and to love and the bold presumption that a lasting bond had been created between them. Linda reached into her pack for a cigarette and lit it without asking his permission. She was meaning to quit, and they always said yes anyway.

3

I WANT TO MARRY YOU

The chief difficulty anticipated by the Fathers is,
in the enforcement of single marriage, to which the savages are unaccustomed.

THE JESUIT RELATIONS, VOL. 18, 1640

THEY WALKED THE WONDROUS AND murmuring city of Toronto among the people, the streetcars and the chestnut blossoms that hung down like fat white rattles from the trees. She held his hand. It seemed to Linda like the sort of thing a woman could allow herself do, perhaps even had an obligation to do at some point in her life. To hold a man's hand in the anonymity of the city. Why not? What could go wrong? The afternoon was ripe and fragrant with the nectar of linden blossoms. American linden, Paul clarified, ominously. American beaver, for that matter too, he told her. The rain had finished, and to testify to his love a rainbow bent now intensely over College Street where the pavement shone silver and slick.

"I want to get married," Paul said suddenly. Almost angrily.

"To whom?" she said.

"To you. Who else?"

"You mean in a church?"

"No," he said. "Of course not."

FOR PERFECTLY NO GOOD REASON, and in defiance of nothing she could put her finger on, Linda did what she always thought was reserved for characters in novels and bad movies. She did something she'd always thought was somehow slightly beneath her. She got married. She entered that place where no thinking person ever went. That she married Paul Prescot struck her as remarkable and even beyond ludicrous somehow. Until meeting Paul she'd preferred men to be caustic and more than slightly unshaven. In university she had dated and dropped an athletic, fair-haired boy for not being dark enough, not drug-addled, not tortured. He quarterbacked the university football team which didn't impress her at all. She had no idea what football was really; some sort of foolish game that men played, for reasons she didn't understand, or need to understand. She had assumed that all her suitors would be eminently qualified as men, meaning that with little effort they could tack a horse, translate Rilke from the German, roll a kayak and pilot small aircraft through large hurricanes. Paul, to her surprise, could only tack a horse.

Despite these failures, she found herself walking down a marbled corridor in the old City Hall building, where the walls were hung with framed photographs of an earlier city; one that was proud of its freshly dug craters. The future city would rise from such holes. They looked like bomb craters to her.

Linda had exchanged armoured heels for a pair of sandals that slapped sensibly on the basement corridor. I am not clacking, she told herself. The world is clacking. The world is clacking itself to death with its sicknesses, with its money-greed and all of its burning and toxic outputs, but me, I'm wearing sensible shoes and getting sensibly married although what the sense was in that she could hardly explain to herself. There was something about the man that assured her, she did not really know of what. She enjoyed the weight of him in bed next to her at night. It felt extremely normal to her.

At the end of the corridor, Paul paid for a marriage licence. "Under the circumstances, I don't think it's necessary to go Dutch, do you?"

"I'm broke," she confessed.

The clerk who processed the forms was, it seemed to Linda, wickedly good looking, broad-toothed, far too attractive to be real. She couldn't take her eyes off him and was suddenly convinced he'd been planted there by cunning bureaucrats to convince incoming brides like herself that their decision to stake themselves to one man was as laughable now as it had always been.

Paul tugged her by the hand down the hall as Linda disciplined herself not to stare back at the clerk. She attempted to console herself in the hope that he was gay. Was she not doing more and more of that? She walked out of city hall, feeling like a girl yanked too soon off Santa's lap.

Paul had expressed a wedding day desire for a dim sum lunch at the Miss Saigon on Spadina, and there, out front on the street, among the Hong Kong umbrellas, the woven baskets and vegetables that she didn't recognize, he changed plans. One of the subterranean deep-throat contacts that he maintained with librarians had made him aware of the original translation of Johann Georg Kohl's *Kitchi-Gami: Life Among the Lake Superior Ojibway* that had been located in the recesses of the Robarts Library. He was desperate to get his hands on it, to touch it, smell it, to feel the grime of old wood fires on the dried pages.

Instead of dim sum, they ate hot dogs off a cart. She was not unwilling, and he was a connoisseur of hot dogs, especially those sold from the street. The hot dog, he lectured her, constituted the cornerstone of Canadian cuisine and he was deeply suspicious of any other food group. "Without the hot dog we are truly fucked," he insisted. Excellent hot dogs, garnished to the verge of sinking, sold to them by a cheerful Ukrainian octogenarian wearing a head scarf over which she had jammed a woolen cap with tassels.

"We just got married," Paul boasted. "Right now. In this world. Can you imagine that? Getting married in this world?" Linda saw that he was grinning foolishly.

The woman nodded. Apparently, this sort of thing happened all the time at the corner of Spadina and Queen, and she accepted his tidings with the steeliness of a bartender. At last she relented.

"You are very lucky. Yes. You are a lucky man. For you have this beautiful woman and the beautifulness of love, yes? Very much you have that. Look after it, yes?" Solemnly she blessed their union with two cans of orange soda. "For you is free," she said.

4

WEST OF CHAPLEAU

The origin and purpose of these deceptively
simple paintings remain a mystery.
SELWYN DEWDNEY, 1962

THEIR "WEDDING JOURNEY" AS HE insisted on calling it consisted of a three hundred mile canoe trip deep into traditional Anishinaabe waters that included stopovers at such romantic hot spots as Ooze Lake, Scum Lake, Black Bog Pond, Missing Horse Creek, and Dead Horse Creek.

"Glue Factory Lake is next," Paul said from the stern. Linda didn't doubt it.

Her neck stiffened on the second day and stayed that way for a week. She undertook twenty-seven portages, not all of them killing, and learned the art of front packing which to her horror meant slapping another knapsack across her chest when her back was already burdened by one. She scratched at ticks, mosquitoes, red ants, blackflies, caddisflies, deerflies, horseflies, mayflies, no-see-ums, fish flies, spiders, herman bugs, curiosity flies, and something that Paul alarmingly called a "dog fly." She didn't want to know.

In the second week they traipsed the deserted paths of a dead bush town called Nicholson. The inhabitants had once slicked creosote onto the black train ties of the continental railway there. That is why the place existed, he explained. Linda was barely listening. She stood in the raw heat and saw that children had been birthed here in the long grass beneath the sun. Their rusted disintegrated toys lay in the dense foliage along with immense rotted cog wheels that no longer turned, tin chimney stacks that no longer smoked, machines that had oxidized and evolved into carbon-rusted fossils in the bush. Desolation and the high burning siren of the heat bugs plowed through the sky. She stood next to her man, her husband now, a pair of mute acolytes staring at the old wooden church made out of knotted deal and barn board, standing in front of them like a grey and ancient person. What modest prophecies had been made from a pulpit of bark, she wondered? That you would come to an end and that you would do it in the deep loneliness of your very own self. That you would seek the support of strange rituals. In the support of a mate. Both of you would stagger hand-in-hand, bowed down by the miracle of waking up together in the morning in the same bed. You would eat much fish and fornicate beneath blankets made of rabbit fur beneath the blinking and countless stars. You would beget and be gone, forget and fall catastrophically into one or more of hell's circles. Let us now sing together, she thought.

Precisely as she was thinking that the church collapsed, the scarred wood, the rusted nails rent already apart by the shifting of the years, all of it fell down in front of them. The structure groaned audibly at first in a faint wind and yielded inward, giving up the dead husk of itself and collapsing into a heap of smoking boards. Two furious crows shot from the trees with an echoing cry of "*Quo vadis, quo vadis*." Then abrupt silence. In the scalding sun the cicadas stilled themselves to mourn this fallen thing.

"Jesus Christ," said Paul, shaken.

SOMEWHERE WEST OF CHAPLEAU, THEY camped beside a remote lake inhabited by giant pike. At twilight the massive fish broke the water, twisted like marlins and slammed down hard against the surface sounding like gunshots. Later, when the sun went down, she lay beneath a display of northern lights that made her cry. "The archangels of God," Paul said. She knew nothing about the northern lights, only that particles, like people, got charged negatively or positively and energy was released. Overhead, the universe drew itself in the shape of a horse and reared through a meadow of stars, galloping to the centre of the sky, legs kicking. Blood-coloured shafts of light flew from the dusty region of its heart and melded into a bleeding veil of green and red, billowing like a boneless thing from the ocean. Linda began to cry. The face of her mother lay in wait for her within the agitated sky, broken, freighted with damage and its own private pathos. In such nights of bleeding celestial splendour, it seemed possible for every human face to be wiped clear of the agony it had known.

Paul draped a blanket around her shoulders and pressed against her with his knees while the fire snapped. With noticeable uncertainty his hand caressed her shoulders. Displays of grief not based on text or prophecy or the violation of the world troubled him. His hands smoothed her beneath the blanket, but she was gone from his touch into a place that was bigger and took no notice of either of them. The curtain of light swung to the earth. Linda was humbled by the stunning size of the sky and the pinwheels of galaxies that rotated into careless infinities. Everything she had ever hoped to be bobbed like flotsam into the red heaving ocean of the borealis; her carefully chosen junk furniture rescued just in time from the garbage truck — away it went like debris stuck to the side of a maelstrom. Her collection of music, the honks of angry jazzmen addicted to heroin, her unsuccessfully re-upholstered armchair, the tenuous friendships, some of them half-remembered, all of it fell away, upward, into the upside-down universe.

USING PAUL'S FISHING ROD, SHE hooked a large pike in the shoals of Wawa Lake and beat the life out of it with a stick. She became a fisher of women, cleaning the great fish under her husband's guidance and tossing the pink and purple viscera of its innards to the cobbles on the shore where the gulls flopped at once, only to be sent screeching away by the high and imperial shadow of a lone osprey floating to the bank. She separated the gnashed labyrinth of the pike's backbone, feeling the curse of its complex y-bone spine and one dead eye. She sawed handfuls of pinkish-grey flesh off the creature's back and tossed them into a spitting black cast iron pan, ate it with her fingers. She had never done this before. There was always someone else who killed her food for her, out of sight in remote abattoirs that smelled of animal terror.

The fish had fought to the very end, slamming the exhausted length of itself against the rock and flailing against each blow delivered to its brains. Linda had no experience bashing out the brains of living fish. With a shaft of twisted root, she smashed it repeatedly and angrily, bringing the ancient weapon down with a sickening thwack against its body. Scales flew from it and clung to her hair. Was it male or female? she wondered. Did it have fishy children it loved and cared for? Or did it eat them too? Did it grieve? Did it prevaricate and commit adultery? Before she'd finished eating the white meat, a bone caught in her throat and she gagged violently so that Paul held her head forward and eventually put a dishtowel between her teeth. The bone came out later in a ball of bread that he insisted she roll about inside her mouth.

For forty days and nights she burned. She'd started out from a Toronto street across from an orthodox church where the sun went down in a blaze of yellow behind the tree tops, where the church bell gonged and where she separated her plastics from her glass. She had ended up north of Pickle River in the cold morning impaled on a layer of roots and grit left by the glaciers. Her body ached. She tramped through cedar swamp and third growth fire slash. She tripped over the roots of pines and cut her face on the boughs of black alders. Her neck stiffened and her skin became covered with insect bites. At times, she felt only intense fury toward that whistling man in the back of the canoe. His shirt was off and his skin seemed to be sucking in the sun like a parched wanderer in the desert. Husband. The man was her husband, she reminded herself. How had that happened? What drugs had he dropped in her drink to dupe her into doing that? She'd been a reasonable enough woman and now she was married? To a date rapist? There was no other explanation. Linda drove her paddle into the water and allowed herself sudden flashes of fury toward her father, that reserved and kindly philatelist who had grown vegetables from seed.

In the morning, she disentangled herself from the smell and the clench of Paul's long draping arms. She got outside of the tent in a hurry and for no reason at all she urinated squatting like a girl child, pissing on the waxy leaves of the blueberries.

"Can you spell your name?" he said, watching her with some interest through the screen. She sucked the air into her nostrils, feeling the tang of its hostility and exaltation and ancient rock. There was no sickness here in these lands, she thought, staring at the dense bush that was as frightening as it was beautiful, even in its sun-infused clarity. She realized that her neck had ceased its daily seizures of complaint and pain. Her neck felt fine.

In the morning, they packed silently and professionally like seasoned Nor'Westers, took to the canoe, and were gone into the silent water. She was water bound, gliding through great glassy pools that in places filled so tightly with water lilies they clutched the canoe, slowing them to a near stop. Paul tried to get her to sing the old French-Canadian paddling ditties, but she would have nothing to do with that. "What?" he said. "Are you too much a downtown girl to sing a little *En roulant ma boule?*"

"Piss off," she said, grinning, and waited for the next predictable argument with him as he tried to improve her forward stroke. "Reach the upper hand high, plant the blade, don't lean forward." She tangled with her ambition to be a life-long disappointment to men, to all of them, him too. Him in particular.

In the mid-afternoon they rested, Paul with his back against ancient granite, sketching with a charcoal pencil in his notebook. He crammed the pages with shaded stick apparitions of men, animals and fish. Stick-figure men with rabbit ears or fingers that showed the spindly length of some webbed creature or a horned beast. He enjoyed the sensation of forming such shapes on a bare sheet of paper. Later that day, at pre-twilight, when the sun cooled noticeably in the pines, he let the canoe up against a sheer granite embankment and stood upright holding the vessel firm to the wall. "Look at this."

Linda rose carefully and felt the sickening quick back and forth plunge of the canoe before it settled upright and steady. His palm was already tracing the figure on the rock, enticing it to come forward, to emerge.

"Turtle," he said. "It's a turtle."

She saw a rusted stain the size of her hand and the colour of very old blood. The pictograph was hardly visible to her but it glowed with antiquity, a granular ancientness like the hide of something prehistoric. Suddenly she saw in her mind's eye withered sheaves of wild grass, snowbound, and bent in stiff winds. The vision had come to her before, the death of someone, of something. She turned her head.

Further down the rock face, on a ledge, a short distance away from the pictograph, lay a heap of human offerings assembled in a pile; a pair of crusty stovepipe trousers folded in twine, a plastic figurine of Elvis Presley wearing a blue jacket, several guitar picks, a black plastic comb, a pine cone, a plastic flower, prayer sticks, a fistful of cigarettes held together by fishing line. Even a dinner set of blue enamelware shone in the heat.

"Makinak," said Paul. "Michilimackinac, extremely significant. The turtle, the ancient symbolic emissary between human beings and the world of spirit. Long living. They carry the weight of the world on their backs, don't they?"

"What is this stuff?" she said. The cairn of offerings reminded her of the white ghostly bicycles wrapped in mourning cloth, covered in plastic flowers and attached to lampposts and stop signs in Toronto, sacred spots where a cyclist had been killed, where life had come to an end in an instant.

"Respect," Paul answered at once. "These leavings are respect. Why not? Or holding time together. Personally, I think what they're doing is giving the finger to Cartesian duality. Someone put them there a long time ago. No one knows when. The paintings, I mean. They make knowledge, it's a way of knowledge keeping, that's what I think. Everything is part of the book." This prospect was obviously pleasing to him. He added suddenly, "They are living things, like books. Living books. They read the dead to us." Linda said nothing. She noticed for the first time that when her husband entered the bush, he became more fit, agile, he even looked younger. He was a shape-shifter, she thought.

They roped the canoe front and back to two deformed cedars that split the rock and picked their way to the top of the ledge. She sat with her legs dangling over a vast precipice feeling the fading warmth from the rock seep into her thighs, watching the serrated blue tree line beyond which lay considerably more trees, more rock, more lakes, and a smear of amber-coloured fog that seemed to chase the sun over the tree line. Linda felt the agitation of a dim wisdom floating very close to her face, like blackflies. It was out of reach, but close. It was not her wisdom. But she would take it. She would take anything that was there. Beneath her hand she felt the rock still warming. Was it hers? Could it possibly be hers, a wisdom that seemed suddenly everywhere? What had she been given to know and to keep and to hold? She knew little of rocks or turtles, nothing at all really. She knew something of microwave cooking, and a course of study that had revealed something she had known since a child: the endless reach and the power of written words. Nothing was real unless it was written down, she understood that. She knew the inhuman catastrophe that lay at the heart of her century. She knew lyric poetry was no longer possible. She grasped the essentials of good grooming but she was not privy, like her husband, to the seven calls of the loon, the last of which cried out to the eagle and said, "yoo yoo yoo, you are the king, not me." She had entered a country of burning sun and impossible winters where on a remote rock ledge people left plastic Elvises beneath a faded painting of a turtle. It was her country, but she had no access to these workings that were strange to her and took place in languages that were unknown. Suddenly Linda was irritated by all of her appalling ignorance. How much of it there was. How stupid she had allowed herself to become.

They set up their fragrant Kelty tent in a vale of club moss, beset by sucking insects that swarmed there until the wind inhaled them away into a place of its own. Well before nightfall, Paul peeled back the moss from a nearby rock face overlooking the water, exposing a writhing mass of insects, musk, and dirt, and beneath that a pictograph, barely visible, the colour of rust and withering in its age. "It has something to do with the cardinal directions," Paul told her. "Usually these drawings follow a south-east to south-west direction. This one's unusual, it has a northern exposure. I have no idea what that means." She watched him trace his body against the granite, pursuing ancient red paint, his eyes intent on the stone and his face pressed to it. The backs of his hairy calves muscled from the rock.

"What is it?"

"I haven't the faintest idea," he answered, and laughed. "I can barely make it out. A horned man? A monster? Do you see a horned man? A monster. Do you see me?"

Truthfully, she could hardly ascertain the drawing at all. Among the rust of time, the algae, and the fungus, the prehistoric granularity of the rock, she had some difficulty making out anything. "A horned man?" she asked.

By ten o'clock, the main force of day had dropped behind the forest. Minutes later the world around them grew dark and cold and they went together into the tent.

POSTSCRIPT 2: THE BRIDGE AT GARDEN RIVER

THE TOWN OF WEBBWOOD CAME up on top of her, deserted and bare. No one in the streets. Not even a tub of dew worms for sale. Then came Massey, the steep, stony banks of the Aux Sable River far below where they'd camped. The tin sheds and Quonset huts and skinny trees, the towering hydro pylons that marched like giants across the land. These things formed the other landscape of the North, the one that no one bragged about or painted or put in photographs or swooned over. The North of rusted air compressors and miles and miles of frost fencing, the crushed packages of take-out joints, empty cigarette packs that skidded the pebbled shoulders of the highway.

Her husband's Westfalia followed the flat green plains of the North Channel as if by instinct. Linda took it all in again as she had before, the sky, the dignified river, the dense green shoreline, the broken barns, such sad affairs left to fend for themselves, the roofs rusted and falling, like forgotten hairdos, she thought.

The Arts & Crafts of Indian People

Trust In Jesus Christ The Saviour

Weegwas Road

She geared down into Blind River, passing the Eldorado Motel on the outskirts. They had stopped staying at the Eldorado Motel on account of the terrible dreams she'd experienced when she slept there. She was in town, then she was out of it on a wide canting bend where the telephone poles leaned toward the river and looked like crucifixes. The wind riffled the grey surface of the river.

The Huron Shore

Les Territoires des Indiens

The Mississagi River meandered next to her, keeping pace with the van. At Garden River she saw the old baseball diamond flooded on the baselines. The bags had been left on the field in the northern way and a bloated and no longer entirely round softball lay near the mound. The road paralleled the train line now and Linda saw the train bridge spanning the river. Across the face of the black metal plates someone had painted in white loopy script *This Is Indian Land*. Someone else had rather carefully painted over *is* with *was*. The old solitudes, she thought. Us them. Is was. Both of them. Her. Her husband. All of us. Someone had tried to paint it back to the way it had been.

Is was is was. Us them us them.

She heard the engine chanting it as she drove deeper into the land:

iswas … iswas … usthem … usthem … iswas … iswas iswas …

5

DOMESTICS

It is increasingly clear to me that the impact of aboriginal values and attitudes
has shaped us more than we will ever dare to imagine.
PAUL PRESCOT: "PICTOGRAPHS, PETROGLYPHS
AND PARADIGMS OF THE APOCALYPSE"

WHEN THEY RETURNED FROM THEIR honeymoon, they resumed their
lives lived in their rented two-storey house directly across the street
from the massive church with its large, forbidding sign that declared
the Annunciation of the Virgin Mary and Theotokos of God.

South of them a desperate, noisy, and multi-generational family
sold a variety of drugs to wobbly, skinny, tattooed men who arrived
on bicycles and shouted or whistled up to the third floor. Linda
watched from her bedroom window, in particular she watched
their scratchy hunger, the foot-to-foot restlessness that knew no
gods greater than the satisfaction of needs. Look at us, she thought,
and watched fascinated because her whole life had been that. Soon
the door opened and a bearded, overweight and this time exceed-
ingly short young man came down the steps and with a swift
Masonic-like handshake dispensed a small bulb of intoxicants and

received payment with the same gesture. The penitent was gone at once, beyond the sign of the Annunciation of the Virgin Mary into the shadows to seek his comfort with a pipe made of tinfoil.

One house north of them lived a man they knew as Karl, and his wife, Mathilde. Mr. and Mrs. Holderlich. A married couple, German in origin, glacial in their features, slow moving, and nearly mute in their intimacy with each other. At one time they had been Weimar Republic lovers. Linda knew the story of how Mr. Holderlich had been found alive in a downed Messerschmitt in the desert at El Alamein and transported half way around the world to Halifax, from there on a prisoner-of-war train westbound; all the signs en route had been covered in burlap so the prisoners could know nothing of where they were. "It wouldn't have helped," he said. "We understood we were south of the Arctic Circle. That's all." Finally, they were removed from the train at a prisoner camp at Neys, Ontario, a provincial park since after the war, one she knew well — the high rock walls where the freight trains canted screaming around the wide bend. There, he had fed a local bear by hand. Lulu, they called the bear Lulu. He would never forget it. From her husband's pictographic research at Worthington Bay nearby, and their camping at Neys, she and her neighbour had that remote watery location in common. Sometimes he talked of the Superior shore there, when he had been a young officer and the spray pounded through the barrack walls. Seasoned Luftwaffe veterans waking up soaking wet in the morning. It clearly impressed him. Enough to return when the war was over. Many of them had returned. In the afternoon, they were allowed outside the camp to pick blueberries without a guard. "Where were we going to go?" he said. He spoke of these times with great reverence, even the blackflies and the rickety tin boats from the Pigeon Lumber Company that took the prisoners upriver on the Little Pic River to cut timber for a dollar a day. They were young men, highly trained and playful, with great skill and energy. At a camp nearby they had built a luge run. On occasions, several of the local Canadian girls from nearby would come up close to the wire fence, and wave.

Now he tended a neat garden with an exceptionally fecund pear tree and was supported capably by a tungsten knee, a pacemaker, a silver walker, and two artificial hips of which he was vociferously proud. "German engineering," he had said to her without a grin. Despite this personal robotic hardware, he managed every autumn to haul himself up a stepladder to harvest each and every pear on the tree, even those that hung over the fence into the backyard she shared with Paul. All this while his wife begged him to come down off the ladder. He was strangely admired for this, although Paul suspected him of vague war crimes and avoided him. "We have all committed crimes," he said. "Some more than others." She was friendlier to the man. The Holderlichs were also loving owners of Rover, a battle-scarred cat of renowned street courage. During the boiling summer days when the orthodox church doors across the street had been wedged open to cool the sweating supplicants, Rover entered the arched doorway without concern and stomped down the aisle of the church, marking the chancel and turning around only to exit with disdain.

IN THEIR RENTED HOME SHE and Paul practised the strange religion of themselves.

He was in the middle of negotiating his somewhat churlish terms with the academy. There were meetings with chairmen and chairwomen and occasionally chancellors, with hiring committees and firing committees and what he was pleased to privately call the Titty Committee at whose meetings strategies were plotted to thwart the ancient lechery of male professors. "We could always gouge out our eyes," he'd suggested in the ornately Biblical cadence that he learned from his father. "It would be a pleasure," answered a battle-scarred humanities professor of Wiccan inclinations, blowing on both her thumbs in preparation for the joy of gouging out Paul's eyes. She'd survived a massive breast cancer and lived her life in the shadow of a son lost to hard drugs. Paul was enormously fond of her. He would miss her as he would miss the raw eccentricity of the true-blue types, their devotion to the Tractarians, or their ponderous musings on Lady Cecily Waynflete, their ability, when drunk, to speak Latin with a southern Ontario accent. Aside from those colleagues, and there were more than a few, he was tired of the very light in the halls and the life-draining that went on inside the walls made of brick and mortar. He was tired of something he could not put his finger on. The sickening indoor-ness of the whole thing. That's what it was. That is what kills me, he told her. It kills every one of us. The damn indoor-ness of our lives. "The indoor man in his head is dead. So there," he announced. He wanted to take his research outside, outside of anything that was known. Paul had long been a somewhat indifferent contract faculty member, a sessional lecturer in a Native Studies program. His doctoral dissertation, written in his early forties, had been deemed indefensible, a committee member had labelled it preposterous, another had warned of racial overtones. Whatever it had been, it was happily published by a downtown firm that eventually sold seven thousand copies of it.

LINDA WAS CONTENT TO DREAM at night, to dream when she napped. She looked forward to dreaming. When she was not dreaming, she freelanced the written word. She ghostwrote an unlikely manuscript: *Eugenta; My Life As An Orphan* by Lydia Smith, a woman who found peace in Jesus after being kidnapped off the Trans-Canada Highway by aliens. Lydia was a small woman, and mild, entirely normal in every way. Linda composed text for an anti-depressant meant for people she believed had every right and even an obligation to be depressed. She edited *Starburst: The Complete How-To of Floral Arranging*. She wrote a children's version of *Kidnapped* at ten cents a word and saw the finished product handed out at gas stations to anyone who filled their tank.

While Linda prostituted herself for petro dollars, her husband finalized a dense study on Pietism and its Moravian origins at the Seminarium Groenlandicum. It was in doomed stories of Moravian piety Paul sought his country, in the company of fellow fanatics, heaving through rock channels in fur-skinned boats, crammed with terrified guides and gibbering missionaries. All of them believing in the impossible.

WHEN WINTER CAME, THEY CLIMBED into his increasingly dilapidated Westfalia and drove to the National Library where he sat for hours pouring over the photographs of J.A. Mason. He was fond of one in particular. It showed a Dogrib medicine man, dressed in black flapping garments as he leaned from the front of a York boat peering into a future that lay somewhere on the Great Slave. His name was Godeh.

"There is a fellow," said Paul, "who possessed serious medicine." She understood that Paul was after that himself, serious medicine. Medicine that could kill a man or make a girl fall in love with him by blowing smoke in her face. The possessor of these arts could also freeze his rival's mouth into a horrible paralyzed grin, or remove the marrow from his rival's bones. The details fascinated him endlessly. "I'm looking for an antidote for science," he told her morosely.

They drove back to Toronto in a snowstorm, the highway subsumed by it in brief intense gusts. The storm stopped as suddenly as it had started and revealed great crusts of white like frozen waves rising out from the dark on both sides of them. Linda sat curled, blanketed, on the passenger side. She was aware of the contentment of driving, of feeling chunks of distance speed softly beneath her while warm air blew through the vents, and the world outside froze. Everything was remarkably still.

He looked at her. "Now this is living. Isn't it?"

"If you don't get us get killed, it's a type of living," she conceded.

"Just be thankful you're not lying in some millionaire's waterbed with a champagne flute between your fingers. That actually happens to some people. What we have is a blessing."

She did not disagree. There were blessings in this world, she knew that. Even if she did not know the extent of them.

He gestured to the land, the pine ridge and the white and snowed-in earth that seemed to scream its beauty at both of them. He was about to go Church of England mystical on her mixed with some Theroux and Hopi Native, she knew it. In a second, he'd be quoting Pauline Johnson at her.

"To be out. Outside, I mean. It's a blessing. The only thing that matters, like the musings of the dung beetle." He looked at her then swung his attention back to the road. "To be outside, outside of us. To have our feet on the rocks, to piss in the bush. To be outside our souls. Go out! I command thee, get ye hence from the lands of the indoor plumbing and the two-for-one cheese pizza. Get ye outside to commune with the trout lily and the white-throated sparrow. Bleat like a leopard frog," he commanded. "Weep like a willow. I command you to weep like a willow."

Linda pretended to be asleep, but felt his eyes on her, and could not stop herself from grinning. He thumped her on the shoulder. "It used to excite you, this kind of jabber."

"Not really," she said. "I was just pretending."

"You drive," he said.

6

LEAVING HOME

SUNDAY AFTERNOON, HE SAT WITH his feet up listening as Mahler's *Symphony of a Thousand* brooded from the stereo. This is what people did on Sunday, he thought, surely. They played a warped three-disc Polygram recording bought for a quarter from the discard table at the local library, the third disc so scratched it couldn't be played. "The Symphony of Six Hundred and Thirty-Three and a Third" he called it. He knew very little about music. He considered the classical composers to be gods of strictly European origins. They were untouchable. Only women could humble them. And they did. More than sometimes. He understood that about the great music of Europe. He had never been to the continent, had no desire to go there.

He watched Linda as she moved from one room to another. She was attractive, the way she moved. He had watched her for some time. He felt he had been watching her since he emerged from boyhood. He had been given eyes for this, for her and for the world. Paul could barely imagine a time when he did not watch this woman as she moved about a room, moving from one to another.

"Rules ought to apply," he shouted. "Don't you think?" He did not have the faintest idea of what those rules might be or how exactly they applied. The basic rules of home and the niceties required of living with people. What were they precisely? What was home to someone who was constantly in motion? He thought of home as a place that was more like a boat with a fifteen-horsepower engine or a book-lined room where a gloomy man drank too much, a place where as a single man he toasted bread, ate boiled eggs, and once a year ran a vacuum cleaner over the carpet whether it needed it or not. He thought of home as a place that a woman had made. Without her, the wind rattled the beams. Paul was almost childishly hopeful that by throwing himself into a sofa chair, putting his feet up and listening to ponderous music on Sunday afternoons he might get into that home by the back door, or fool himself with imitation, maybe fool her too.

Linda brought in tea in chipped cups. Everything they owned was chipped. Neither of them noticed or cared or even had a sense that it was possible to care. To have a cup, to have something in it to drink. Enough was a feast, he insisted long ago, sipping on some hot drink. They sat like opposing potentates who were unsure of their realms, on different chairs, not needing to speak. He had an afternoon flight to Regina, followed by a taxi ride through the wide city streets that would be framed by elm trees. From there, he would proceed north up Highway 11 in the company of a Pic Mobert resident with the unlikely name of Joe Animal, a man she'd never met and had begun to suspect did not exist. Joe Animal? Really? But why not? She'd grown up with a girl named Mary Christmas. Strangely, she believed she had once dreamt of the man. The two of them were standing side by side above a dream pit on the north shore of Superior somewhere extremely remote, looking down. From an oblong-shaped tin she was tossing ashes into the cobbled pit and held the container toward him, so that he might do the same, but he shook his head. "I suppose I shouldn't be doing this," she said suddenly. "No," he said. "You shouldn't, neither should Paul." The man said nothing else. He didn't have to. She understood somehow that this man standing next to her was Joe Animal. This was the man her husband planned to join up with along with a third person from the Canadian Rock Art Association, an ambitious name for an organization with neither a mailing address nor a telephone, and administered by an eccentric high school teacher paralyzed on his left side following a stroke. From there, northbound to Weyakwin, Patuanak, La Ronge, by freighter canoe up the Churchill River to the Hickson and Mirabelli lakes, into the big flat water of the Mirabelli, and the pitted rock faces and the pictographs. There were places there still, he had told her, that when you put your foot down on the earth, you were the first white person to have ever done so.

Linda wasn't going. He had not asked. It wasn't a point of contention with them. She'd made a pact with herself never to be the needy wife, could not in fact imagine a fate worse than that. To be a wife was concession enough. Consciously, Linda had engaged in a strategy to treat her husband as a live-in stranger who shared a house, a bathroom, a bed. The bed was the easy part and, increasingly, a past that swelled with each day. A husband, she had decided, was someone who deserved to be treated with politeness, aloofly. In general, she thought the strategy to be working. Although there were cracks in it. There were cracks in everything, she told herself. Even heaven had a crack in it.

She embraced her husband at the door. She put her arms around his hulking presence and kissed him, squeezed his ribs, and felt him take her up into the vortex of his own excitement over a journey about to start. Linda stood in the doorway and watched him depart for the airport in a limo that had pulled up in front of the house. Solemnly, followed by a grin, Paul made the sign of peace through the open third of the window. In the faint bulbous residue of blue exhaust, the window closed tight and he was driven beneath the old Norman castle of a church where the Virgin Mary was annunciated, out of the reach of Rover's scorn, and beyond her. Beyond their city. He was about to take to the skies and the rivers. It felt like betrayal; she had no reason why it felt that way.

She heard the phone ringing already as she closed the door.

7

JOE ANIMAL

An officer of the Mounted Police told me that when on duty near the International Boundary Line he had heard there was a wonderful cave some miles distant, containing Indian pictures. This he visited and found stone couches within and drawings upon the wall. Conversing with several Indians he was told that two young men had gazed upon the writing and consequently they were killed.

JOHN MCLEAN M.A. PH.D., 1888

THE MAN WAS WAITING FOR him on a sagging dock on the Churchill River where the pike hung in the weeds like transmissions of energy, quivering green and slender in the shallow water. An old hide-coloured freighter canoe with a twenty-horsepower motor knocked against the dock. The man who stepped out of it was mustached and beer-bellied and his black hair hung from under the same tattered tractor cap he always wore, on which an expanding stain of sweat was working its way. The cap had an air of impregnability about it, so did the man. *Red Man Chewing Tobacco* was stitched in gold letters across the cap. Paul had never seen the man without it and was not entirely sure that it was physically possible to remove the cap from his head. It was not possible for him to conceive of

Joe Animal without this tractor cap. Beneath the rim of the cap, a hand-rolled cigarette rested on the man's lip and hung down like a line of spittle.

"You look great," Paul offered.

"Don't I," said Joe. His forehead showed large as a rock face and he leaned in as if he intended to crush Paul with it. The man's lips were ample and floated on his face with no apparent means of being fastened there. To Paul, the entire face resembled an old baseball glove that he'd owned as a kid. He was tempted to remind the man of that. Despite the individual wreckage that made up the parts, the face was comforting and familiar like a well-used map.

Paul strapped himself into the lifejacket that Joe handed him and positioned himself carefully in the bow of the freighter canoe.

"Where's Raphael?" asked Paul. "Is that his name, Raphael, that guy? That weird guy? I thought he was coming with us."

Joe Animal spat his cigarette end into the water. "Raphael was in the hospital. Only now he ain't. I called. He's dead. He got the pig flu. Or that other one. His wife told me. She's not doing so great either."

"Jesus," said Paul.

Joe nodded, but said nothing. There was nothing to say about it. They paddled without speaking. Paul would have spoken gladly, his companion not so much as a word.

After an hour, Paul attempted to provoke the man into language.

"The trouble with you Joe is that you're not phlegmatic enough. In the old days you couldn't read about a Native who wasn't phlegmatic."

"I wouldn't know that," said Joe Animal. "Seeing as how I can't read." It was a falsehood the man was unusually insistent about. For a moment, Joe Animal was tempted to repeat to Paul, once again, that he was the lone and illegitimate descendant of the Earl of Sandwich and an English show girl. He'd read about such a girl in a half-burnt magazine that he'd found in a hunter's camp near Hawk Junction. The magazine was actually called *Hot Chicks in History* and stated, on absolute authority, that the young woman possessed the finest legs in all of Europe. Duels had been fought over her. Men mortally wounded in the fog at dawn. Her name was Eliza Vestris, she was a nineteen-year-old actress and her legs had been cast in plaster by a sculptor. "Such a leg," said the sculptor, "is always sure to fetch a high price." Joe liked the sound of that. He had good legs himself. There was a woman who had told him that, years ago. He remembered. He came from a long line of men and women with good legs.

The freighter canoe thumped alongside a world of green, abundant green, a vast green hemorrhage of trees that reflected in the chill and now almost purple water. A heron drifted over top of them as still as an aircraft. To Paul, it felt like there was not the slightest deviance from green, the universal green textured differently in the trees, the marsh grass slightly less green, the leaves of the birch trees darker green than the marsh green, the green world, the wedges of green, the greenness of his wife's thumb. There was nothing that Linda couldn't make grow. He thought there was something brilliant about that. Suddenly he missed her immensely. He had made a mistake, he thought, coming here.

"Everything's green," he said lamely.

"Green," said Joe. "Yep."

At nightfall they camped in separate domed tents, both of them snoring viciously and in tandem while the stars shot over top of them.

IN THE MORNING THEY WERE on the river again. The water had darkened. The cliffs rose in steep and black formations, straight out of the water, icebergs made of stone, and the rock tripe hung down in sheets, dark and vulva-shaped. *Windigo cabbage* they'd called it. Famine food. Paul had tasted it. Franklin's men had peeled it off the rocks and eaten it on their journey back from the Coppermine. Half the men starved, others took to cannibalism, Franklin ate his boots instead. Two centuries earlier, on the U.S. side of Superior, the Jesuits had eaten the rock tripe and gone mad. Father Menard, irascible, hateful, holding a cross in an outstretched hand, actually running through the woods in an effort to convert *les sauvages*. Chased them into their own homes. Paul had written about Menard; he vanished out of La Pointe in a desperate search for souls, his body never found. For a moment he considered what it must be like at the end, to be broken like that, eating rock fungus.

They moored the outboard at the rock face. Paul took his camera and began to snap the rusted blots, a canoe the size of his fist, inhabited by three stick figures and what looked to be a cross; an X figure joined at the top and bottom, two dots that might have been eyes or suns, blind eyes, he thought, dead suns. The figures were in the shape of an hourglass, and possessed five fingers. He put the camera away.

"What do you think?" he said. He expected no reply. There was the click of a cigarette lighter, and then Joe's deep and remote voice.

"What they drawed is what they dreamed. That's what I think. I know that. What do you know?" The man paused for a long exhalation in which he watched the smoke leave his mouth and begin its journey.

Paul stood and made a sweep of his hand to indicate how the painting would be composed, here, in this spot in a craft like this one, a clay paint bowl in hand, a finger for a brush. Most likely a finger. He was only guessing. So much of it was guesswork.

They drifted a few metres, clapping gently against the rock, until they reached the lines. Three rust-coloured lines stacked horizontally at eye level. Joe Animal spoke: "That first one up there, eh, that first line. You know what that is, right?"

"No. I don't. Neither do you."

"I do."

"Who told you? Was it one of your cousins? One of your many cousins?"

"That's right. Cousin Clarence." He pointed. "That first one, that's the Canadian National Railway."

Paul looked closely at the horizontal stain three inches long welded to the rock. It was a tally mark, nothing more, he was sure of it. He had no idea what it tallied.

"The second one. That's the Canadian Pacific Railway. The third, you know what that is?"

"The Trans-Canada Highway," said Paul at once. It would have pleased him enormously to appear knowledgeable in front of this Native from the Pic Mobert reserve, a man he had come to know, against the odds. A man he probably did not know at all. "The Trans-Canada Highway," Paul repeated. "The Highway of Hope."

Joe Animal shook his head and grinned. "The third one is the end of the world," he said cheerfully.

8

RENDEZVOUS

SHE STAYED AT HOME PRUNING tomato plants, monitoring the yellow roses, saying good morning and then good afternoon to Mr. Holderlich, who made his regular appearance in the backyard. She made phone calls and pitched story ideas to editors who were rarely interested. She was rarely interested herself.

Mostly she leafed through the *Dictionary of Canadian Biography*. Her father had gifted her with a new volume every year since she was twelve. Their creamy yellow covers had foxed and turned a red brown over time, but the spines remained solid. Even if her spine did not. Her entire collection occupied a bookshelf in the living room, from where it radiated authority. Inside each of those volumes, the words lay packed and dense as plankton, swarming always without exception toward the death of a man. The books were full of men. They all died in the end. They were all men of the book. Even her. Through the years of her raw and often undressed youth she'd developed a consoling passion for those hefty volumes, and wondered if her father did not have some personal motive in insisting that she have them. To give her something else to do in bed? Her father had been an indifferent lover. She knew this because her mother had told her, had told her several times in fact, once suddenly, blurting this to her in his presence, viciously. He hadn't said a word. Linda was barely thirteen, and had tried to die within herself in the moment. Her mother was unfolding fast, the bottles crashed, the evenings died in agony. The mornings could barely be roused into life. Her father had loved his wife to the bone. Linda, too, she told herself the books had been a way to solidify her character, to make her upright, filling her with facts. To give her a spine. Many spines. Given that her own life was such a mess of longing and dreams, of jealousies, fears and obligations, reading those confident biographies was medicinally soothing to her, men like Claude Guitet who got up in the morning and "consolidated France's position in the New World." Why hadn't she got up in the morning and consolidated France's position in the New World? She considered it a major triumph to get up in the morning and consolidate a cup of coffee, without which there was no chance of her consolidating anything else, especially herself. In Linda's experience, the historical imperative was likely to take a back seat to the dry cleaning and was accompanied by the guilt of having, for the second time, cancelled an appointment with an embittered and perhaps unstable woman who had agreed to re-upholster her favourite armchair. Only afterwards, entombed, stone dead, written up in a book, set in type, and laid out in columns, would her life, or anyone's life, appear to have made any sense at all.

SEVEN DAYS INTO HIS ABSENCE, Paul called her from a lonely truck-whipped phone booth at a gas station on the side of the Trans-Canada. She heard a dark, vast country echoing on the line. He had come down south to the Lakehead. She heard the passing horns of immense trucks. Was she up to anything? Would she like to come up? Meet him. Why not? A rendezvous, an assignation. "A French weekend," he called it. Come on up for a French weekend, it was only a day's drive. Okay, two days. She could take the bus to Thunder Bay if she didn't want to drive. They'd sit up on Hill Street and watch the freighters limp out to sea. The strip malls, the railway sidings. A massive Finnish Breakfast at the Hoito? Maybe watch a baseball game between the Thunder Bay Border Cats and the Traverse City Pitt Spitters. What wasn't there to like? Are you coming? Why not? Please? Linda? Darling? Come.

With a small suitcase and basket of green Bartlett pears harvested with permission from Mr. Holderlich's tree, she stood in a ragged line of passengers in the blue fumes of the Bay Street Bus Terminal. Like all of her fellow travellers, she was lost in the terminal loneliness of bus stations. Seedy men shifted from foot to foot, clutching racing forms like letters from someone who had once loved them. Pigeons flew in all directions through the sooty rafters. Every few minutes the great muster of her country crackled through bleak speakers mounted in the ceiling; *Greyhound Coach number one fifty departing terminal gate five to Vancouver via Parry Sound Sudbury Espanola Heydon White River Pancake Bay.* Such names, such places. They sounded like a gorgeous litany of lovers to her, of muscled thighs that stretched for more than two thousand miles. A journey that ended in a place called Hope, British Columbia. All journeys should end there, she thought. In Hope, in the mountains where the cold air smelled of the pines breathing.

Linda sank into her seat and pressed her forehead to the glass. She slept briefly until Toronto was behind her. Soon, outside the window, she saw off-roads leading to port towns that were unknowable, where the sun dissolved into streaks of fuchsia. Barely legible signs stuck up from the earth; *the wages of sin is death.* "Are," she thought. Surely the wages of sin are death. It was the copy editor in her. Was she ready for the coming of Jesus? Sure, she was. Why not? Come on down. Bring your wife. Home-cooked meals and the guaranteed repair of small engines? Fine. *Pizza, hamburger, mini golf and the coming of Jesus.* She wasn't ready for any of it.

Linda sat up front, down one seat from the driver. A sign bolted above his right shoulder sternly prohibited the transportation of *caribou heads and stuffed game animals.* Another sign directly above it informed her it was against the law to engage the bus driver in conversation. The fine was two hundred dollars. Despite this prohibition she soon realized the driver was speaking to her in a steady even monologue that required him to swivel his head in her direction and leave it there for alarming lengths of time. She watched the twin headlights of the oncoming traffic shoot close and then vanish behind them.

"You don't hunt, do you? Me, I hunted. Yessir. Not no more but I used to. Used to get myself a deer. Just one. Only one. Every year." He swivelled his head away from her, checked the road, found it satisfactory, swung back. "So I got me this critter lined up. Put a bead on him. Fired. Bang. Folded that animal right up. Folded him completely up. He's spinning through the air, hits the ground. I goes over. Knife out. I'm ready to slit that critter's throat. What's he do? Shakes his head, gets up, goes running off. Goes running right off. You forget how strong an animal your deer is. Yessir." He gave her a knowing look before turning away. Linda leaned deep into her seat, smelled the faint medicinal smell of long-distance buses, heard the soft exhalations of human life and gurgling babies, the tinny sound of headphones plugged to ears, and was gone, gone into a fast coma-like sleep. She dreamt that the particles of the road were breaking up in front of her, the trees shattered like frozen things.

The rivers ran with tar and pizza boxes floated down like wreckage from a lost civilization on its route to the oceans.

AT THE SUDBURY BUS TERMINAL, Linda snapped awake in time to watch a man with his fly unzipped get on drunk and stinking, listing to starboard and muttering darkly about the end of the world which, he announced, was also sick and tired like him. The bus was a third empty, but despite this indisputable fact he sat beside her. "Today's my goddamn birthday," he said apparently to her. "Just got outta the hospital." He appeared to view this disclosure as an invincible pick-up line for he immediately dropped a paw upon the knee of her right leg.

She wrestled with a desire to smash his face into a pulp, but instead stood up and resituated herself in the gloomy rear of the bus. Some of the passengers had fitted white surgical masks to their faces and stared at her sullenly as she passed, as if everything was her fault. Linda was no longer sure of the protocols. She never had been. Did the wearing of the mask mean the wearer was sick and attempting to protect you? Or was it the other way around? Was she the sick one? The infector? Were they protecting themselves from her? From Linda Prescot *née* Richardson? Protecting themselves from what was inside of her? God help them if that's what they were trying to do.

Linda set herself down in the aisle seat next to a woman of considerable age. Skeins of white hair fell from a scarf tied to her head. She was reading a folded paperback edition of *Tales of An Empty Cabin*, by Grey Owl. Linda warmed to her. Paul owned that book somewhere. They exchanged mute introductions performed with short nods of the head and movements of the mouth that were not smiles but close to smiles, the unspoken promises of equanimity and respect. The woman seemed to be expecting her.

Linda couldn't help herself, "My husband has a copy of that book. But I've never read it."

"Oh," said the woman. "Look." She turned the book over to show off the Karsh photo on the back. "He wasn't a real Native, he was a phony. Like everyone, but he was good looking. My god he was handsome. He looks just the way we want our husbands to look forever."

"He kind of looks like my husband," murmured Linda, "except that my husband is older. And doesn't have as much hair. Plus his hair is blond. Blondish. In fact, he doesn't look like my husband at all." She laughed. "In fact, my husband's going bald and looks nothing like that man."

The other woman laughed too. "That is very remarkable, for he somewhat resembles my husband. In the details of the face, I mean." The older woman laughed again. "I am talking now of many, many years ago of course. That man. I met him on a dance floor when the bombs were falling. Oh, they were falling the way the leaves fall here in the autumn time. It was London you see. The Blitz. I was a student. Falling like rain I suppose. Bang bang, boom boom. That is how it was. He said to me, 'Would you like to dance? Please would you like to dance with me?' He sounded like a count. For all I knew he was a count, I was seventeen years old. We danced to Al Bowlly on a dance floor in London while the bombs were falling all around us. They put thick curtains over the windows you see. He was Polish, from the borderlands. His English was very good. Better than mine really."

"He asked you to dance?"

"Yes, I danced with him. He was a pilot. A brave pilot. A fighter pilot. An excellent dancer. He kept a tin of wax in his pocket, for his shoes."

"You didn't have a chance."

"No. No chance at all. He had blue eyes. So it really was not fair. We went back to my room that night. Straight to bed. Everyone did back then. I had a roommate, a Belgian girl. She just picked herself up with a blanket and went into the other room and slept on the floor."

"It's not fair about pilots."

"No, it's not."

They sighed together over the grief that airmen had inflicted on women.

"Regula, my name is Regula."

"Linda."

"You're not wearing a mask."

"No," said Linda. "Neither are you."

The woman smiled. "He had blue eyes, my husband, and was very handsome. Still is, at eighty-two. Although I must say that I have become a bit tired of him." The woman looked out the window and saw the pitch black. "We've been married for sixty-four years and I'm getting rather tired of him. He says no all the time. You see? He sits in a chair, his chair, and says no. No I don't want to do that. No this no that. What is it you want to do? That's what I ask him. He has no answer. He wants to sit in a chair. I'm not going to be one of those old ladies who sits in a chair and has nothing to do. Can you see yourself doing that?"

Linda shook her head.

"Well exactly. He can sit in a chair if he wants. I was in Toronto visiting someone. A gentleman friend. Widowed. A diplomat. Former diplomat. Though his mind is going now. Still, he has a wonderful laugh. We went bowling." She fell silent for a moment before adding forcefully, as if speaking to herself. "I'm not going to sit in a silly chair, really."

They talked effortlessly in the dark in low voices in time to the motion and muffled by the night that pressed the windows. The woman told of her great journeys and migrations, Switzerland, the littleness of things that finally wore her down. The apartment she'd waited four years on a list to live in and how it suffocated her. She felt the great size of her youth and she and her Polish fighter pilot sailed to Canada on a converted cattle boat, the *S.S. Columbia*, nine days on the Atlantic, up the St. Lawrence, and finally to the towering silos of the Lakehead, Thunder Bay.

"I wanted to go somewhere where there were Natives. Real Natives. Indians and Finns. Finndians." She laughed. "Don't ask me why. So Thunder Bay, why not? Oh, it was very exciting, the most exciting thing ever, really. I was so young. I was on a great ship. I saw whales in the St. Lawrence, sunning their backs, turning in the water. Then we got here and the big freighters, the big grain silos, big, everything big, so big."

She stopped talking and looked out the window. "My second week here, at the Lakehead I mean." Her voice was barely audible. She cast her eyes to the seat in front of her to a dark spot that she seemed to be familiar with. "I was walking in the woods by myself, I loved to do that, I still do. I heard this howling, it was a bear you see, and I'd never seen a bear before, of course not, and this was such a small bear, it was the size of a dog really, no bigger than a dog, and it was caught in a trap. Oh, my goodness it was crying. They do that, you know. It was crying like a baby. I could see it, the teeth from the trap were in it, the blood was everywhere in the snow, and it was crouched there like a baby crying and crying. It wanted its mother. It must have been there for a long time, I don't know how long. Terrible. That is the country too," she said, turning away to hide her face in the boreal black of the night.

They slept fitfully side by side, warm in the company of each other, snuggled in the unfolding miles that sped past through the dark. At Nipigon, the bus turned off the highway, down into the village, and heaved to a noisy stop at a red brick restaurant. Already it teemed with the pre-dawn energy of timber men and mill workers, fuelling up on strong coffee and fragrant scorched meats. The caustic accents of mid-country, white skin, a confident heehaw of laughter and raw talk. The room they sat in was a low-ceilinged angular art deco construction from a different age, the waitress tall, young, gum chewing, her hair in pigtails. She recommended something she called a turkey melt sandwich and leaned in to them and whispered conspiratorially with a grin, "We melt those little suckers right here."

The two women ate in silence, hungrily, like penitents, and returned to the bus, content in the bodily proximity of each other. They were driven out into the grey morning landscapes of water and rock, the swale of twisted vegetation preceding the straight hundred-metre drops to Superior. On the other side, the vast dark reach of the Nipigon River, crowded with its furred mountains, stretched on forever north to the enormous lake. Sleepily, she remembered Nipigon, their trip there, she and Paul and the lake, the enormous dimensions of it, the haunting beaches made of green sand. Shakespeare Island. The Katatota. The sense she had then of the unlimited-ness of herself, of her life, of the man she was with who chauffeured her around the great earth and shared her bed. Linda slept and saw the flashing tan legs of a man running and charged with sweat. He strode a desert land holding a jar of water stopping to sprinkle it on the parched earth. She awoke, afraid that she had dreamt this dream before. She had always thought there could be no greater punishment than to dream the same dream night after night.

They arrived with a clank at the Thunder Bay bus terminal and in the glinting steel of buses and hubcaps and the haze of exhaust they took their leave from each other. Linda presented her companion with a pear from Mr. Holderlich's tree. For a moment the woman held the fruit up to the light, as if examining the properties of a fine claret.

"Thank you, dear. What a pleasure to sit with you. To pass miles with you. There are so many of them, aren't there? So many miles. I want you to have a marvelous life. A big life filled with big weather and big life. I know you will. You have no choice." She leaned in and kissed her on the cheek. "Such a choice is not given to us is it?"

9

THE SLEEPING GIANTS

… when I am in great danger, and on the point of dying,
then I shall collect all my family around me, and reveal to them
the entire history of my dream. And then they will hold a great feast.

CITED BY JOHANN GEORG KOHL, 1860

SHE LEFT THE BUS TERMINAL in a cab driven by a man of stony aspect
with a large cauliflower ear on the right side of his head. A boxer,
she thought. With a past. Everyone had a past. Everyone had been
beaten up in the ring. "Prince Arthur Hotel," she announced and
he accepted this information from her gloomily and set forth
beneath a sky that opened into scattered blue holes through which
a more cheerful universe seemed to be going about its way, indifferent to them, to her in particular. They did not speak a word.
He drove with a studied casualness paying no attention to the
road and allowing his gaze to linger intently on grey buildings, the
closed curtains. The streets were empty of people and possessed
their own loneliness.

Even before she exited the cab, she saw her husband through the
doors, standing restlessly in the ornate amber-coloured lobby of

the Prince Arthur, its massive chandelier curved above him like a cluster of stars. She assessed the man without his knowledge, feeling a strange childish excitement in doing so. She saw him move from foot to foot, prey to his restlessness. He stood there, looking half-made like a man waiting for his wife to come out of the bathroom. When he saw her, he snapped and moved swiftly across the floor. "Let's eat," he said. "Not here."

"Shouldn't we kiss first?"

He laughed foolishly. "You're right."

Their lips pressed, only half of them, his own parched by the wind and sun, the hard cracks pressed against her lips. Perfunctory kiss, she thought, like a handshake between people who trusted each other to the end of time. She accepted the polite passion of her husband and was briefly annoyed with it again.

They found a restaurant close to the water, a tacky interior filled with formica and old neon signs and what looked to be a glazed thirty-pound stuffed walleye hanging on the wall. The waitress deposited two cups of strong coffee in front of them. "Special is fish," she said. "Fish."

"Where does the fish come from?" Paul demanded. The young woman pointed her finger across the highway to the black water. "Out there," she said curtly. "Where do you think?"

Paul smiled hugely.

Soon they were gorging on enormous fillets of lake trout that curled over both edges of the plate. They ate passionately and without speaking. She thought that in the week and a half away from her Paul had turned vindictively handsome, something she found oddly annoying. His face gleamed with an intensity she had not seen for some time, tanned and weather-beaten as if a freshened veneer of his self had been blown on to him by the wind. His lips were cracked by sun.

They finished their meal and walked back to the hotel on streets that were uncomfortably empty and garish with shadows that seemingly danced to music that couldn't be heard. A crowd of people stood outside a makeshift vaccination clinic not saying a word, all of them wearing white masks. A few young men, sullen with drink, directed mean looks at Paul: it seemed they were furious with him for being in a woman's company.

In the hotel room Linda crossed to the window and stationed herself in front of it, staring out at the long low formation of the Sleeping Giant as it rose up out of the harbour. The mountains and mesas outlined a sleeping god, one that would sleep forever, she thought, with some envy. The ridges glinted in the lapping surface in the light of the moon, or a passing satellite, and she understood that a few elusive cougars still hunted and copulated out there. Paul stood behind her and they stared together from the fifth-floor window at the wild and random mix of dark sky against the city and the great lake. The world was so very big. Beneath them, the Canadian National shunted rolling stock from the Soo Line. The black rail yards skirted up against Cumberland, still furious with trucks hurrying to their destinations. She saw no one at all. The city was empty of people, it seemed, and repopulated by trucks and cars and trains that boomed as they hitched and unhitched. Five thousand acres of sheet roofing and warehouses and hydro pylons stretched in front of them without any walking souls, only crows lifting off and settling down again.

"A lot of crows," she said.

"Yes, the taunting enigmatic crow. From their mighty flapping wings come thunder and wind, comes lightning. Look at them, they sit out there waiting for the world to be given back to them. Good luck with that."

Linda was not particularly in the mood for the apocalyptic musings of Paul Prescot.

"Did you miss me horribly?"

He looked at her mystified. "Sorry, were you away?"

Despite herself, she chuckled. He did too. They had for years over this particular gag.

"If you must know, I was at home having criminal sex with Mr. Holderlich. What a filthy beast that man is."

"It's all legal now isn't it? You don't need to worry."

"He tied me to a table and took pictures of me. Fed me nothing but pears." She pulled a pear from the basket only to have Paul snatch it impulsively from her and chomp into it before grabbing her around the shoulders and steering her from the window, pushing his lips to hers, forcing the broken hunks of fruit from his own mouth into her mouth, sloshing pulp between their teeth. Linda thought she was about to choke.

"Jesus," she gasped, and without warning slapped him across the face hard enough to make her palm burn.

Paul rubbed the side of his face, focusing his fingers on a spot above his jaw line on the left. "Careful. My teeth are bothering me," he said. His teeth were always bothering him. Linda felt foolish in her brutal naked drama and irritated with him. With herself. Sex, she thought, the desire of the body, her body. It was a joke that God played on men and women. On her in particular.

"Sorry," she said and was angry with herself for saying it. Her husband tried to embrace her tentatively now and she felt that a dull wall of intimacy had thrown itself up between them again. An old wall made by Scottish rock builders and Presbyterian damnation. She'd had enough of it. There were times she felt her country was made of it. Even herself.

Paul wiped particles of pear flesh from his face and kissed her full on this time. They staggered as one toward the bed, collapsing to a stiff and ostentatiously luxurious mattress set beneath a pine-scented air freshener and the glow of a Mediterranean sunset painting. She cast a rueful look at it on the way down to the bed and witnessed the familiar colours of cosmetic hell. *All ye who enter into such a place.* Then she was wrestled beneath him; the pressing of his body was warm and familiar and respectful. She had no use for so much respect. She did not collapse on bed sheets or appear unannounced at a man's door to be respected. She rather vaguely desired the hot exhalations from a forest floor, something a little more volcanic. For some reason she thought of a cougar, with its lithe body, roaming the mesas of the Sleeping Giant, desperate for a mate. Sniffing the air for her smell.

They aligned together with her hips hounding his hips, her body seeking his in search of something to press against. Below them, on the black roads of the city, the traffic confounded their turmoil and moaned in a language of its own. The hissing dominion of eighteen-wheel trucks rose softly through the window; all of them loaded with brandy and furs as they rushed away from her, west to the terraced city of Duluth, to the storied peltries that lay beyond Pigeon River.

Linda lay on the bed in a cord of light that shafted into the room. It was warm to her, like the glow from a kerosene lamp that was seeking them out, settling on their limbs. They lay together as man and woman, *manwoman*, she thought, or the other way around. It felt as if they were welded to each other and she settled into the mix of him and her, her chest against his back, her arm over his. It was what they did best, inhaling together, exhaling together, rather like two valves pumping in unison. It made them work.

Soon Paul rose up from the bed and paced heavily to the window putting his hands on the sill and preparing, it seemed to her, to launch himself like a falcon into the sky. Despite his bulk he looked momentarily lost there at the glass, and uncertain where to throw his gaze, uncertain where he would ever land. Linda lay without motion, aware of her contentedness; needing nothing, hungry for nothing, knowing nothing, at peace with nothing, moving through her mind content to breathe and exist beneath moons that were invisible to her. There were so many gods, she thought. Some of them were in this room. All of them had names she couldn't pronounce. Her body was content to lie upon a bed. What was it she did next? She didn't know or need to know. Everything felt to be in place, as if her life had settled into the seats of an auditorium to watch a performance. Behind her eyes, pulsating webs of northern lights seemed to be falling. Animals she didn't recognize hove their wings in front of her, buzzed furiously and shot away. The wings were woven of bulrushes. Even her most indifferent kiss could turn any one of them into a prince with shapely legs and a gold crown. There would be castles to live in.

"I traced a dozen pictographs," said Paul suddenly. "Something is happening." She saw him at the window, staring into the distance. "The sicknesses, I mean. It's not getting any better. I don't think it will stop." She shut her eyes again imagining him as she had seen him before with the sky over top and him intense at his work, pressed against the rock, touching the tip of a Comte crayon onto the pictographs, applying a sheet of rice paper over top of that. The crayons had been her idea and, in the end, produced an entirely acceptable reverse image of the pictographs without impacting the original.

"You should have been there," he said, looking at her. "Why weren't you there?"

"You didn't want me. You wanted to copulate with spirits. You were being mythopoetic again. Probably you were banging on a drum. Were you banging on a drum? You were having an affair. With that Animal person? With a drum?"

Paul turned and re-examined the reflection of himself in the window and was unsure of it, doubting its authenticity. He saw two waves of blondish fur turned that way by the sun and white sprouts of hair growing daily, to his annoyance, not to hers. In fact, Linda awaited his *éminence grise* with some impatience.

He turned from the window and crawled into bed with her again, slow and tired and well fed, shifting his way next to her the way a bear enters a dark den. His hulking form with its worn contours pressed against her on the mattress and immediately Linda tumbled into sleep where she found herself examined by the glossy eyes of a caribou. "You intend to kill me with your fire and your electricity. Kill me," said the animal. "Take my casement for protection. Sunder my spirit from my frame. Eat my meat for strength. Your clan is in desperate ways. I give you my bones for your labours and you shall not want. Your clan is in desperate ways, tell me why have you done this to yourselves?"

Linda woke up suddenly and saw her husband's sunburnt back rising from a chair like a porterhouse steak that had spilled over the sides of a plate. A stout and well-thumbed binder lay open and upright on the desk in front of him. Over her shoulder she discerned the outlines of the pictures he had traced at Hickson, Mirabelli, and Red Lake and many of the other places of their wanderings and of his wanderings. She saw the anthropomorphs, the man with the rabbit ears, the lines, the circles, the approximated animals, animals that no human being had seen but in dreams, tally marks and the abstract renderings that formed the bulk of Canadian rock art. His notebooks spread out on the table and he was writing in them, the pages filled with arcane jottings on Native medicine. His arcane thoughts. His attempts to enter a world that was denied to him. The better world.

Paul turned to face her. "Something has happened," he said

cheerfully. "I believe we're being touched by a civilization that is fantastically alien to us but is part of us. It's in us," he said, staring at her. "We are becoming something else."

POSTSCRIPT 3: THE DARK SOO

IN THE FAST INVADING DARK near Thessalon, she searched the incoming road for a skid mark she knew would be there but to her surprise wasn't. She'd put it there on a dreadful night some years ago with Paul asleep in the passenger seat, the right front tire banging flat, a fox family on the asphalt, the mother haunched and stone-still as the hunk of steel came for her and her young. Linda had gone into a hard, shuddering skid that left her heart pounding and the van half off the road in the dark. The foxes were now a smear of fur and pulp on the tarmac like those photographs she'd seen of human shadows imprinted against the wall at Nagasaki after the bomb. Paul sick with it, vowed he'd never again drive a car or eat meat or slam the door on a Jehovah's Witness or engage in any evil. While they changed the tire, turkey vultures and dung hawks wheeled over top of them and the smell of beached fish and seaweed rose from the shore. Linda saw nothing there anymore that reminded her of the stain of their brutal passage. She wondered if it meant she'd been forgiven.

By dark morning hours, she'd made the bypasses and green traffic signs that cluttered the outskirts of Sault Ste. Marie. An hour later the rain had nearly ceased and she let the van roll down a nameless unpaved road. The machine stopped for her beneath a mantle of spruce that dropped fat pearls of water on her windshield. She had always known that in such places lurked the drooling axe murderers who wore hockey masks and waited to chop her into bits. They had always waited in such places, she heard them rustling like skunks in the soaked underbrush waiting for the woman she had become, the lone woman, a woman alone. She rolled the windows up against the flies that rose despite the rain and snapped the sleeper to the sky and to the impossible stars, climbing into bed with her clothes on and the mangy old Hudson's Bay blanket pulled across her, scratching at her chin. The cricket-clamour and patter of rain on the roof guided her at once into her dreams.

10

KENORA: THE FIRE

LINDA OCCUPIED THE MORNING BY herself, penciling a stack of free-lanced manuscripts in front of the fading velvet wallpaper of a third floor room in the old Kenricia Hotel in Kenora. The entire sprawling joint was now a firetrap on the verge of being shut down, but it remained sporadically open somehow, a jewel in the north with its striking interlocked white bricking; it stood as proud as a castle on the skyline of the old town. The room she and Paul had rented glowed with the ghosts of bootleggers and American gangsters who had once lived large in it. The very broadloom blossomed with history, including, she had discovered, cigarette burns from another era.

Outside, the bush planes landed and lifted and droned carrying fishermen and mineral prospectors deep into the woods. She heard them as she worked. Pilots dropping their planes onto the bay, taxiing to the long pier by the town laundromat, and hauling a bag of filthy bushwhacker clothes inside for a wash. Taking off again when the laundry was done. Beneath her, Main Street bustled with sharp air and western oil money. She stood by the window and watched swaggering men visibly on the lookout for a big score, the trophy pickerel or natural gas deposit, or diamond vein. Fortunes were getting made out there while she fiddled with a stack of writings that depressed her endlessly, including an incomprehensible self-help book for vegan dog owners called *Feeding Fido; Meat-Free Meals for the Dog You Love.*

When she'd had enough, she put her work away and pulled on a sweater; it was time for her unofficial, unpaid secondment to the nonexistent offices of the Canadian Rock Art Association where she would compile her husband's enthusiasms into mind-numbing manila folders containing mostly lichenometry data. Today she would not do that. Today, instead, she went down the stairs into the northern street. Despite the presence of overweight carpetbaggers and bushwhackers packing chunky wallets, the intersection of Main and Princess showed many boarded-up storefronts and yawning windows. Spindly decorative trees sprouted from concrete boxes along the sidewalk. A torn yellow sheet suspended in the window of Francine's Watch and Giftware store stated ominously, *Everything Must Be Liquidated. Everything!*

She took the long sweeping walk around Kenora harbour, in no hurry, inhaling a premature Arctic chill that came down off the Ungava land mass. The wind moaned in the hollows of her face. She stopped periodically, on the lookout for the sturgeon she'd seen earlier, its grey and white body basking out there in the water beneath the sun. But the fabled and enormous fish refused to rise to the surface. She saw instead Husky the Musky, a giant muskellunge tourist attraction made of papier mâché, painted green, mounted near the beach at the lakeshore, frequently vandalized, its mouth open extremely wide, as if frozen in horror.

In an hour, she had walked the lakeshore and entered the fifth floor room of the Lake of the Woods District Hospital, filled with light and scored by the symphony of a game show that blared from the television. By the window of the lounge, Priscilla Prescot sat humming the same snatch of a forties swing tune she'd been humming the day before. The serene royalty of the crone affixed itself in a halo around her. Ninety-six-years-old, glowing with a faint and dignified absence. Several of her teeth were missing now.

"Lillian," Priscilla said softly.

"Linda," she corrected, as she had done before, but the woman ignored her and pressed a button on a control panel imbedded into her chair that made the television go black. "Oh, my dear, why is it I should be going on like this? It is time for me to be over with, isn't it? I've lived too long Lillian, too long. I've done everything there is to do. Everything except this. Really." She gazed distastefully around the room. "My teeth are falling out," she added with grim pride.

During the span of her rather enormous life the woman had traipsed the largest diocese in the world, the naive and often stunned companion of the Reverend Joshua Prescot D.D. during those vigorous years when no amount of liquor could bring the man down. From the Attawapiskat to Kapuskasing, from Matagami on the Quebec side to Missinaibi in the hard bush above Iroquois Falls, she had negotiated the immensity of it. In the aftermath of one of her husband's binges, she had helped him transport a grand piano fifty miles down the Chapleau River, straddling it across two Peterborough canoes that had been lashed together with her own stockings. Silk stockings sent to her without her husband's knowledge from an admirer who was killed in a tank battle at Aquino. Such stories once abounded and now she was forgetting them, every day.

"Did I ever tell you the time —"

These sudden discursive turns of the old woman's memory delighted Linda. They were like birds carried by a wind that had stopped blowing, beautifully plumed birds that never ceased their singing.

"No, tell me please." It felt right to her that she should end up at the bedside of an old woman attending to memories from an earlier and different world. A world that was never coming back. She sensed the comforting presence of things that existed and were entitled to be forgotten in the passing of time. "Tell me," she urged. Tell me everything I have wanted to know. Tell me everything. Everything there is. Everything that has ever happened. I want to know. I must.

"Manitoba, it was Manitoba. I was your age. Younger even. Much younger. I was standing in front of the Hudson's Bay store, Josh was inside, Paul wasn't born yet. And the fur brigade came down because that's where they got paid at the Bay store there. They all got paid there. And that's what they did, they went in and got paid and then they got drunk. I mean they got drunk. We forget how drunk men can get. Maybe timbermen, back in the day, they used to get drunk like that but really, my goodness. They made the stuff themselves. Moose milk they called it, lugging great jars of it about everywhere. Get drunk, stay that way for four months. I remember they started being sick, they started puking. They went to their knees by a ditch and they were all throwing up. This was at the Osnasburgh House, way up there. And here were these men lined up and puking themselves a regular storm. And that was it, you see? That was the last fur brigade ever. The very last one the Company ever hired. It was all over. I was such a young woman, a girl really, I had no idea. No one did. Here were these men vomiting in a ditch and three hundred years of history was coming to an end. That's what it looked like. Men puking in the snow beside the ditch. Sometimes that's what history looks like. It all ends my dear, everything. It just comes to an end like that." She made an effort of snapping her fingers but very little came of it.

Linda sat in the light, staring at her mother-in-law, and stroking her right arm. She was so feeble, barely ninety pounds of her remained, her hair so white, so drained of lustre, her skin translucent as parchment. She knew this feeble woman had travelled ten thousand miles by dogsled and half as many by snowshoe, or perhaps her mother had; Priscilla's stories and her mother's stories mingled now in Priscilla's memory. One of them had somehow played an advisory role in the late revisions of E.A. Watkins' *Dictionary of the Cree Language*, and had been present at the last treaty gathering at Naongashiing to which she'd travelled sixty miles by canoe through a maze of islands, each inhabited by its own spirit, while baby Paul lay in the middle, diapered in a bag made of moss that had been slowly baked to make sure no insects remained alive in it. The boy lay between the thwarts of a canoe, staring up at the sky. His mother wore a pair of beaded moccasins sewn with sinew and embroidered with porcupine quills. Of course, Priscilla was not old enough. Her mother's memories had become her own. That woman had been friend to Edwin Turner, the first Indian Agent of Keewatin District, a small energetic man who conducted his official affairs from a small ketch. In a series of lengthy and passionate letters, he'd convinced a fading Italian diva to board a tramp steamer and come to Canada to be his bride. For the next twenty years, as he nosed his way through the countless bays and inlets of Lake of the Woods, his game Italian wife planted herself in the bow of his ketch belting out Verdi's *Rigoletto* to tone-deaf trappers who fried bannock in bear grease, staring up through the trees as her mezzo-soprano soared its way into the boreal twilight.

The old woman drifted from the mist of those greying afternoons and flitted in and out of decades that were gone, barely remembered, touching down on brilliant days; at twenty-two years old, volunteering at Chorley Park military hospital in Toronto. On burnished wood floors she helped amputated veterans acquaint themselves with their artificial limbs by dancing with them. She forced herself to smile as their hard prosthetics continuously stabbed her toes. They couldn't feel a thing, and she clenched her teeth against the pain, looking out the window at the leaning trunks of the white pines of the estate. She smiled strangely. Only the vast land and her marriage had made sense to her, and that not much; the loud and burly form of Joshua Prescot, the minister, her husband drunk or sober.

"Dearie dear. Sometimes I don't know if who I am is what I remember or what I've forgotten." For a moment she was gone into that other world that increasingly belonged only to her, where men paid a dime for a dance. At least that is what she thought took place there. Fireworks over top of them while couples clenched below the lights of the fairground.

"Tell me about the fire. You said you would."

The woman sighed. It was necessary that she begin positioning large memories, untangling them like fishing line from the scramble of the hours and years that had piled up on her. "Well," she said. "It started in the bush didn't it?" Linda was not meant to answer, only to sit, to listen, learn, and one day, from the rooms of her own great age, to remember them, maybe repeat them. "It starts in the bush." Priscilla waved her hand at the window indicating that for all she was concerned the great conflagration was out there still, moving toward them, extinguishing everything, even her memory, especially her memory. Memory was the only thing that burned really. "Eight miles an hour, that's what my father said, forty miles wide, shaped like a horseshoe. The fire was moving at eight miles an hour and you could hear a noise, the flames, cracking things open and burning up all the air. A great whooshing wind, like war it was, and after three days we knew it was heading for us because the animals started to move. Right into town, they came over the railway tracks down Second Street, and they had to cross a bridge to do it, the bears and the wild dogs, the skunks, snakes and no end of deer. Even fishers, there were two fishers, side by side, and I remember that because I'd never seen a fisher before. I only ever saw one after that either, and it was stuffed in a museum. Every kind of animal, the streets were filled with them. I was seven years old and I was with my mother in the Kresge's department store, and she touched me on the top of my head and said 'Look there' and right in front of us was a deer, a big buck with these spreading antlers, and it stood with its feet splayed looking extremely foolish, the way a deer does when it's standing on the highway. Very ungraceful, standing on a wooden floor next to this great bin of women's underwear. Second floor. It had come up the stairs you see. These tiny wooden stairs."

Priscilla Prescot sighed mightily and shifted on the pillow. "That husband of yours, dearie? My son. Is he here?"

"He's in the archives at the museum."

The woman's dark little eyes aimed themselves worriedly at her. "You watch out for him. He has mighty ideas. My bloody goodness." She laughed herself into a wet and alarming cough and then came out of it. "He saved the world, my son. In a dream. Twice I've had that dream. The same both times. Paul is in it, all painted up like a Hollywood Indian and the world is on fire and turning into ash right in front of me, and Paul puts his lips up close to it and he whispers something to it, and then I wake and everything is all right. I know it is. And there's Paul smiling at me. Oh, he was always one for the ideas. You watch, one day those mighty ideas are just going to wear him right out. He always wanted to be something that boy. He'd rather be a porcupine, I think, or an otter. God knows."

Linda looked blankly at her. Her mother-in-law had always expressed the belief that Paul was in some special need of being taken care of, but was never so tiresome as to suggest that his wife ought to be the one who did it.

"Is he drinking?" the woman asked.

Linda paused. "No, not now," she said.

"He'll get himself all worn out like his father. Bad hearts, the Prescot men, I mean they have good hearts, but they don't have strong hearts. I believe somewhere they have little holes in them. And bad teeth too, they have bad teeth. Have you learned that? They won't get them looked after, will they? No they won't. They're too busy with the business of God and the meaning of life to spend an hour in the dentist's office. They're out there, re-routing rivers and leaving their mark on history or whatever it is they're doing, meanwhile their teeth are all falling out."

She shook her head and both of them, as if in agreement not to speak any further, turned and stared out the window. Together their eyes lingered on the grassy lawn below that plunged to the darkening surface of Lake of the Woods.

11

LORETTA RAMSAY

The cup of life will almost be spilled.
The cup of life will almost become the cup of grief.
THE PROPHECY OF THE SEVEN FIRES

PAUL STOOD IN THE STREET watching the northern sky shine with a clarity that cast a visible outline around the town of old Kenora and everything in it, the wires, the frames of the billboards, the sooty rooftops, even the branches of the trees. The sun had climbed to mid-sky a long time ago and refused to move any further. He took a final longing look at all of it before ducking into the clammy press of Ned's Diner, a classic grill and soda bar of the kind fast vanishing from civilization. Paul had resigned himself to the idea that there was nothing he could do about it. All civilizations collapsed. Even his, especially his.

He took his place inside the restaurant alone. Linda was back at the Kenricia, sound asleep, and he felt suddenly estranged from her, a feeling of drifting away from her, and wanted her powerfully now to be beside him. He felt a strange anger that such a feeling could exist. Paul sat down and scanned the place. Generally, he allowed himself a broad standard for judging northern restaurants, there must be no animal guts on the walls and the cook must not be drunk. Or rather the cook could be drunk but he must not be waving a carving knife at the waitress or the customers.

On the wall in front of him hung a red Coca-Cola sign, dented and probably salvaged from an overgrown baseball diamond. The booths were straight-backed, and upholstered in crushed horsehair. Men and women in polyester jackets stitched with dream catchers, recovery wheels, and the names of remote reserves sat staring out at Main Street through windows clouded with steam. The place smelled like pea soup. A sign propped against the cash register stated *We Support First Nations Hockey*. On the wall hung an ancient poster of Janice Joplin in mid scream. Next to her a framed embroidery of Reinhold Niebuhr's *Serenity Prayer*.

"God grant me the serenity," Paul read, before lowering his eyes to the menu. An Italian place at one time, still was, he thought, frequented by Anishinaabeg mostly. A noble Greco-Italian-Canadian-Ojibwe joint that proudly served spaghetti "Italian Style" with an order of fries on the same plate and a small Greek salad on the side. His multi-cultural country, he loved every bit of it. Every mouthful. Two sodden orders of *poutine* drifted by at eye level and he had the powerful notion they were being taken out back and slung to the bears.

He first saw the young woman sitting on a vinyl stool at the counter, tracing a length of her hair behind her left ear with a pencil. She had a notebook open and was sketching. He was undone by this gesture. The neck, the neck, he thought. To neck with someone.

He spread his own work on the table, a sketch of a man with rabbit ears and a pole-sized phallus. He pretended to shuffle papers beneath other papers, glancing again at the young woman, regretful of her, somehow, that she even existed. Her face … it was impossible to him. Faces like hers lit up the world. Because of faces like that, he thought, men invented the compass.

Paul arranged his papers on the table, folded the menu. It was time for food and appetite and he was pleased to see her slide from her stool and advance coolly toward him, aggressively even.

"Pickerel. You have pickerel?" he said.

"We have pickerel. One or two left."

"One or two?"

"The cook has one or two," she said crossly. "The season's ending. Pickerel season is ending."

"Yes, it's ending. Everything is ending. Pickerel, please. Mash instead of fries, no gravy, coffee later. Thank you."

She wasn't paying attention to him. Her head tilted, the hair fell in knots over her left shoulder and he saw that not all of it was black. She was staring at the papers on the table. "Those are pictographs." It was almost an accusation.

She bent close to the table and he could smell her now; it was as he suspected, patchouli oil, the ancient somewhat sickening scent that had once drifted from head shops, poster counters, and the skin of wild teenage girls with loose long hair from decades ago. He was surprised that it still existed.

"Port Coldwell," she said. "Those drawings are from the pictographs at Port Coldwell.

"Hickson Mirabelli," Paul said.

"No."

Paul laughed. "Yes. Hickson Mirabelli."

She looked at him almost furiously. "They look like the ones at Port Coldwell."

"How do you know that?"

"I've been there. I've worked with them."

"Worked with them? You're an artist then? A magician?" She

made a display of astonishment, as if he had made an observation that distinguished him from other men. Something secret had dropped between the two of them, for a moment he felt that.

"I'm here for the summer, I study in Toronto and yes I am," she laughed. "An artist. How did you know that?"

"Because you're working in here. Because of the way you look," he added recklessly and regretted it at once. She didn't seem alarmed. She was used to it.

"Tell me about it, your art," he added quickly. "I'm interested."

She examined him intensely. "I work with aboriginal motifs. Exclusively. Native rock, pictographs, petroglyphs, those," she pointed at his papers. "That's wild."

"You're First Nations?" It was a misstep, he felt it as he said it.

"Yeah, well," she took up the menu. She was gone, pointedly gone ten minutes and then she was back with the food, the pickerel streaked with gold grill marks, the potatoes steaming. She put the food on the table. He saw that her face had the power of a sun, and that everything existed within it.

"I'm supposed to be Cree, way back on my mother's side. My name's Ramsay, very old name. *Très* distinguished." She made a disgusted flare of her nostrils to indicate what she felt about the whole business of that. He'd been forgiven, he could see. "I'm the distant offspring of someone famous. David Ramsay. He wrote a book in 1807 called *The Life of George Washington*. But he was shot. He was shot three times in the back by a man he didn't know. Just walked up to him in the street, kablam, three times." She laughed oddly. "He was a lunatic. A hatter. A mad hatter. They were all mad because of the mercury. I'm mad too," she said, and smiled.

Paul nodded. "You got off to a good start."

"What do you mean?" Suddenly she was cold again and noticeably suspicious.

"A good start. To be an artist. Or a shaman. To be mad. It's all the same."

This pacified her. "What are you?" she said suddenly.

He was surprised by this sudden attention, flattered even; it felt like she had shone a bright and marvelous light on him.

"I thought you would never ask. It so happens I'm the world's leading authority on aboriginal rock art, east of the Rockies." He flourished a cracked leather pouch from next to his thighs and unzipped it, withdrawing a copy of *Pictographs, Petroglyphs and Paradigms of the Apocalypse*. He laid it on the table.

"Hey," she uttered. "I have that book. I've read it." She turned the copy over, and quickly surveyed the picture of Paul Prescot, a younger Paul Prescot.

"You're that guy."

"That guy. Me."

"You're not a fucking anthro are you? Or an art critic?"

"No, I'm not," Paul assured her. "I promise."

12

AFFAIRS OF THE HEART

His survival, apparently without much disfigurement, was credited
to the application of native remedies: immediate submersion in the lake,
a purgative recommended by the Ojibwa leader, Ayagon,
and the treatment of his burns with swamp tea and larch-pine salve.
DICTIONARY OF CANADIAN BIOGRAPHY VOL. VIII

BY WINTER, HIS WORK IN Kenora was done and they were back in the city in their rented home living their rented lives, lying in bed with books in hand, her with her cream-coloured dictionary packed with men who invariably died. The hall light threw a cube of white through the doorway and onto the wall by the bed. Tenderly, even with reverence, he stroked the dark mole that adorned the back of his wife's left shoulder. He was aware that at various points in her life that mole had been the source of considerable attention from mankind, or at least men, thrusting itself out against a background of unforgivably white skin. It floated on her like a lost contact lens, offering the possibility of sight to any man who could claim it. It had been stroked, sucked, kissed, bit, scratched, photographed, analyzed, philosophized and masturbated over, and now absently, in ever tightening circles, Paul searched out the ridges of it, patting the air around it as if the thing itself was not connected to her body. Decisively he pulled his finger away, only to return it, beating a tap on the surface of the mole this time, keeping beat to whatever came next. He knew what was coming next. He dreaded it. He was not the sort of man these things happened to, he had always known that.

Out the window, an unstained sheet of snow bedded the tree branches and dragged them downward to the ground thick and pristine. It was as if a new world had fallen upon the earth, hiding the old one, hiding its wounds. In the basement, the furnace coughed and began asthmatically to breathe through the vents. The Greek Orthodox Church chimed in the cold. Four times the bells sounded. Four clarion calls into the night.

Paul got up abruptly and left the room. Linda remained on the bed counting the chimes while he went below and made tea for them. Reaching over, she pulled his notebook off the bed table and saw that he was glossing George Nelson's letters on the Cree and Northern Ojibwa religion, *your lands are distressed, keep not on the rivers.* Paul had underlined this heavily.

She rolled away and went back to her own book. Her plan was to read every volume of the *Dictionary of Canadian Biography* before her life ended. She had advanced beyond the Ms of the seventeen sixties; Mineweh was dead, knifed in his tent, his famous silver tongue made silent by death. Montcalm awaited his defeat. She was skipping now, randomly turning the thin pages.

Paul re-entered the room, quietly like a butler, stooped over a tea tray of all things. She had not seen it before. She didn't know they owned a tea tray, or what part of the basement he had dug it up from.

"Lin," he said, vaguely. He so rarely called her that.

His voice rose huskily and freighted. She hardly recognized it.

"I've met someone." That's all he said.

There was a pause before a slightly insane snort escaped her. She only half-prevented herself from laughing out loud.

"What do you mean? We meet people every day."

It was a mistake to speak. It wasn't even true what she said. She did not meet people every day. She met them in books. People who were brought down with a musket ball. Linda sensed that everything she'd taken for granted was on the edge of being over with. An enormous knife had fallen between her and her life. It was gone with those few casual words. Everything that mattered was made of words. Paul had met someone. A large-looming someone, a Biblical someone. Had he met her on the Red Road, the true path? Or maybe it was the road to Galilee, or the laundromat?

"I'm sorry, I don't know how else to say that." He looked at her pleadingly, "I don't know what to do."

His words knocked into her. She was suddenly startled that he could do this to her, that he could still knock her at all with words, or with anything. She'd thought that the knocking moments of her heart were behind her in regard to her husband. This man, this strange and stupid miracle that he was. She had taken him for granted, she realized that, like a tree that had always been there that she could climb and find shade beneath.

"You don't know what to do?" she repeated. And then again, more softly. Linda understood perfectly well it was not the loss of a ferocious passion that made her heart knock. It was the understanding that if Paul in a moment of frankness felt compelled to confess to an affair he was having, then maybe she had an obligation to confess hers too.

13

ARTHUR GRATTON

... He had a great fluency in speaking and a graceful Elocution that would have pleased in any part of the world. His person was well made, and his Features, to my thinking, resembled much of the Busts of Cicero.

DICTIONARY OF CANADIAN BIOGRAPHY, VOL. II, 1701–1740

THERE WERE REASONS SHE DID not want to confess about the man she was having an affair with, but the most troubling thing was that her affair was somewhat stupid, even to her. She did not perceive of Arthur Gratton — that was his name and she enjoyed the feel of his name in her mouth — as bumpkin-stupid in the manner of people who sat in restaurants and jeered at the government and mocked people with educations. He belonged to an elite order of intelligence marked with postgraduate degrees earned abroad. It was a confident stupidity; incisive, urbane and it manifested the cold side of the city, of any city. Arthur Gratton, she had come to realize, was one of those scathing incisive people who carried powerful electronic devices in their briefcases and could demolish a man's reputation with a flick of a key. She understood that such men had no idea how to dress a deer or weave a fishing line from bulrush fiber or, for that matter, make a menstrual pad out of it, as Paul insisted he could do and, in fact, had attempted to do for her north of Superior, failing rather catastrophically. Instead they could eviscerate a public servant or a politician in an afternoon and be having a drink by dinner. The man wrote articles for keenly intelligent magazines, appeared on television and spoke hotly and intensely, with wit and arrogance and a noticeable jawline. She enjoyed seeing him on television, it made her giggle. Men always looked foolish on television. The way they tried to appear smart, smarter than someone else. It seemed so important to them somehow. These men with their privileges. There were so many of them; women, too, now, in their scary makeup, the ranks swelling every day. It seemed to Linda she couldn't get up in the morning without their heads ballooning and shouting from televisions and radios, desperate to opine. Desperate to make people like her giggle. They were so desperate to say things. They would never grow old, their teeth would never drop into their soup. Their heads were stuffed with opinions. She despised them all. She had in fact spent her semi-conscious life in flight from such men, every one of them, and now she was shacking up with one, something she found both nauseating and arousing.

Linda had examined her excuses for getting into bed with this man and put them down to the demands of her body which she rarely questioned. In many ways he was the polar opposite of her husband, even the bipolar opposite, she sometimes thought. Arthur Gratton was selfishly, compulsively, and perversely hungry for her. He wanted her in every way possible, wholly naked, part naked, he would take her fully dressed if he had to. He had said as much. It was a type of compliment. He once cheerfully confessed that he fantasized her revolving on a rotisserie for all eternity. A small electric rotisserie. He controlled the speed, and direction. He wanted pictures of her, sketches, her breasts, toes, fingers, the fur on her ears, he wanted binary parts and fragments of her, the totality of all her fragmented selves, and from these fragments he had constructed his Venus; Linda Prescot, *née* Richardson.

She quickly accepted this as the way it should be. The man was arrogant, but he was aggressively and faithfully starving for her which for some reason she found agreeable. He had fallen so deep into the habit of her that she had almost, without knowing it, conceded him status as an acolyte of her flesh. She even took his phone calls in the middle of night when her husband was away. He was away more than ever. She didn't ask. She wondered if she cared. She loved her husband; she would never be capable of hating him. She listened to Arthur's panting, she tolerated his obsessions, she was one of them.

She knew of Arthur Gratton that he had grown up in a fanatical Christian sect in a small town in Saskatchewan, population eighty-three and declining steadily. When he was a boy, his father had been decapitated by a salting truck on Highway 39 and Arthur was bused home from a Moose Jaw public school to find his living room packed with sect members writhing on the floor, speaking in scabrous tongues. The event was a "fire fall," he told her, performed in its daemonic intensity in front of Arthur in the hope of indoctrinating him. It didn't catch. He had recoiled in horror. By the age of seven he was a skeptic. He didn't believe in the transfiguration of the Lord Jesus Christ, or the divinity of hockey teams. He was a critic of Santa Claus, debunking the great man from lecterns behind which he stood like a pint-sized Lenin. The boy climbed on his desk and urged his classmates to wipe the department store pixie dust from their eyes. He denied the existence of Santa Claus and for this was expelled from school, run out of town by liberal orthodoxy, he insisted. He was virulent toward even the vaguely spiritual or the mysterious. His dreams were not worth the fathoming and vitamins were a hoax, massage was a fraud. He wanted yoga banned. He left his first wife because she booked an appointment with a chiropractor. "I lost her to a cult," he told Linda sadly. Whenever he was having drinks with a woman, he told this story. Chiropractic and voodoo, it was the same. As far as he was concerned it was all part of a gooey New Age conspiracy to turn the planet into a politically-correct neo-fascist Pilates class for postmodern vegan feminists who would all spout postmodern nonsense in favour of the marginalized voice. The margins were for losers. He was in favour of the centre, the voice of fact and truth. His voice, the voice of himself uttering the tenets of a world that had lost control of its utterances. "That's me," he said. He made it clear he would have no truck with an alternate universe that had been birthed from a moiety of muck returned from the sea by an otter or some other creature. She despised him slightly and she quickly had grown tired of sparring with him.

Arthur Gratton was also the vain owner of a hard body buffed on treadmills that churned beneath screens scrolling 24-hour news. It didn't hurt his cause that he had a deep and noticeable dimple and a streak of white hair that showed quartz-like on a head of trimmed locks. I am a simple woman, Linda told herself. I desire simple things. Even simple men. She enjoyed the simplicity of their bodies. He was tall like her husband, but wider at the shoulders than at the middle. He was muscular and responsive. He did fine in some passionate and empty way, and she understood that while Paul sat disconsolate on the bed beside her, she had no desire at all to make a marital confession of her own.

POSTSCRIPT 4: INTO THE MOUNTAINS

IN THE EARLY MORNING WITHOUT ceremony or ablution she took her place behind the wheel and resumed her path north up the highway over the Goulais River and into the rock and the mountains. The great cavern of the north opened white as ice, and she drove up, up, as the old Westfalia dragged and droned. *Black Dog Road*, a sign read.

The van drove by feel now, independent of her, stroking the grey asphalt, entering into the tops of the trees, climbing into the vapour of the clouds, coming out the other side into a lagoon of blue sky where an eagle flew perfectly straight and without effort. She was among the eskers and skinks and the black dinosaurian skin of the mountains. There she looked down and took in cold Superior, strangely purple in the moment, and immense, flexing to the road where old billboards lay, long toppled in the blueberry mantle like soldiers fallen in combat. At one time each of those signs had shilled a restaurant or stopping place that now no longer existed. The paint was curled and bubbled now. She drove past husks of *Stop Here* places with *American Plan* and *TV* and *Vacancy*, bare boxes of sagging boards standing on grey concrete slabs. Stubbles of stone foundations. Overgrown parking lots breaking up as the thistles threw back the tarmac like pastry. One after another the motels, some not even boarded up, had given way to the club moss, some abandoned in a single fateful afternoon, the car packed, the owner gone south for good. The great and foolish promise of the north come undone. *For Sale* signs nailed in place thirty years ago curled on the walls from which the paint had long decamped. Linda bit her lip. At one time a groaning confusion of love had filled those places; the songs of smoky-voiced crooners on solid state radios, the newlyweds, the tacky negligees made of chiffon, the price tag still attached; adventurers, the travellers, the runaways, the sigh of trucks on the highway. So many of them. Of us, she thought. So many of us. Now rain pelted through the holes in the roofs and the porcupines gnawed the cladding, as if they had all the time in the world.

In a moment it was all behind her, yanked backward by the passing of her country.

14

DRESSING QUICKLY

*The Seventh Prophet that came to the people long ago was said to be different
from the other prophets. He was young and had a strange light in his eyes.
He said, "In the time of the Seventh Fire, New People will emerge."*

THE PROPHECY OF THE SEVEN FIRES

LINDA LAY ON A HOMEOPATHIC Swedish-made mattress that belonged
to the ex-wife of the man she was having an extra-marital affair
with. That the ex-wife was attending a crystal healing conference
in Seattle, and that Arthur was here in her absence to feed an
anti-social Himalayan cat and to sprinkle dried shrimp-bits to a
Madagascar cichlid that stared at them from behind the glass of
an aquarium, said something to her about the state of the man
she was involved with. His back faced her from a desk where he
sat sunning himself in the rays of a computer screen.

"Arty," she tried. It amused her to level silly and even idiotic
lover's nicknames on the personage of Arthur Gratton. He did not
approve. "Arty-poo."

"Fuck off," he answered, without looking up from the screen.

She pulled some sort of painfully authentic quilt over top of her and whispered hoarsely. "Arthur, who was it who turned your cock to stone? Did you ever consider that."

He looked at her, almost angrily. "What is it that you're trying to say?"

"How is it that without the benefit of cocaine you have the ability to achieve rock status and stay that way?"

"Because I am the king." After a moment, he added, "And you're the queen." He was entirely intent on the screen, as if some final answer was to be found there. What he was looking for. There was something terrifying in the way that men looked at screens, she thought. As though life existed there.

"No, not me," she said. "It's because of you. You've had your cock turned into stone by a wizard. Face it."

"How would you know that?"

"How do we know anything? I read it. It's written on the rocks near Spences Bridge, British Columbia. We were having a fight one summer, so Paul took me there. Why not? All these stones covered with writings. Some horny beast was having his way with all the girls until one day a pissed-off father who happened to be a sorcerer turned his cock to stone." He had also, if she remembered correctly, turned his wife's vulva to stone as well. She thought it best if she skipped that part.

Arthur squinted at the limpid surface of the screen. "Where was this?"

"Spences Bridge, population twenty-five. Franz Boaz was there a hundred years ago. He made cylinder recordings of the Nlaka'pamux people speaking."

Arthur tapped a key and made a flourish in the manner of a pianist. "Who would come up with that? For what reason would any thinking person come up with some story like that? Why would anyone waste their time writing it down?"

"It's a folk tale. It comes out of the primeval mud of your unconscious."

Arthur leaned back with his hands crossed behind his head and put his feet up on an abstract piece of furniture that resembled a circumcised mushroom. Evidently it had no practical use whatsoever for his feet slipped off of it at once. "What if you have risen from the mud, what if you are mud-free? What if your use for mud is to hurl it into the face of the hocus-pocus industry? What do you think this mud is?"

"Icky mud," Linda answered at once. "You're not in touch with your icky mud. It haunts you, Arthur. You've become a screen person. You're all screened off. It makes you sterile. If you need to know, it's a legend, it comes from an understanding that can't be reached by thought."

"Ha," he grunted. "The great feely fraud of the century." He frowned at her. "You're implicated. Your husband is a practitioner. Your mind has gone soft. Nonetheless I find you extraordinarily attractive."

She was suddenly tired of the way they went down this path. It had been funny, she thought, at first. There had been wit in it. A teasing competitiveness that frequently led to sex. Now it was only annoying. "There still is a peace that surpasseth understanding, whether you like it or not," Linda said. She wondered if she was trying to convince herself. Arthur consented to squint at her.

"There is just one piece that surpasseth understanding." Arthur spun in the chair and braked in front of her, clutching himself. "This piece. I thought that you of all people would know that."

The way he sounded in the moment reminded her weirdly of certain fishing nets she had read about. Fifty miles long some of them, dragging the bottom of the ocean where they scooped up every living thing that had gone there to hide. She hauled herself from the ocean floor and began to dress. He watched her. He did not approve of women dressing. "You really should not put on your clothes," he said. "It's a misstep. It is civilization itself going in the wrong direction. Trust me."

She was dressed, preparing to go, flummoxed with him, eager to be somewhere else. How much of her life had been spent moving from one room to another where different men lived? What would Paul say? He would say, "'We murder to dissect.'"

"Pardon me?"

"'We murder to dissect.'"

"That's a bad thing?" Arthur knew he should let this go, but was unable. "If Banting had not murdered those cuddly puppies and dissected them? He did it down the street in that lovely grey brick building with ivy growing on it, by the way. The puppies screaming in the basement. If not for that you could be having a seizure right now instead of being here with me. 'We murder to dissect?' I like that. Did you make it up?"

"William Wordsworth, the poet. Remember? The people who once legislated the world. 'Tintern Abbey.' Read it. It will help you."

"I'll read it," he said. He made it sound as if he'd already done so.

"You won't read it," she corrected him. "You'll keep invading people's privacy in the hope of finding dirty underwear or a porn stash. You'll find it too; welfare mom doing outcalls, a councillor with the crack-addicted daughter. You'll keep putting your nose into people's messes until finally they jump in front of a subway train, and then you'll get an award for doing it. You should be ashamed of yourself."

"This may surprise you, my dear, but I am ashamed of myself and furthermore I know all about Willy Wordsworth. Didn't he screw his sister or something? Weren't those Romantic guys always doing that? I trust they were ashamed of themselves."

"He did not screw his sister."

"No?" Arthur sounded crestfallen. Then he brightened, "I'll just say that he did," and laughed.

SHE SHUT THE DOOR BEHIND her the way she put down a newspaper or snapped off the television, dirtied by a hunger that coursed through her body and seemed to have no interest in ever being satisfied. There were no stories. No children. It was an adult building. Filled with adults. Only adults, acting the way adults acted. There were ornate light fixtures and sex performed the *ultra luxe* way with no risk of infection or fertility. There was the gassy sound of electronic equipment murmuring through the carpeted corridor from behind firmly shut doors. Muffled music made without the touch of flesh on gut or lyre. Muffin music, she thought. We are being muffined to death with such music. She was mad. There was no doubt. Mad as a muffin. The entire world had become a pathological and diseased muffin. She stood alone in the elevator reading a hand-written piece of paper taped to the console; *WARNING*, it read. The raccoons were rabid and another earwig infestation had entered the parking levels in the basement.

15

APARTMENT

There is a most evil custom among the Savages.
Those who seek a girl or woman go to her to make love at night.

THE JESUIT RELATIONS, 1639

PAUL SAW HIMSELF IN REVERSE in Loretta Ramsay's mirror and didn't like what he saw, the stooped and dim outline of a thief in a room that was not a woman's room, only a chamber filled with a young person's confusion and ephemera. The sensation of being spied upon touched him and he searched for the source of it. He found it finally in the form of a stuffed teddy bear on the floor in the corner, dressed it in a child's T-shirt, *Homeland Security Fighting Terrorism Since 1492*, shown on the front of it.

For a moment he listened to the city outside meting out its confusion of cars and the hysterias of young people. He heard students who were either singing or screaming or committing violence against one another. Arguing about Hegel and young women. He heard the swish of vehicles and the distant punctuation of car alarms that sounded mournful as trumpets. He heard the great Babylon of the city at night.

On the walls of her apartment hung posters of musicians he'd never heard of and was glad not to have heard of, tall, skinny men with violent names and dark sunglasses. Indoor people. A poster of Malcolm X wearing black shades and machine gun, he recognized. It seemed like something from a movie. In her window hung a massive dream catcher of feathers and deer hide. He wondered what nightmares had been caught in it. He didn't want to know anymore. It was not his business. There comes a point in a man's life when a young woman is no longer his business. He thought he knew that.

She lay on a mattress supported from the floor by four plastic milk crates. That tradition strangely had not changed from his own student days from so long ago. The smell of oil paint pressed every inch of the room and her canvasses and boards leaned against the walls randomly. Paul stared somewhat wildly at the stark depictions. He saw again the figures knifed in their sleep, the tortured expressions of mouths, eyes flashing open in colour, others in black and white. Children suffered violent death in her work, one after another. It was the children, always the children where the murders went to nest. The boards pressed against every available space in her apartment, stacked three and four deep. Suddenly he resented the bravado of them. The bravado of other people's pain. What did she know? Of murder. Of anything, even children. What the hell did people think that they knew anymore?

Paul looked at her, but could barely comprehend how far away she was from him. All of the miles he'd tried to compact into his own life, all the bridges and portages he'd crossed, the solitudes he'd tried to tread, the trails, the car rides. They all flapped away from him like bandages come undone. He stood in a bathroom that felt hostile to him, his urine splashed on the porcelain, a dreary rain of failures. He did not want to turn to where the mirror was. He didn't want to see his own face. His despicable face. It had begun to look like a shoe. A man had an obligation to be handsome, he thought. He had failed.

He flushed the toilet and went back to her room where she was up and unmindful of him, squatting undressed on the floor. Her hair, her impossible hair, fell down in a tangle against her shoulders and her vertebra flexed like a ridgeline of rock, shining and silver. He would not look at her.

In a white ceramic bowl, the red paint pooled, her fingers sunk knuckle-deep, withdrawn to stroke the board, finessing rivulets of red from the eyes and the mouths of her figures. He continued to watch her. It had always looked like this he thought, in the dark caves at Chauvet it looked like this but darker, the vapour of glaciers hung in the air, at Altamira, at Lascaux, at Creswell Crags, at Agawa, at Peterborough, Ontario, someone crouched, someone infested with insects, someone holding a torch or a stone bowl filled with animal grease while the partner picked vermin from their lover's hair. Without a paintbrush or a pencil, without paper or practice, a man or woman, forty thousand years ago brought a charred stick to the surface of a cave wall, or his finger, more likely it was his finger, or her finger, and rendered the first painting on the planet — an animal, a horse in profile, or an aurochs in perfect detail, roaming the forests of what would become Poland, showing the very tremor of animal life that throbs beneath the hide.

Paul looked at Loretta Ramsay doing this as she squatted on the floor. The two impressions at the small of her back. He heard the low hum that came from deep inside her throat as she worked. A pop ditty that was as unfathomable to him as cave songs. He understood that a rushing herd of animals thundered past him, like traffic in the city. He turned away. It was not too late. Not midnight yet. He watched her, wanting her to turn and remain in the shine of the streetlight. He thought if he looked at her again, he would turn into stone.

The phone rang, and she allowed her concentration to break. She turned his way and Paul saw she'd painted red and horrendous lips around her own. The effect was as shocking to him as the gash of a wound on her face.

"Look at you," she laughed. "You have been mad and drunk all winter."

"What's the matter with you?" His words knocked against the walls. What's the matter with you? He didn't know who he meant exactly. She was already gone into the kitchen.

"Megwetch," he heard her speak eagerly to someone. Her laughter foamed back. The brilliant bottled sound of her voice had been opened. It flowed for someone else now, someone tattooed and wearing a gold ring in his left ear, though Paul was skeptical the man had ever sailed the China Seas or crossed the equator. For Paul there existed a special place in hell reserved for men who wore a gold earring without having shipped the Asiatic seas, sailed a submarine, or survived the sinking of their ship. Nobody knew their traditions anymore. They just swallowed everything like plankton.

From the other room, he heard her speaking in a voice of extreme intimacy. He'd had that voice directed at him. Only him. Only her. She could take it away in a moment. Her voice lowered and he understood that she was pointedly excluding him from the passions in her life. She had once aimed that brightness at him. Now it was aimed elsewhere and he despised himself.

"I'm not doing anything." He saw her wipe the red paint away from her mouth, damping at it with a cloth. "I'm just hanging around. What are you doing?"

I should cough, he thought. Or burp loudly. Instead Paul moved across the room, stopping at her desk which was a wooden door set across two sawhorses. He'd helped her carry it up from the trash out front of a hardware store at the beginning in the sun when they couldn't stop talking to each other, when every word was rich and blossomed with discovery.

The desk was now heaped with books and the elaborate constructions of her confusion. A white forgotten bra, flattened, a scattering of hair clips, strips of moose hide, a great boxy computer that didn't work, earrings, pencils, a velvet-lined flute case but no flute, fishing wire, a gram of hashish in tinfoil, a shoe, a scattering of articles clipped from the paper, all concerning the one she was on the phone with. She talked of him increasingly, he was a thin man of considerable height who had achieved notoriety for smuggling six dozen jelly doughnuts through the lines of the Canadian army at Akwesasne and giving them to a garrison of Mohawks. He was the one who had shut down a gravel pit, closed a road. Barricaded a rail line. Paul shuffled the clippings. The photo showed a tall man with long hair and a melodramatic nose — Joseph Maracle, of Tyendinaga, in all his power, *Aboriginal Protester Surrenders to Police. Mohawk activist found guilty. Leader of Highway shutdown faces twelve-year sentence.* She would do anything for that man on the phone.

"I'm not doing anything," Paul heard her say. "What are you doing?"

Nothing. She was doing nothing.

The excitement coming out of the next room blew palpably through the hall. He remembered suddenly the way she bit her bottom lip; it had appeared to him as the most breathtaking gesture he'd seen. She'd told everything, her family, her "fucked up family," as she put it, her lovers, many of them despicable, the exalted position of art in her life, a stranglehold she had called it, a stranglehold. It reassured him that there were still young people in the world who were getting strangled by art. She gloried in art, she gloried in the vision that allowed her to see through hypocrisy in all its stupid ways. She was on fire with herself. Karl Marx to techno pop, from College Street to Kenora. There were times when she was nearly overwhelmed by the brilliance of things and herself.

He shut the folder on her rebel and lover. Insurgent, the reporters called him, activist. They called him a terrorist, or a Mohawk, or Mississaugan; coded words to indicate other, Native, that impregnable thing. He was of the people, first people, Paul had come in second. Or third. He was not impregnable. She was talking on the phone to a man who founded his race beneath the snow-bent boughs of pine trees and stole the sun from a woven box. He was also, according to reports in the news, in default on support payments for three children and facing public mischief charges for pointing a fishing spear at a redneck during a standoff at a Caledonia condo development.

He heard them chuffing in the laughter of their excitement with each other, and prepared to leave this place in his humiliation. Quickly, foolishly, he tried to reassemble her clippings to the order they held before he had mangled his way through them. There was nothing to keep him here.

His knuckles dragged the table skidding a sheaf of papers off a clutter of other papers. He saw exposed a black and white reproduction of a watercolour he had seen before, a James Peachey work of a Loyalist encampment on the banks of the St. Lawrence. An officer mooned importantly in front of a young woman in the foreground. Behind them a row of neat white tents stretched against the shore, a pretty, transitory city made of canvas, and above it the solid detailing of the clouds. The reproduction was dull and barely discernible in places. But the title glared. DAVID RAMSAY, MURDERER. The article was stapled together in the top left corner. That staple astonished him, an act of fastidiousness that was remarkable in the tangle of her life as he knew it.

David Ramsay — Indian Killer.

The piece had been photocopied from a forty-year old *Beaver Magazine*; Paul recognized the formal typeface and found the byline: Smithers Donaldson, a University of Calgary professor who, if he remembered correctly, was dead, had collapsed following a lecture on the apocalyptic mythology of the Pawnee ten years ago. He had met the man.

He heard her from the kitchen. She would be at the table, her legs folded, her arms wrapped around her knees, an image that was stunning to him. David Ramsay — *The Indians captured him and tied his hands to his neck.* She'd underlined the text. He saw that half the article was underlined. His gaze slid from one underscoring to another; *we have reason to believe that David Ramsay has passed beyond the reach of God Almighty.... the subject of our present visit is the murder of eight of our Indians three of whom were killed at Kettle Creek.... 'After killing the first Indian I chewed thirty balls of lead.... I thought it a pity to shoot an Indian with a smooth ball ... after killing and scalping the woman....'* Paul looked up slowly at the painted boards slanting against her wall, the primitive rendering of a face torn into two — *he evidently performed the same atrocity on her children, one a mere infant* ... agonized mothers with bellies sundered, the children uncomprehending and amputated. The knife was highlighted with an almost photographic intensity. *After which he took a hatchet and killed all of the sleeping ...*

The page turned here; Paul was about to finger it, but stopped. I'm the distant offspring of someone famous. Serving him a plate of pickerel, she'd said that to him.

The distant offspring of someone famous.

Mad as a hatter, mad from all the lead.

After killing the first Indian I cut lead and chewed above thirty balls, and above three pounds of Goose shot. For a moment he saw a mouth of blackened teeth, stinking with rum or brandy or both, gnawing through three pounds of lead, spitting the ragged bits into a pouch.

Mad as hatters. *Within the space of three weeks he killed . . .*

"What are you doing?"

She'd put down the telephone and stood in the grey darkness glaring at him.

"I don't know what I'm doing," he said truthfully.

She came to the table and covered up the David Ramsay article. "You have to leave. Someone's coming over."

"I'm leaving," he said, feeling suddenly foolish, even idiotic, as if he had thrown everything away.

In a moment she was back at her painted boards, crouched again and swaying. He heard her humming a song that he did not find comprehensible and finally he closed the door behind him and she disappeared.

16

END OF THE WORLD

LINDA KNOCKED AROUND THE HOUSE in the long days of something she didn't have a name for. Her marriage, she thought, or life. It seemed important to attach a word to it. The end of time. The time in which words and worlds lost their meaning. The bottom of the ninth. Two out. Her husband was in or not, he was drinking or not. She found the sticky rings of his spent scotch glasses over his scribbled notes: *the command for the final destruction of the world is in the hands of the four gods of the directions.* At the bottom of the page he had written, to himself, *See all notes on Pawnee apocalypse predictions. Do!*

A postcard came in the mail addressed to him, an invitation to an opening at a Spadina Avenue gallery. *Medicine For A New World (works on rock and Masonite by Loretta Ramsay (Waunathoake.)* Her photograph was on it. The young woman was dressed in black and white, adorned with shells; a tan face, narrow, piles of black shining hair. *Loretta Ramsay Waunathoake crisscrosses the country of the human heart. Her ancestral blood traces to Deseronto's landing at the Bay of Quinte, a family line that begins with a Fort Hunter Mohawk and an unknown missionary at Tyendinaga. She is a Time Keeper of the Eastern Door, and her work avenges the crimes that call to us from the past and haunt our dreams.* She read the card with some distaste. The opening was to take place in a second-floor studio warehouse above the Miss Saigon restaurant where she and Paul had once intended to eat their first matrimonial lunch.

She felt dismissive of all them, Loretta Ramsay, the jaded movie stars who announced themselves one quarter, one half, or one thirty-second Native. Everyone so desperate to be something else. To be authentic. She got up from the sofa and went to the fridge where she removed the postcard, holding it in her hand as she had several times before.

Paul entered the room with a small plate heaped with eggs. He was extremely fussy about his eggs, like Descartes, he told her, and brought them up to his chin with disapproving glances, before wolfing them down.

"A presentation of her most recently executed motifs," she read out loud to him. "Can you tell me why artists have to execute their paintings? Why can't they just paint the damn things? Why must they execute them? Like Louis Riel for god's sake. Execute, really." Paul wiped the yellow scrabble off his lips. He had no answer, he was gone deep into his own place, that existed in the spaces of his grey eyes.

SHE DID NOT ATTEND THIS gala. She missed the Loretta Ramsay (*Waunathoake*) opening. Paul attended. He did not expect her to come, but he asked. He thought it was what adults did, to ask. She remained at home on the sofa, like a life raft, the television barely audible; a stream of flickering blue agitation glowed from the face of it and filled the room. The most cherubic of newsmen wearing a considerable amount of eyeliner reported that birds were dropping from the sky above Swan Hill, the tiny corpses scattered on a highway in northern Alberta, like tufted sticks. It had to do with a marketplace in Shanghai, he said, where birds were kept in small cages. Like go-go dancers, she thought. What ever happened to go-go dancers? They had all gone-gone. They had dropped from the sky. Like the birds.

With a blanket over top of her, she spent the evening leafing the *Dictionary of Canadian Biography Volume V*; *Craig, Creighton, Cruikshanks, Curtis, Davan, Davies*, and *Dease*; *Educated in both Ireland and France, John Dease became a doctor* ...

Doctor Dease became a doctor and was dead like the rest of them. Before you could say "Doctor Dease, please come to emergency," he was dead. If you have been written about, she brooded, if your photograph has been taken and somebody is looking at it, you're dead, you belong to the legions of the shades. When you die, she remembered, you turned into a star. It was an old Pawnee idea, according to Paul. The idea calmed her. She would take her place among the stars.

PAUL CAME HOME AT MIDNIGHT with a cautious bearing, smelling of wine. "I'm drunk," he announced and went upstairs singing and then gargling in the bathroom, a cavernous noise that had grown comforting to her. The gargles, groans, and giggles of their life together comforted her, had always comforted her. She depended on them, took them for granted. She heard him shut the bedroom door. She could join him. Go upstairs and get in bed with him and be nearly content in the familiar warmth that brooded from the both of them and had for years. Instead, she remained on the sofa with her dead friends about her, rustling from the past in the great dictionary of the dead. It was the formality of those written lives that comforted her. They lay there on the pages of history in their grim Canadian glory, stumbling across half-eaten human hands staked to a fire pit outside Sault Ste. Marie, knocking ice off their own bodies with an axe handle, starving to death, eating their tents and fur diapers that had been "beshit in a thousand times," eating buffalo testicles, and fried eel *sagimate* that caused a man to piss a hundred times a day.

She closed her eyes and read her life:

> **Linda Richardson**; *a woman of exceptional intelligence and beauty, spent the last days of the final millennium on the sofa in the aftermath of an unsatisfactory carnal affair with smartass journalist Arthur Gratton, while her husband, Paul Prescot, the world's greatest authority on aboriginal rock art (east of the Rockies) made a fool of himself chasing after the hope of renewed youthfulness in Loretta Ramsay (Waunathoake) part-time waitress, painter, artist, who had assumed a Native background in an increasingly common search for authenticity.*

Good luck with that. Authenticity. Nobody knew where it was anymore. She smiled, somewhat gloomily. Her eyes grew leaden. **De Bonne**, *had a successful but unremarkable career, in 1803 was empowered to hear cases involving crimes committed at sea.* **De Burgo** *(see Burke)*. She didn't. **Decoinge, François,** *one of the best fur traders the North West Company ever had.* **Dejean** … **Delancey***, poisoned by a disgruntled female slave.* Who was that female? They never made it into the book, those disgruntled female slaves. Was there another kind, she wondered.

The words, so many words, tiny, microscopic, thick as plankton. Her father had gifted her with a galaxy of words. More words than she could ever read in a lifetime. Like music, more than she could possibly listen to in her allotted years. She went back over the last lines that had passed blearily in front of her eyes; **Demasduwit (Shendoreth, Mary March, Waunathoake)** Then she rose and checked the spelling against the card magnetized to the fridge. *Waunathoake.* A saintlier woman than me would find this funny, she thought. Or contemptible. She returned to her moorings on the sofa and read the page and a half of text, *Waunathoake, b.c. 1796 married Nonosbawsut and they had one child who died as an infant, 1820 at Bay of Exploits, Nfld.* It was an old story she remembered somewhat, a story that had been expounded breathlessly in a classroom from her childhood by a grey woman with large ears. Her classmates had called their teacher "the elephant lady," and she had terrified them with a dramatic digest of dubious interpretations of aboriginal history in particular; "Eskimos" who lived in snow houses, said "mush" and had babies by rubbing noses together. Indians who tied Brébeuf to a stake, cut out his heart, and ate it. Linda had thought of this as her first sexual act, the erotic beginning for her, having her heart hacked out of her chest and held up to the sky by a boy with dark eyes.

The Elephant Lady was wont to enlighten them, day after day it seemed, with what she called "The Last of the Beothuks," a phrase that to Linda had the ring of one of her mother's musicals to it, and was rendered with some lip smacking. Beneath a framed portrait of Queen Elizabeth in a blue dress and a pearl necklace, the Elephant Lady subjected them to an eager account of a people hunted down for sport, until the last one of them was dragged from the forest to spend the final year of her life in a cage where folks lined up and paid money to see her. She could not avoid a notion of this woman as the original go-go dancer dancing in a cage to psychedelic light.

As a school girl, she had accepted the story without skepticism. She wasn't sure exactly how it differed from the last of the Mohicans, and soon it blended into a vague school board doctrine that held Hurons to be good and Iroquois bad because they ate Father Brébeuf's heart without bothering to cook it. "This is what he suffered for Christ," moaned the teacher, "for these Indians, ransomed for the Son of God's blood!" The woman clutched her skinny self and stared at them, her fingers indicated it was all their fault. A strange heat filled the room and Linda suspected there would be no end to having her heart cut out and eaten by boys.

Twenty years later, she had read her husband's article *The Archaic Dorset And Beothuk Peoples of Newfoundland*. The Beothuks, according to Paul, had largely died of tuberculosis, their lungs gone, or they had been killed in clashes with trappers and European fisherman, and frequently they had died in an ongoing war with the Mi'kmaq over resources. One of the last of them, a woman known by a variety of names, was kidnapped by a British raiding party who then killed the woman's husband for having the audacity to want her back. His killers were placed on trial, acquitted, and his widow led a short and dreary life as a domestic servant before she died horribly of tuberculosis.

Linda lay on the sofa listening to the heavy substance of her husband crushing the mattress above her, groaning the bed legs against the old floor of the house.

Waunathoake, she read it again, alarmed that the rise and fall of the green phlegm in the woman's throat was taking place in her own throat. The woman, heaving on starched sheets hour after hour in a room lit by lamps, wondering what was happening to her body, her baby dead, her people, her man? Linda let it all collapse beneath her eyelids, a desolate Labradorian landscape of stunted trees, eight gaunt men, black rags against a sky without sun, guilt-ridden bodies, murmuring recitations of prayer, having arrived at the end of life really. At last, they lay the woman's body on the ground hoping that some of her people would claim her, surrounding her with gifts of sewing needles and musket balls.

Linda startled awake, unsure of where she had been, then retrieved the heavy book from beside her, and finished reading the tale. The story ended with a last remaining band of Beothuks who gathered up Waunathoake's body and lay it next to her husband's. Years later a group of white men in a failed attempt to make contact with the Beothuks found her resting place, a few shredded bits of black cloth whipped in the wind, the crows raving and hollering over top.

Linda got off the sofa and stood in the room staring out the window at the illuminated dome of the Greek temple. One thirty in the morning; it burned a warm amber from inside. Ghosts, she thought. Every building in the city was filled with ghosts, crouching beside the furnace, where the skis were held together with frayed string; Mississaugan women groaned in labour, or tossed glowing hot stones into woven baskets filled with water. The spirits of people who came before her, the laughter of their children, the barking of skinny, tethered dogs. They struggled to be remembered. They could not stay hidden. Their whispers came up from the earth, and through the floorboards and lived in the air. They whispered to her.

Waunathoake. Loretta Ramsay. Linda Richardson.

Standing rigidly in the room, she was suddenly angry. She longed for the thrilling life as much as anyone, often two shots of Bushmills or a puff of hash did the trick. In a pinch she could un-shelve her dust jacket first edition of *Under the Volcano* and open it anywhere, "*where did we go … in what far place did we wander hand in hand.*" In more extreme cases, a tall man with a navy tattoo…. Aside from men, books, and television reruns of *Dr. Quinn Medicine Woman*, she was not sure what she had the right to ask for. Certainly not to wrap herself up in suffering that wasn't hers.

Linda attempted to calm herself. So what if someone had given herself a Native name? People did. She could do it. **Linda Prescot**, née Richardson (Thanadelthur, Pocahontas, Madonna, The Iron Lady) *daughter of a sultry Basque flamenco dancer, disguised herself as a boy and was* *hired on as carpenter's helper to Cook's fateful voyage to Vancouver Island where she was kidnapped by the Swampy Cree and forced to become North America's first exotic dancer.* She again reminded herself, without pride or shame, that she was the bone-white progeny of ancestors from the coal pits of Northern England and treeless enclosures of Scotland. She had little desire to be otherwise.

Let the other ones do that. There were so many of them now, so many sparky young beauties running around. The world couldn't get enough of them. The media fed on them. This one had appropriated a name freighted with misery, a self-dramatizer. What was more contemptible than self-drama, she thought? Enough went wrong without it. All she had to do was wait ten or twenty years and she'd find herself covered in enough of her own bruises, she'd have no interest in parading around in someone else's. Or even have room on her body to put those bruises, she thought.

Linda waited a few moments until the heat subsided in her and then went to the sofa and slept.

POSTSCRIPT 5: ROAD KILL

SHE TURNED IN AT A paved lot on the banks of a crashing river and ate tuna fish sandwiches outdoors in the sun. The fish tasted like tin, not even fresh tin. The air was rich with the smell of fir trees. Ten minutes later she was back on the highway over the Batchawana, past the *Kozy Kabins*, boarded shut, and into the anonymous forest tracts.

Up front of her, through the windshield, she saw a commotion of some kind; then it became clear. A moose had wandered onto the highway and been horribly T-boned there. Now it lay obscenely wounded and enormous, like the end of the world she thought, lying on its side, unable to get up. As she sped toward the spot, she saw an emergency vehicle with a flashing yellow light parked next to the animal, a slender man in a brown official-looking shirt crouched on the highway administering the rites of a bush religion it looked like, murmuring consolations and holding his hand piteously against the warm flesh, stroking the fur. Linda thought that the man was crying, she saw it. His face was stricken. The animal too, she couldn't bear that, to see the stricken face. She was about to cry herself. Her own stricken body. The suffering of animals. She couldn't tolerate it. What had they done except refuse to be human? To love their children? The beast was too magnificent to be dead, it mustn't be dead, she thought. *It must not be dead. He had to save the animal.* She told herself wildly that Paul could do it, he could save the animal. He would pull some arcane knowledge from a hat and cure it. The man out on the highway in the brown shirt. He could do it too. There were times when she had faith in what men could do. The brown wool waved in the wind, whipped by the passing vehicles. In a moment it was gone, she saw it in reverse in the mirror. Gone. The ash was in her throat. In the fleeting appearance and disappearance of that dying animal her grief took hold of her. She was in grief for living things that wandered from the wilderness, or into it, and were struck dead by forces that made no sense to them. She grieved her husband.

17

ERRATIC

PAUL CAME DOWN THE STAIRS in his housecoat, barely cinched at the waist, thudding heavily and erratically, like a boulder come loose from the side of a hill. An erratic. She had married an erratic. I wanted erotic she thought, and instead I got an erratic. She lay tenaciously on her side on the sofa, as though on a life raft, with a tattered comforter tugged over top of her. Her eyes were open, Paul saw the flecks of bronze in them. He also sensed that her eyes had been open all night, looking through everything. Looking through him in particular, looking through the holes in him, the empty holes. A volume of her *Dictionary of Canadian Biography* lay open, face down on the floor. He felt suddenly stupidly jealous of it. Steady snow came down outside the window.

"Good morning."

"It's snowing," she answered.

"Yes, snowing." His fingers went to his face as if to take the stubble off his jowls. He saw snow coming down, swirling, hesitant to make contact with the ground, apprehensive about landing. He blinked at her. "Is there coffee?"

"Did you know Loretta Ramsay is the last of Beothuks? The very last one. Forced to wear hoop earrings and attend gallery openings at which she is gazed upon by middle-aged men like you. It's a sad story. Very sad."

"Coffee," he repeated, carefully.

"Infected by a very common and virulent strain of guilt, she's forced to dance half-naked, night after night, in downtown night-clubs, high on designer drugs, until she avenges the crimes that call to us from the past, and having done that she drops dead in the front seat of the car of a married advertising executive who is driving her back to his penthouse condo in the hope of sleeping with her. Very sad story. 'The Last of the It Girls.'"

"I gather there's no coffee?"

"It doesn't bother you?"

"It bothers me," he said. "No coffee."

"It doesn't bother you that your friend is traipsing around under the name of the last member of an extinct tribe? That's too pathetic."

He went to the window and examined the familiar stern outline of the church, lit up with floodlights, every window in the place fiercely lit. The church resembled a surreal birthday cake offered up to an indifferent child, a child who did not like cake at all. "Fortress God," he said, and turned quickly on her. "How do you know she isn't? How do you know she's not the last surviving member of some doomed tribe? A Transformer, working medicine we don't know anything about. She's after something, like everyone. She's been put here for a reason. Like you. Even me."

"The woman is a fake. She's wearing dream catcher earrings. She's wrapped herself up in shells, she's ..." Linda felt the intoxicating rush of a full-blown rant coming on her. She was good at ranting, it was a skill she had picked up from her mother, who had levelled elaborate curses at just about everything, including an upholstered chair. "She is really that most despicable of things." Linda thought she might be shouting, but was pleased to determine she was speaking calmly. "An artist. Don't you get the sense that even the gods are sick of artists? How many times can you piss on Jesus Christ or smear menstrual blood on a wall? Or talk about your process?" She was up now, peering again at the postcard on the fridge. "Behold the artist," she said. "Fakes. That's what it's come down to."

"Nobody's a fake," he said suddenly. "Not even God. I had a dream last night, I'm sure I did. I just can't remember it. You tell me is that the same as not dreaming? Did I dream? Did I save the world in a dream I can't remember? Did I just dream me doing that? Or her? Or you?" He stared intensely at her. "Who are you? Loretta? A Ramsay? Or anyone? You as much as anyone are the last of your kind. You're the last and the first. You have no choice. You were strung up on a cross. Your husband was shot dead in a raid." He turned to the window, to the snow that fell as soft as a child's blanket and to the amber light that burned from the church.

"Paul," she said softly. "You should be careful." She did not understand why she had spoken those words. He gave no indication of hearing her but in a moment replied, "We should all be careful."

18

THERE'S SOMETHING WRONG
WITH YOUR WATER

... when the world has been befouled and the waters turned bitter by disrespect...

THE PROPHECY OF THE SEVEN FIRES

IN JANUARY, HE LEFT THE house with a throbbing toothache while the church looked down on him with disapproval. The bells refused to chime anymore. He remembered when they chimed. What man could ever forget when the bells chimed? Or the woman who was involved? Four times that day they hectored a solemn diphthong as he lugged two suitcases into a cab and drove away to take rooms in what he hoped was a fleapit, at the Waverly Hotel.

"Take rooms." That's how he put it to her without a wince of shame. He would take rooms, like Beau Brummell. He would take rooms next to the mission for the homeless, the funeral home and across from the madhouse where they put 10,000 volts into the brains of lost street poets. He would pay his penance. That's how he put it to her. He would take rooms in the bleached edifice of the Waverly Hotel where paranoid drunken poets hauled meagre belongings from room to room in the hope the RCMP was spying on them. He would live as he had always thought he wanted, the way a man should live, among the salt of the earth, a dropout with a past lounging beneath smoke in the scrubbed white lobby where a television hung from the ceiling, broadcasting clips of war, shootings, and spoiled rivers. He would drink cheap wine with the refugees from the Six Nations and stay drunk all the time.

In fact, it was too late for any of that. The Waverly had flipped management on a daily basis and was now a tottering strip bar from which the dancers stormed out unpaid and cursing on Friday afternoon, kicking over chairs and giving the middle finger to the manager. The salt-of-the-earth poets had performed their last righteous *delirium tremens* on the stained mattresses, and were now dead and forgotten.

LINDA DIDN'T KNOW WHAT HER husband did in that place. Or much care. She stayed in the house alone, a monastic, confiding only to Rover even though Rover did not belong to her. He was merely on loan from the Holderlichs the way men were on loan. Not for the first time she longed for a child, a chattering and thoughtless infant that she could gibber agreeably with. She shut that thought down very quickly. She dusted off old vinyl LPs and played them. She perused an art book on Arshile Gorky and imaged herself married to the man. *Goodbye my lovelies* he'd written to his wife and daughter before snapping his neck.

Against her better inclinations she read too much Manrique in translation but couldn't remember whether the river that flowed into the sea was death. Or whether death was the dried-up river that no longer reached the ocean because it was dammed by a hydro project. Or was love the river and life the sea? *Nuestras vidas son los rios.* She slept again. She woke, she shuffled from room to room, fell into a river that was life or love or death. She came ashore brimming

with confusion and undertook a dismal and semi-conscious campaign of going to bed with people. It was not difficult to meet men.
She began with a silent, forty-year-old polymath with haunted eyes
and subject to sudden bouts of narcolepsy of which she was envious.
He was an authority on the Russian ghetto and the writings of
Mordecai Specktor and the recipient of a court decree that allowed
him to see his six-year-old son on Wednesday evenings and alternate
weekends. After him, she crashed into a bearded and articulate
Cypriot named Aris, short for Aristides, who clung to memories of
a war about which she knew nothing and insisted on photograph-
ing her naked. (Kids Fridays, Saturdays, and alternate weekends.) "I
will maintain you like this forever," he promised solemnly. "Great,"
she said. "No thanks." Then she stopped.

IN THE MORNING, JETLINERS DREW contrails in front of the sun. She
advanced toward an apartment building that towered above the
trees. She passed the locked doors of jazz clubs and locked bicycles.
She sought the man's name on a gleaming glass screen in the lobby.
It was there with the Greyhursts, Greenes, and Gluckmans, she
saw her finger pressing a button beside a number beside a name.
"Come up," he said with only slight annoyance, as if he had willed
her to this spot by a spell. She went up. She walked a cloistered
hall of carpets, with ultra-moderne light fixtures jutting from wallpaper and rapped at a door. The glass eye glared at her. Let me in,
she thought, and immediately he came to the door and opened
it. His shirt was unbuttoned. "I don't really have time to fuck you
right now," he said.

"Still, it's gallant of you to say. I need to pee." She went directly
to his bathroom, a stainless cubicle that reeked of his up-to-date
masculinity. She came out and parked herself on a cold leather
sofa. Around the room his belongings had been arranged in

fastidious heaps, Soviet-era paintings neatly hung, generals encased in medals on canvas, the brutalists and the Vorticists, the victors of Stalingrad, the purged, the unpurged, law books arranged authoritatively on built-in bookcases. Tiny figurines of twentieth century dictators arranged like chachkas. His apartment was small, deliberately small to ensure it could never be shared with anyone.

"Do you have any idea what time it is?" he said.

"No, I don't." Behind Arthur's head she saw a shelf on which a stack of micro-cassettes rose up in a precise towering structure, almost to the ceiling. He had two televisions going. News crawls slid from left to right across two screens. A seventy-year-old farmer had been pinned five hours under a pregnant cow, berries had gone dry on the bushes and were falling like shot. The bees had gone missing. She'd heard it before. The world was going away. Like the bees.

"It will rot your brain, Arthur."

She watched him suck in the screens like an endless and shimmering mound of cocaine.... *Sex fiend teacher reinstated after lengthy trial*.... It seemed that Arthur was swelling in size with each fragment of news, each morsel of information. As the bombs went off, as each catastrophe pushed the previous one away, his head shot closer to the ceiling; a foul gas entered the membrane of his body and inflated him. She knew of these creatures, she'd read of them; Paul was a minor authority, or claimed to be; Wendigos that roamed in her land. Insatiably stinky beasts that ate human flesh and were afflicted with a hunger that grew worse the more they fed.... *Concert pianist bites hand of flight attendant*.... Feed me. Linda felt the apartment growing cold around her. The skin on Arthur's face pulled itself more tautly across the bones, the hollows became more sunken. Suddenly he was unclean, he suffered from suppurations of the flesh. His body had grown to preposterous heights.

"It will rot your brain," she said, with no idea what she was referring to ... *Avian flu threat requires extermination of 50 million birds; experts....* How much is fifty million? ... *Annihilate them all says assistant deputy minister....* Annihilate what exactly?... *Headless man found in topless bar.* Lying now on the leather of Arthur's couch, she longed for the days when headless men could be counted on to be found in topless bars.

"It was beauty," she said suddenly, sitting up.

"What?"

"It was beauty that killed the beast. There's your story Arthur, it was beauty that killed the beast. It's always beauty that kills the beast."

From the twin screens the words, the images, the faces, the noise, the experts, the villains, the bugs, the vaccines and victims crawled into the room. *Annihilate them all ... put your faith in ...* She closed her eyes ... *birds drop from the sky while seventy-year-old sex fiend teacher bites off finger of flight attendant playing Mozart from beneath pregnant cow, film at eleven ...* She went to the sink and tried to wash it away with a long glass of water, but the water stank of the swamp, of an industrial swamp, and tasted of rust.

"There's something wrong with your water."

"What do you mean my water?"

He came to her side, took the glass from her hand, sipped it and pursed his lips like a professional wine taster. "Perfectly good city water." He was dubious though. He'd lost any sense of what water was meant to taste like. Was there supposed to be a tang of fish in it? Surely the fish shit in it. Where else would fish go to shit?

Arthur finished snapping on his shirt. His briefcase made its way into his hand. He was prepared to impose himself on the day. There was work to be done. It was not her work. It was work for him.

"The door locks behind you," he said. He seemed worried she might not leave. He would return ten hours from now and find her still here, having washed his laundry, wearing an apron and popping a casserole into the oven for him. His life over.

"Yes. The door locks behind me. I understand that."

"Good." He smiled. "Have a nice day." The door swung shut. A black door. The man had a black door with a white cycloptic hole in it through which he scrutinized his visitors. The door closed with a crunch. She was cast away. Like Robinson Crusoe. It struck her as wrong that she didn't have a goat. She had a man, Friday. It was in fact Friday. But she didn't have a goat. Every woman should have a goat. Instead of tragedy she should have a goat.

The day was threatening to unroll in front of her. She was unrolling herself; she knew the signs; the lack of rain outside the window, or hail, no pestilence of frogs. The day was not doing anything except being sunny and sickeningly beautiful. Like the most perfect day possible. Even the birds were going at it. She missed her husband, her ridiculous husband who did not satisfy her. She reached into the pocket of her jeans as if to find him there. She missed a life of monotonous travel over long roads, the smooth blacktop. The miles piling up. Their windshield time together. Rivers whipping underneath them. She missed the folds of Paul's body where she had gone. She missed the way he scratched himself. She missed his pronouncements, the pompous ones in particular.

She took up Arthur's phone and punched in the number for Bulwark Books.

"It's Linda," she said breathlessly. "Linda Richardson." In speaking her name, she felt she had uttered an extraordinary lie. "Vanessa, please," she said. "Vanessa Wainright." Vanessa was the sort of name a woman should have. A Vee name with its hint of Veritas and Verisimilitude and Virtue. If only her name was Vanessa, she would not unroll. The world would not burn as quickly as it burned.

"I'm sorry Vanessa's in a meeting. Oh, wait, no she isn't, one minute please."

Finally the music clicked off.

"Linda? There might be a seed catalogue that needs proofreading. It's all I have."

19

WHO ARE YOU?

"Tolerant to Black Rot and Downey Mildew, the Arcadia broccoli is one of North America's finest stress tolerant hybrids, and provides impressive yields with good dark green colour and outstanding side shoot development...."

BETWEEN THE BLACK ROT AND the development of side shoots the Holderlich's cat came through an open window and gave her a rather chilling look before slinking out of the room. Apparently, she didn't cut it. She no longer made the grade. There was no other audience, just mirrors on the walls of the rooms and a critical cat. The page proofs glared at her. She pushed them aside, stood up, and just as suddenly sat down.

Unlike the Arcadia broccoli, she felt herself intolerant to Black Rot and Downey Mildew. She felt Black Rot and Downey Mildew had infested the airwaves and the lint in the carpet, that she herself was a breeding ground for both of them. She was alone in a house with a growing residue of mildew, black rot, and a streetwise cat that didn't belong to her. There was no audience. No children. There had been a cone biopsy, a second one performed in a white room in a hospital downtown. It came back to her very suddenly. Mostly she was unconscious. Squamous Dysplasia. The drugs came on and she'd thought that squamous dysplasia was located in British Columbia, and that she had gone there to hide from a bad relationship. The anesthetist possessed a bloodshot eye. The doctor had spoken to her. Please. This is very important, I need to tell you this. Are you clear? She was clear. Everything was clear.

To her husband her complications had been a much-longed-for get out of jail free card. During their journey home, after her release from hospital, he found it difficult not to skip through the streets beneath the white chestnut blossoms. To not look relieved was an effort. He largely viewed children as shrunken adults with little experience on the trail, deadly on a portage, and ignorant of carbon dating or geothermal physics. This did not stop children from adoring him, following him, and stalking him. To his alarm children and small animals routinely mistook him for a combination of Francis of Assisi and the ice cream man.

She closed her eyes and at that moment the doorbell gonged and she went to it automatically, like a sleepwalker. No one was there. A box sat on the porch. She did not have to sign for anything. She brought the box into the kitchen table and opened it. Fifty copies of a paperback issue of *The Apocalypse Already; Rock Writing and the End of the World*, by Paul Prescot. The book had been an irritant, a secretive little project that, for the first time, he did not desire her assistance on. It was barely more than a revised version of the "Legs That Walk by Themselves" chapter from *Pictographs, Petroglyphs and Paradigms of the Apocalypse*; a closer look at the rock painting site on Coldwell Peninsula.

She slid a copy from the surface and opened it:

The apocalypse enters water as e-coli, and enters the intestines of domesticated fowl in the form of type A avian influenza that will demand their slaughter in the growing millions. Prepare for a new virality. Prepare for the age of the virus.

They enter our ears in the songs that do not belong to us, but are penned by men of the indoor variety who refer to what they do as "music." This is not music, but the death of music, songs are not chanted from the origins of our dreams but rather excreted from the rust of our machinery ...

She closed the book and held it between her fingers. The volume consisted of 126 pages; her husband had paid several thousand dollars to have it printed in an edition of five hundred. A hundred of those copies had wended their way to academic journals, to curators of sombre museums. The rest would be in a box like this. She held the book in her hand, unable to stop herself from reading. She had never been able to stop herself from reading. The cover showed the Legs That Walk By Themselves, a pair of legs painted in red ochre, and a prophecy woven in wampum, later spoken to an assembly of elders by an eighty-nine-year-old man, grandfather William Commanda; *that at the waning of this fire there would come someone holding the promise of great joy and salvation, but that promise would prove to be a false promise.*

Her husband's linking between a telling of the Seven Fires prophecy and the aboriginal rock art of the Canadian shield was a stretch that had caused him some professional embarrassment. He'd identified that promise as science, ("a system for killing people remorselessly") and linked it to a host of diseases that he saw predicted in the hybrid of human and non-human symbols defining Canadian rock art. The microbe in the pig or the bat that went into the human. The false prophet was any book he happened to disapprove of, which was most of them except the 1887 edition of *The Iroquois Book of Rites* translated by Horatio Hale, and anything by Pauline Johnson. Paul had demonstrated to his own satisfaction, if no one else's, that the armies of sickness and greed would amass and one day be defeated, or not be defeated, in a battle taking place in a dream. That dream would unfold on a holy landscape, the rock of the Coldwell Peninsula somewhere between Dead Horse Creek and Black Dog Road, ten miles down from the truck stop diner at Neys. The promise would be a false one. Death would come on the air and in the water and the blood of the bird and in the heart of the pig and the brains of cows. A great pestilence would appear out of the open pits of the old Congo. The machines getting smaller and smaller. The animals killed. The children with small machines in their hands.

Linda realized she was wearing her husband's bathrobe. This disturbed her. Why wasn't she dressed in her own clothing, building her own story, dream by dream? I am, she insisted to herself. I am the teller of my own story. She loomed over top of the page proofs of *Vesuvius's 26th Anniversary Seed Catalogue*. A popular improved coreless variety with excellent quality and good flavour. Vegetables, she wondered? Or men? The improved coreless variety. There was no shortage of the coreless ones. She heard them on the radio and television, eagerly holding forth. *A popular improved coreless variety with excellent quality and good flavour. Sow early and follow with a second planting . . .*

Yes, sow early and follow with a second planting. Perhaps a third planting. Then throw the whole bunch of them into a ditch and see what happens. Maybe they would flower.

From outside the window, the squirrels screamed at her. Who are you, they chattered, You don't know who you are. You are not Native, not Aboriginal, not the first of people.

She had no idea who she was. She had grown accustomed to being defined by what she wasn't. Non-Native, nonchalant. Increasingly nonsensical, often to herself. She was not *of* the people. All those Indigenous language words for people did not apply, did not take in her tribe of drunks and civil engineers and audio technicians who watched television, did crossword puzzles, and increasingly sat in front of computer screens scratching themselves. She was *chimookoman*. She knew the term from Paul's writing, or thought she did. It meant, to her knowledge, "non-Native," which to her mind described just about everything she knew, but it didn't place her. She was non-everything. It struck her with some force that without Paul she was alone in the world and that without her, so was he.

Linda forced herself to sit again at the desk and took comfort in the knowledge she belonged in the chair. The chair was made in China or assembled there. She belonged in it. This was something. It was better than nothing. She belonged with those who ate spanakopita on Danforth Avenue and sold spice from roti shops on Queen. She was an itinerant member of the pale tribe cast out from the coal pits of Manchester and the enclosures of Caledonia, a literary caretaker of the Heirloom carrot: *Sow early and follow with a second planting*.

She fingered Paul's book. The war, she read, the outcome, would take place in dreams. Of course it would. She had read it all before. When it was over, a boy would appear. Paul had learned of this boy from his ethnographic readings. A boy with shining eyes. She read on: *Who are we and what are the chants that move us from one dream to another? What are the stories that made us possible before speech? Who sings us into existence now that the song has been reduced to a ditty sung by a teenager executing doubtful martial arts kicks?*

It made her smile, his ranting. It was tiresome, but it was real. It had a stink to it. Whatever he was trying to sell, it had her Heirloom carrot copy beat to hell, even if the Heirloom did have flexibility in the field and long term storage capabilities.

She turned the book over and confronted his face in black and white. The face was as common to her as an old rug, one that was constantly on the verge of getting tossed out but had faithfully managed to keep her feet warm through many winters. She expected such a face to be fringed by a grey beard in a counter-attack against his receding hair. While she was thinking, the telephone rang.

20

YOUR EX-HUSBAND

Picture writing is the lowest stage of writing in use amongst men. It is crude and cumbersome. Many tribes of Indians still use this method of conveying their ideas, though many others, to their credit, have learned the language of their conquerors."

JOHN MCLEAN M.A. PH.D. 1888

THE DEVICE BLARED ACROSS THE spaces of the house, incessant, filled with needs. It brooked no possibility of going away or dying unanswered. She rushed headlong toward the machine, despising herself for doing it. Answer me. The world is collapsing, female snails off the coast of B.C. are developing male genitalia. The ice caps are turning into circumpolar toxic slushies, and your marriage has split on the rocks like an overstuffed oil freighter. Answer me. Respond to my needs.

She rushed headlong to answer the ringing machine, not because she wanted to, but in response to the desperate neediness of the technology itself. The world was so full of desperate and lonely telephones, desperately lonely machines, all of them on the verge of suicide, ringing furiously into empty rooms, hungry for contact, calling out for phone sex, for pizza, for anything, wanting to be cradled, longing for something, for a connection, or any sort of hand to hold them. A human hand.

Answer me.

She hustled on at the urging of it, her feet encased in a pair of Paul's enormous wool socks. The rest of her remained wrapped in his white bathrobe. Linda got to the machine and put the plastic to her lips. An idiotic voice sounded, *her* voice, *hello*, it said, the way idiots answered the phone. She was mortified. What sort of idiotic person answered the telephone by saying hello? "Yes," she tried, and this was worse. Yes was no improvement. Yes was cursed by its hissing snake sound at the end and its geisha-like subservience. Yes was crazy. She realized with horror women had been answering telephones since the last ice age and all they had to show for it was someone else's stained bathrobe and a pair of horribly itchy wool socks that didn't fit. No, she thought. No was the only appropriate response to the telephone. Everyone on the planet should pick up the phone and politely, firmly say, "No."

A blackness, filled with pricks of white, hissed in her ear before it gave way to a man's heavy voice.

"'Five years have passed. Five summers with the length of five long winters.'" There was a pause at this moment for heavy breathing then the voice resumed. "'And again I hear these waters, rolling from their mountain springs with a soft inland murmur. Once again do I behold the steep and lofty cliffs that on a wild secluded scene impress thoughts of a more deep seclusion ...'" The beefy voice ended. "Pretty good huh? Tintern Abbey, William Wordsworth who did not sleep with his sister. Unlike like Byron who did. As for William Wordsworth and his problematic penis, he went off wandering lonely as a cloud and impregnated some French hottie, correct me if I'm wrong, Annette Vallon of Calais who had his baby. Meanwhile Windbag Willy runs off to spend six weeks with said sister at Windy

Brow Farmhouse where he wrote scads of poetry and took long and meaningful walks. With his sister. Settled down by the fire. With his sister. But no hanky panky right?"

"It was beauteous evening," Linda answered, "calm and free. He was trying to burst his mortal coil."

"Oh, I'll bet he was." Arthur cleared his throat and went on. "'That time is passed and all its aching joys are no more, and all its dizzy raptures. All its dizzy raptures.'" He interrupted himself with a groan. "Did I mention that I have an overwhelming desire to have thee?"

"Who?"

"Thou. You. Thee thou and you. And your sister. Do you have one? Sweetheart," he breathed again. "It is only thee thou and you that I desire so sweetly —"

"You'll have sex with mud," Linda said abruptly.

"I will not."

"You will."

"You're naked?" he said.

"I'm wearing my husband's wool socks and his housecoat."

"Your ex-husband."

He made the point of reminding her of this. To her it did not ring true. Paul was not her ex-husband. He was like carpet, the air in the house. It would be there even if she wasn't.

"Sweetheart." This time the word was made clinical. "I have your ex-husband's book. His latest. It came to the office in the mail. A remarkable piece of nonsense by the way. Would you object if I ruined the man? Ruined him completely I mean? Nothing personal."

Linda had a vision of the cold room she'd live in when she was ruined too. All the pornographic places of her mind exposed on the front pages of newspapers. It was all her fault. Her filthy mind.

"What are you talking about, Arthur? I would have thought you'd had enough of that. After that man. The one you wrote about."

"That guy had too many problems," he said, carefully.

The man was a school teacher, or had been, who got himself stuck in a back room of the world wide web where he called himself Peter Pan and detailed vivid fantasies about boys. Arthur had uncovered him, disrobed him and left him beneath a headline that stated *Sex Teacher*, or *Teacher Sex*, she couldn't remember. She remembered that the man's school had fired him and that he had swallowed a massive amount of oxycontin and had gone into a coma.

"He was a perv."

"*You're* a perv," she said.

"Yes, but I'm a perv for women and that makes me normal. Like pie. And you're just saying that because it heats you up. You're naked, you're on the phone, and if you don't have sex you'll become one of those burden-to-society women who write novels and go on about their creative process and appear on talk shows."

His voice drained at once of its moaning and became cool and inquisitorial. "Did you know there is someone who insists your husband is a fraud? Other than me."

"The entire British Columbia Rock Art Foundation insists my husband's a fraud. Even my husband insists he's a fraud. A real genuine fraud. Not a fake fraud, a real one."

"It's a woman. She outs him as a fraud. Some artist-type. Her name is, get this, Wan … Wana …

"Waunathoake?"

"Yes," he said. "You know her?"

"I don't know anything."

"She said she did them. The paintings on the rocks. She said it was her who painted them."

"So?"

"She says all those ancient rock paintings that your husband wrote about? Guess what? It was her. She did them, the big one anyway."

"The big one?"

"On Lake Superior?"

"You don't mean the Agawa Rock? Someone wrote a description of the Agawa Rock in the eighteen-thirties, I spent a month in a canoe staring at it. If she painted that thing Arthur you really have a story."

"It's in his book, in fact it's in both his books, *Pictographs, Petroglyphs and the Paradigms of the Apocalypse*. It's all over his new book too; *Apocalypse Already*, I've got a copy. Self published, how quaint is that?"

She heard the distant thunk of a book hitting the floor. Apparently he'd dropped it.

"Chapter Five, the legs that walk by themselves. Are you ready for this? 'The legs that walk by themselves, an essay on the end of the world.' Really, I'm not making this up. Have you read this?"

"Are you interviewing me Arthur? Because I could interview you. I could get you to talk about your handcuff collection."

"Legitimate research. I was given those at a police conference. This woman. Her name is Loretta Ramsay, I mean it's also Wanny-wooky-wawa or something, but it's also Loretta Ramsay. She says there are pictographs on some Lake Superior outcrop. Port Coldwell? The ones your ex-husband wrote about. His theory is based on those paintings. Am I right?

"On the advice of my attorney I have no comment to make at this time."

"Well, guess what? She painted them. It's what she does. It's what she says she does, listen to this, 'a Time Keeper at the Eastern Door.' That's what she calls herself. What exactly is a Time Keeper at the Eastern Door?"

"Don't ask me, Arthur. You should talk to my husband about it."

"If she wants to call herself a time keeper why not get herself a watch? 'A Timekeeper at the Eastern Door, her work seeks to avenge the violence and injustice that call to us and haunt our dreams and history.' She says she painted the rocks at Port Coldwell years ago when she was still a teenager. Your husband dates them to the sixteenth century, or earlier. That would make him look foolish. Even more than foolish."

The telephone clung to her ear like a fungal conk on the side of a tree. An empty hiss spewed from it. The machine had never evolved she realized. It formed in the primordial slime a billion years ago, and it remained there, an organism for spreading lies and loneliness around the Earth.

"It never evolved," she said.

"What?"

"Nothing. I don't know what I'm talking about. Neither do you. Neither does she. Have you ever seen a rock painting, Arthur? You can't fake them."

"You can fake anything," he said cheerfully. "You can even fake the fakes. Trust me. She signed the damn things. L. R. She signed her name."

"Those letters came later. Centuries later, Paul thinks some trapper put them there in the early eighteen-hundreds. A French-Canadian named Robitaille. Leroi Robitaille. L. R."

"That's what he says. That's not what she says. She says she painted those letters with crushed ochre and a special fluid from the swimming bladder of a sturgeon, and that she painted them from the blood of the suffering. Your husband says that those images are ancient and predict the end of the world. Have I got that right?"

"Ask him."

"I would if I could find him. Every time I phone his house, I get you. His loving wife. You are such an easy person to have an affair with really. Your husband is always out trying to start an Academy of Rain Dancing or something and there you are at home. I've made some inquiries about getting it tested, the paint, I mean. There's a chemist from the college, a former park superintendent up there in Terrace Bay, works at a community college as a chem professor. He knows the site. He's going to go out there and take a few scrapings so we can date them."

"Scrapings?"

"I've talked to him, he's willing to take some scrapings for the lab. That ought to settle it."

She could tell that in Arthur's mind that it was already settled.

"This is not going to be good," said the voice.

"No," she said.

"For your husband I mean. Your ex-husband."

"Do you want to know about my husband?" she said suddenly. "When he was a child, he never played cowboys and Indians. His mother told me. He played cowboys and Metis. Guess who won?" She had no idea why she was telling this story. She hung up the phone and watched four pigeons shoot like bullets outside across the frame of the window.

21

LORETTA RAMSAY

At length the grown-up daughter began to beat the war-drum, mutter
wild songs and question destiny, or, as they term it, "dream." She had a dream,
in which it was revealed to her that the only method by which to obtain
consolation — that is revenge —, was by sacrificing her lover."

JOHANN GEORG KOHL, 1860

WITHOUT KNOWING WHAT SHE WAS doing Loretta Ramsay began her search for herself in the crevices of her body and the body of boys and young men. Later, she searched in men, older men. She enjoyed their bulk. It was the first place she thought to look. There had been a mother, but she didn't look there. As far as she was concerned her mother was dead, even though the woman lived in a bungalow on leased land belonging to the Golden Lake Band where she watched television and scissored coupons from newspapers delivered to her door every day.

There had been a father, but he was gone. What she remembered of him was a room, darkened with the shut door indicating he had been there in the first place. Sometimes that door opened and she saw a man who looked like him in the darkness, looking for something on the floor, his wallet? For her? He had a face made of stone. She knew someone else was in there as well. Her, sitting on the floor. The room remained dark, but sometimes the door opened and she discovered that by force of her own mind she could make it close.

There had been a father. For a time, he drove the freight trains but his trains had the habit of jumping track and ending up in a farmer's pasture or in a field of mustard. He drank and he gambled with a group of men who came up from Minnesota in a black car and went back over the border with eighteen years of his savings. After that, he became a lineman on a lightly-used section of track, and ran several trap lines up the Goulais River, taking out pine marten and mink. Sometimes a fisher pelt brought in two hundred and fifty dollars and he'd be gone from the house for weeks. She delighted in his absence. She wanted her father to be dead and frequently said he was dead. His ship, the U.S. Coast Guard cutter *Mesquite*, broke up on a reef in Lake Superior while retrieving signal buoys, he died attempting to rescue a shipmate. She liked the sound of it, and the way it swelled her presence.

Through the years, she saw a succession of counsellors and juvenile probation officers, and social workers and a gentle forensic psychologist with a Sigmund Freud beard and pipe-smoker's cough who felt obliged to remind her, softly, that her father had shot himself on a railway siding between Kenora and Thunder Bay over a gambling debt. Surely, she had some feelings about that? He also felt obliged to remind her that her father had been a bigamist in the manner of more than one railway man; possessing a family outside Kenora, and another far down the line, under the same name but slightly different spelling, in Weyburn, Saskatchewan.

She searched for herself in old alleys of brick or in grotty highway underpasses, drinking wine with two boys from the Pays Platt

Band, twin brothers, one of them deaf and subject to savage teasing. She fell easily into drink and drugs and music that left her ears ringing. For four months she clutched a soggy paperback by Carl Jung and read it emphatically until her eyes swam. She searched for herself on dance floors fired by strobe lights, in rooms of sullen, skinny men who wrote poetry and survived on Jamaican weed and *The Diaries of Anais Nin*. Mostly she searched with crayons and markers on any surface she found. She found herself in the eyes of men desiring her. She told lies easily without expecting them to be believed by anyone, or caring.

There had been a grandmother, Glen, a schoolteacher who for ten years had taught school in a passenger car of the Canadian Pacific Railway that stood uncoupled on a siding by the sawmill outside Keewatin and was heated by a coal stove. Every morning the deer came to the windows to muzzle seed from the hands of the kids. She had seen photographs: Glen unfathomably pretty with hair up top and held in place by pins. Through those pictures, she discovered she had a fondness for old things, for looking things up, for the archival nature of everything. She examined pictures of the warm faces of the Cree kids, grinning next to the blond braids of girls who were not Cree and whose eyes were as big as plates.

Glen put the money away for her after her father was found in the snow. During the years of her mother's retreat into beekeeping, and a range of wilder therapies that saw her confined to an orgone box and screaming "mother" while writhing on the floor with people she'd never met before, her grandmother took care of her. Glen believed the dark was coming and that it was a woman's duty to turn the lights on. She died of pulmonary thrombosis, seated in a chair with a *Reader's Digest* turned face down on her lap. There was a will. She'd put away money for Loretta's schooling.

The young woman came to the city, filled with notions of

snobbery and homosexuals and criminals who didn't know how to quarter a moose or dress a deer. She entered Toronto at the end of a twenty-hour bus ride across the Shield. In Toronto she met snobbery and homosexuals and criminals and cold people. But she also met women on the way to the bingo who walked the streets in flip flops with their hair in curlers while clutching a ferret in their arms. She met grifters and sharpers and Eritrean cab drivers who had been tortured with burning cigarettes and showed her the scars. The city took her in. She felt the eternal greatness of cities, that they accepted you as you were. They accepted her. Even in misery. The city had no interest in what had happened to her. The noise, the clutter, the banging, the shouts, the fresh rolls, white cups of coffee in the morning, clattering pigeons, Farsi and Hebrew, Portuguese, Italian, Pashto, French, choruses of languages she was free to not understand. She feasted on the city and it feasted on her in turn: she sprawled in the lounges of the Ontario College of Art with a nineteen-year-old girlfriend who'd made love to a Basque bomber on a trip through Spain with her parents. She was aware of the young men, their laughter, their shoulders, seated together. She had a classmate whose father had been murdered by Mossad agents. She let an elderly poet touch her thigh. "Remarkable," he'd uttered, with great conviction, "Remarkable." The city needed her. It fed on young women, grew flush on them. She knew that. The city would starve to death without her. The subways did not run, the streetcars stalled without her. Without her the city simply would not go.

She teemed with herself and laughed a great deal and stayed out late. She was nineteen. She sat in cars driven by men named Kenneth or Tyler. Sophisticated men, she knew not to trust them. She came to accept the shadows and complexity of the city. She felt secrets and ghosts pressing her on the subway platforms and in the coffee stalls. She rode streetcars and lived on Chinese noodles and all-day three-dollar breakfasts. She studied at the New School of Art, under a Mohawk painter named Robert Markle and every Wednesday afternoon they all got drunk after class, sometimes before class. The whole class got drunk. "What kind of Indian am I," Markle asked them. "I've never climbed a tree and I hate fish."

"I want you to look at your work," he told his students. They smelled the beer and the cannabis drifting off of him in sheets, it was not yet nine o'clock in the morning. "I want you to look very closely at your work and try to understand why it's such shit." He burped and went out to use the toilet.

When the streetcar lurched beneath her, or the birds woke her in her bed, she forgot that she was searching for anything or anyone. She stood in front of the Chaim Soutine canvas at the art gallery and watched the colours spill into each other, like the fogs that came up off Lake of the Woods. She missed only the land, the landscapes that she saw when she closed her eyes. She loved the fog, the city fog too, when it rained. She smelled homemade wine fermenting in the basements of entire neighbourhoods. She watched loud men drop hard ceramic balls on sandy bocce courts. Reggae music cracked through pulverized speakers from second floor windows without curtains.

She was an artist. She worked as a waitress in the lounge of a fitness club downtown to make money. The money left as easily as it came. She wore a red Danskin, a red skirt, and pantyhose with a tinge of blue in them. Men looked at her. They gave her money. One afternoon a man with black hair called her to his table. "Here, beautiful," he said, and reached out and held her forcibly around the wrist. She thought he was going to break it. With his other hand he daubed a piece of bread roll in the steak juice on his plate and smeared it along the inside of her forearm. When he finished, he flicked the bread to the floor at her feet. "You can pick that up if you want, beautiful." His friends laughed, some of them were embarrassed but held their drinks and laughed again in an embarrassed way. They were rich and successful men. She went into the bathroom and looked at herself in the mirror before removing a lipstick from her beneath her belt and tracing her face on the mirror, a quick vague outline that she examined for a moment and then drew four squiggly power lines, like snakes, or thunderbolts, from her head to the exterior of the glass.

She lived by herself in a room with high, arched windows above a pizza parlour that catered to students. She painted on blocks of Masonite that she found stacked behind a hardware store. She read the poems of men who threw themselves off bridges and the decks of steamers. She read the poems of women who had killed themselves. She read the visions of Black Elk, she read Carl Jung on the visions of Black Elk. She read *Pictographs, Petroglyphs and Paradigms of the Apocalypse* by Paul Prescot. She sought herself out in libraries and in the blank cream-coloured interior of the provincial archives building behind the hospital.

It was in that place she came to herself. Under the gaze of a smiling, watery-eyed security guard who followed her step by step through the room where she found the origins of her raven hair. She found it on the banks of Loch Leven in a fifteenth-century monastery already in need of repair.

Loretta Ramsay sat on an upholstered swivel chair as the sickening lurch of the microfilm unspooled in front of her, the snapping click, the rewind, the knobs and dials, the click, the rewind, the stomach-wrenching spool of text across a grey screen, skidding to a stop at some useless place. It was like she was guiding a submarine underwater. Click. Stop. Turn. Click. There. Ramsay. More Ramsays. She uncovered Ramsays who emigrated from Scotland in the fifteenth century having lost their Culdean faith and its Druid origins. Ramsays who settled in Burgundy where they became Ramezays and entered the nobility from the fiefs of Boisfleurant and La Gesse. They came like pestilence across the Atlantic, riding wicked ships, she saw them, she rode with them in their sickening quarters, in sickening storms, the vessels listing so steeply that the lanterns hanging from the ceiling knocked against it. Claude Ramezay landed in Canada 1685, married the daughter of Pierre Denys de La Ronde and began to write nasty letters to the French Governor. He incurred massive debts, proved himself a military incompetent. His son died in the wreck of the *Chameau* off Cape Breton Island in 1725. Two decades later, a man named David Ramsay laid siege to this same island. He was a ship's boy in the Royal Navy. It was an age of war and violence and slavery. These are the first traces of herself.

This is him, she decides, she knows, she had always understood that such a moment was coming. The man in her dreams in which the blood pours into the soil. The cause of those memories in which her mother is on the carpet, holding her hands to her face. The shut door. David Ramsay. All of those murdered women. The missing ones. The ones found dead. She feels sweat on her back. Her stomach is in turmoil. What is happening? She sees a face looking at her from the dark blue screen. Her face. The eyes are too big, they see too much. She sees a time, only yesterday, she was a girl, sketching Ronnie Whiteloon on a rock on the shore of Lake of the Woods, thrilled by the romance of Ronnie Whiteloon. Her heart is sticky with boys. She hangs around the perimeters of tribal pow-wows, swaying and dancing in the clockwise circle, sniffing at sweetgrass, smiling, observing herself as much as others.

Then she found her family name on the genealogical rolls of Lake Erie settlements going back to the 1780s. Her forerunners built the

Port Dover Road out of rough planks. She read carefully: *"instructions and constitutional rules pertaining to the alienation and dispossession of Indian lands."* Her first sisters jounced along that road, pregnant, in groaning wagons —*"no lawful surrender of land from Six Nations to the . . ."* One of many migrations undertaken by people with common names.

Then he appears, the man emerging from the woods with a hatchet in his hands. She begins to dream him. Not every night. Not every time. He was in her. She comes from him, he who is not human. She saw him. In the woods. Standing over them with the moon on fire.

22

KETTLE CREEK 1771

In the fall of 1771 Ramsay undertook a trading expedition with his 17-year-old brother.
They travelled from Schenectady, N.Y., to the mouth of Kettle Creek,
on the north shore of Lake Erie, and from there went some miles upstream
to winter with a group of Indians, mainly Mississauga Ojibwas.
Exactly what happened during the winter is not clear.
DICTIONARY OF CANADIAN BIOGRAPHY, VOL. V, 1801—1820

THE FAMILY SLEPT HEAVILY ON mats made of cedar bark. The night-hawks soared over them and plucked moths from the sky. The oldest slept at the end, his face blackened in grief for his mother. A wound in the shape of a crescent moon had hardened on his face. A Potawatomi had put it there with a stone.

The man lay in the slumber of Ramsay's English liquor though he preferred French brandy from the paddler Racicot, whose nose had been taken off by a bear. To Racicot, he happily gave otter pelts in exchange for French brandy. The pelts went out in canoe brigades all the way up to the Sitka and the Russians, the men singing obscene French ditties they'd taught to the Indians who sung them well enough but did not comprehend them. They could not fight, the French, but they could sing. The brandy he drank with his family. He preferred it to Ramsay's watered-down English stuff.

David Ramsay lay ten yards away on the dirt with his hands bound. His brother, drunker than them all, shivered in a coat that was too big for him. He had done nothing wrong, the Mississaugans had not thought to bind him. David Ramsay's breath burned with his own rum, diluted with water from Kettle Creek. That is what they called it, the traders who filled their kettles there. It had a name. The Indians called it something else. They did not know what the Indians called it.

"Wake up," he hissed. His brother lay beside him, a boy, wearing a British coat.

"Wake up you Gordie bugger!"

The boy grunted.

"I who was ready ... struck him with a spear upon the breast, and following my blow, rammed him through ... he called out that he was killed ... I turned about and struck that person with the shaft of my spear. By the light of the moon which shone bright I saw another Indian come to the door ... I sprung out and struck him with my spear in the breast, and killed him also."

DAVID RAMSAY, 1772

IT HAD BEEN A NIGHT in July, the full moon was in the sky. The one they called Wandagan appeared in the door of the post at Niagara. He spoke words in English and Mississaugan. He wanted rum. You want rum, said Ramsay. He took the spear and pushed it directly into the man's throat. The two women entered behind him, both of them drunk on Ramsay's watered rum. He killed the first one with a hatchet blow to the skull. The other woman put her hands to her mouth and Ramsay struck her with the blade. The bodies barely moved. Wandagan's children came toward him. He reached for the skinning knife, then thought better of it, he would not waste its edge on children.

"WAKE, YOU BUGGER. WAKE UP!" Ramsay awoke from the memory of his spree, and tasted his own blood. His hands were tied with a leather thong.

"You buggers!"

He shouted into the night and into the face of his former commandant who had ordered him confined to the guard house at Montreal in the hope of having him hanged. Buggers, he shouted at his brother who would not wake. Ramsay grunted and slapped his bound body on the earth.

"God almighty." His brother's snores became thick, abortive snorts. With difficulty Ramsay managed to loose a stone with his foot and to kick it at the boy, splashing dirt on him. The boy's eyelids fell open: a look of ripe astonishment on his face.

"Brother!"

His brother's voice came to him from the forest with the bleating of mosquito hawks, and the peeping of frogs from the ponds and swamps. Crickets screeched in his ear like mad fiddlers. He saw his brother curled on the matted grasses, bound hand and foot. The occurrences of the last two days came back to him; the Mississaugans appearing from the vines. One of them steps forward and says in perfect English, "You have been mad and drunk all winter" and strikes David at the knees with a club. They knew already about the killings at Niagara. The leader, the speaker of perfect English, the one with black paint on his face, looked at the young Ramsay and gave instructions to imprison him. David they bound hand and foot with thongs, tied his hands to his neck and kept him pinioned like that for several hours. He remembered a fire, the gutturals of their speech with its rough Ks and short booming grunts. The rum came out and he saw the thick, squat keg of his brother's supply. The Indians had passed it among themselves like a pipe. The one painted in mourning had approached them with the keg. "Drink with us or you will be stabbed," he said.

Young Ramsay realized then that all of this had happened only moments ago, hours perhaps. His brother was bound hand and foot and hissing at him.

"Wake up, damn you. They left the knife." Ramsay jerked his chin toward the belt, a wide scarlet *centre fléchée*, woven on the fingers. His brother fumbled at the sash until he located the dirk hidden against the buckskin. He had it out beneath the moon, a glorious dirk, forged in the shape of a diamond. Ramsay watched while his brother cut the thongs at his wrist and grabbed the dirk from his brother's hand, severing the bond that kept his sore and bloody ankles together. He looked up and saw a heathen night.

"Watch, boy!"

He crept to the insolent red man, the one who had spoken like a trained parrot. "You have been mad and drunk all winter," Ramsay mimicked. After he finished, he released his hand from the mouth of the Mississaugan. and moved to the other men and then to a woman and straddled her sleeping body. He had killed women before.

He looked across and saw his brother on his knees, vomiting, attempting to speak the name of his saviour. Around him the people lay on their woven mats, curled against the night. Ramsay put his foot into the first man and turned him, heavily. The children did not move. Their size alone enraged him, the size of their eyelashes, smaller than the fingers of a squirrel. Both of them were awake and silent. One of them made an effort to crawl off. Ramsay looked up and saw that the clouds in front of the moon had burst into flames.

23

THE BURNING CHURCH

Frontenac asked Outoutagan, "a bad Christian and a great drunkard,"
what he thought liquor was made of. The Ottawa is said to have replied
that "it was an extract of tongues and hearts, for when I have had a drink,
I fear nothing and I speak like an angel."

DICTIONARY OF CANADIAN BIOGRAPHY VOL. II, 1701 TO 1740

LINDA FELL ASLEEP WITH VOLUME V (1801 to 1820) on the bed, beside her where Paul would have slept. The short and pathetic life of Jacob Overhosler, an illiterate Canadian farmer falsely accused of treason by his envious neighbours, punctuated her dreams. "You are to be hanged by the neck, but not until you are dead, for you must be cut down while alive and your entrails taken out and burnt before your face. Your head is then to be cut off and your body to be divided into four quarters." Great, she thought. Have a nice day. The poor soul blended into Ougier, Peter, 1775, who insisted the Newfoundland fishery was on the verge of collapse, and then committed suicide to back up his claim. She paged backward into Ouabachas (*see Wapasha*) chief of the Santee Sioux. Osborn, Mary, "you are to be hanged until dead dead dead and afterwards your body to be dissected." O'Hara,

Felix, "a sensible well-informed man." Her disembodied neighbours flitted before her eyes; O'Donel, James Louis, (March 18, 1811), burst into flames while sitting in a chair."

When she fell asleep, the rats were there again, crawling through the rusted gears of a ruined machine. She saw the letters L.R. tattooed on a man's hard belly; his eyes opened, blinked, and sent out two shafts of light that danced on the ceiling above her. Help me, he said. She was almost positive that's what he said. Help me. Help all of us. For God's sake. We must put out the fire. But why did his voice sound like tin?

The cough of the walkie-talkies broke in on her harsh and loud, punctuated by static. She lay in bed listening to the urgent voices of men doing what they're trained to do. I'm awake, she thought, and to prove it she watched the red emergency lights flash against her ceiling. For a moment they seemed to have the ability to hypnotize her. Then she was up, wearing Paul's housecoat, she moved to the window and saw that the church was on fire, the Dormition was over, the Virgin had erupted in flames. Dark billows of smoke crept upward from the building, flashing into orange and uncurling behind the stained glass windows. Flames ignited the old window frames, guttering from the dark alter, and raced from the chancel into the night. Fire burned in the body of the church. She saw Corpus Christi set aflame by a candle. Linda watched, paying her ancient tribute to fire as the smoke escaped from the ceiling and poured upside down into the night, like black water. The roof shimmered for a moment, trembled, then at once blew open, shattering into tiles and glassy splinters, hurling black shards into the night on a column of flame and cinders. Her bedroom window became too hot to stand beside, the heat radiated through the glass and burned on her forehead. She watched as the church crashed in on itself and flamed in a bonfire of walnut banisters, oak panels, and pine spindles, a shower of incandescent ash circled upward into the night.

The phone rang. Her phone. It sounded like music. Like a song she'd heard before. She wasn't surprised. There would be a voice on the other end of it. Help me I'm on fire. My consciousness is burning. Please help me. The world is burning.

The telephone rang with a melodious patience that suggested many years of shared history, a song in search of itself, unhurried, even resigned. Her arms drifted in the dark to the bed table, not really an arm, a thing remote from her, an appendage belonging to someone else. She felt the press of plastic on her ear.

"Hey."

In the street, the firefighters manoeuvred frantically, shooting water at windows, smashing them beneath the force of the jets.

"The church is on fire. Fort God is burning. Didn't I tell you that would happen, I mean, sooner or later?"

Paul laughed.

She heard a dull cheer in the background. It would seem Paul was whiling away his life without her in a dubious Irish bar along with the audible gibberish of a half dozen televisions.

"Are you all right?"

"The church is on fire. I'm watching it on television."

"Yes," she said. "You're all right?"

"I'm fine. I'm drunk. A little. Not Peter O'Toole drunk. What are you doing?"

"I'm proofreading a seed catalogue. I'm watching the church burn." Another film crew had arrived and debouched expertly from the van. She watched them leap out of their vehicles, wielding walkie-talkies. Cameras were cocked and aimed at a woman in a long leather jacket holding a microphone. She knew the routine: first the fire. Then the filming of the fire. Then the commentary.

"It looks like Christ's blood," she said suddenly.

"What?"

"It looks like Christ's blood streaming in the firmament." She had a vivid picture of what this looked like, a flood of rich red fluid, thicker than blood, searching the land, arcing the sky, like a comet.

"Ah, the firmament." Paul cleared his throat. "That old thing."

"Your books came," she said. "A box came, they're here."

"Good."

"There's something else. I was talking to someone."

"What? What did you say?"

"Someone called. From the media. Someone's looking for you."

"Who?"

"Some reporter. I don't know. I can't remember his name."

"Was his name Gratton? Arthur Gratton?"

"Yes, that's who I think it was."

She heard her husband laugh.

"The guy's an asshole. You think I'm an asshole? This guy's a superior form of asshole. He has a doctorate in being an asshole. What did he want?"

"He has some questions," she said quietly. "He wants to know about the L.R. site at Port Coldwell."

"Good. Questions are good."

"I don't think so. He says the site's not authentic. He thinks L.R. stands for Loretta Ramsay and that she painted the entire site. It's bogus. The whole thing is bogus and that you've been taken in. You've been had, Paul."

"He said that?"

"She said it. She wrote a letter. Some sort of manifesto, I don't know, she sent a copy to him. Not just to him. Those paintings you wrote about, the Port Coldwell ones? She painted them. It was her."

They were silent, linked by a telephone wire, staring at different glass surfaces. She heard the squawk of radios from the street, the hissing disquiet of the place where Paul was. In front of her, a telescopic hose unfolded upward over the flaming roof, and she watched as the water burst furiously from the nozzle.

POSTSCRIPT 6: PIT STOPS

THE GREAT FALLEN MOOSE DISAPPEARED behind her. It had taken forever. Then the van took pity on her and pulled over to the shoulder
of the highway for Linda to cry. Her head collapsed to her chest,
her upper body rocked the seat as her grief sought to rise. She felt
herself dissolving into an old hippy van, Paul's only possession. The
acid cleanse of tears washed her face. Then she started up again,
sobbing evenly now, driving into Hemlo, where the gold waited
in the rock. She was driving, she realized, in the aftermath of
the great fire, the Wawa Four, or Five, she could never remember
what number it was. There were so many lately. The branch-
less trunks stuck up like pins from the charred land. In spots the
black earth still smouldered, giving up puffs that danced like
veiled figures.

Black Creek.

Swedish Creek.

The miles snapped behind her. She drove outside of time on a road that went forever.

AS LINDA DROVE, SHE WAS aware of herself once again standing in the blue-ish basement in the Thunder Bay coroner's office that towered like a castle over Red River Road. The coroner apologized for wearing a medical mask and admitted eagerly, without her asking, that he was having trouble with the northern winters. "We are Bangladeshis," he said suddenly, happily. His entire family was having trouble. He wore enormous black-rimmed glasses. Her husband lay on a steel tray beneath the lights, a thin strip of flesh sliced from his left thigh, the wound showed there. Self-inflicted, performed with a Swiss Army knife, the knife she'd presented him on his fiftieth birthday. "Would you know ma'am, please, why he might do something like that?"

In the veiled window a white-frocked assistant sprayed down a gurney, a soothing hiss. Low Muzak on hidden speakers. The room smelled of vinegar. Light was coming in from somewhere.

"It is not necessary for a woman to engage in the ritual of self-mutilation," she said quietly. "Is it?"

"I beg your pardon?"

"In a quest for vision, it isn't necessary, just a man."

Just a man. The coroner had removed his glasses but not his mask.

"There is a peculiar thing, ma'am, I must say so, it's not the tooth. A very impacted tooth, and infected yes, infected very much. It is that your husband's legs, the bones, the major bones, I found empty of marrow. Almost completely empty." He had no idea how this could possibly come about. "There is an insect," he said without conviction, "that will do this. It has a Latin name. But this is an insect of Brazil. Not of here." Had her husband been lately to Brazil? No, her husband had not been to Brazil. He would not go south. Only north. There was no meaningful way for her to say this to him.

24

THE NEWS IS THE ONLY THING IN
THE WORLD THAT NEVER CHANGES

The Glue the Native saves out of the Sturgeon is very strong and they use it
in mixing with their paint which fixes the Colours so they never Rub out.
JAMES ISHAM 1740

ARTHUR'S PIECE APPEARED THE WEDNESDAY morning of a news week
in which a Tallahassee housewife cut off her husband's penis
with a pair of fabric scissors and was immediately offered her own
television show. As a consequence, Paul's public crucifixion was
less public than it might have been: *Toronto Artist beats Academics,*
Aboriginals to "Ancient" Drawings. Linda read that stinging quartet
of barely coded words; Artists, Academics, Aboriginal, Ancient.
Arthur's piece insisted that the Native Studies departments of
North America were in a tizzy. The dean of Trent University's Native
Studies program made it clear that any relationship the university
may have had with Paul Prescot was on a part-time, contractual
basis, and in the past.

"*Mr. Prescot has never defended a doctoral dissertation, nor is he currently*
employed as a professor at this institution. He has once or twice appeared as a

sessional instructor and guest lecturer, but beyond that he has no affiliation with this department, or any other," clarified the Dean.

Loretta Ramsay was photographed squatting on the floor with a bowl of paint in one hand, tracing thick lines on a board with the other. "Loretta Ramsay (Waunathoake), is committed to creating a living art within the context of her people." According to this "young iconoclast," she'd rendered the pictographs on Port Coldwell as part of a campaign to "atone for the horrors that the conquerors visited on this Island and on every one of us." Yes, she stated, Paul Prescot's books, especially *Apocalypse Already*, were based on her own rock paintings. They were what she called "healing bandages applied to the wounds of a technological world. It doesn't surprise me," she went on, "that researchers insist on seeing my art in terms of war and destruction. It's what they know. It's what they're comfortable with, and what they're taught."

Linda read on. It seemed for the last ten years, Loretta Ramsay had been inscribing her figures on the rocks of remote Ontario landscapes; "Sewing them," as she put it, "on the bleeding world." These claims were backed up by the authority of Walter Prendergast, a scientist with Beta Analytic, Inc., and leading expert on mass spectrometry analysis. Why leading, she wondered? Why not just expert? According to this leading expert, the substance he examined was no more than twenty years old, probably considerably less than that. "A good facsimile," he said. "The giveaway was the bonding agent, vegetable oil. The kind you can buy in the supermarket. It's a lot easier to find than sturgeon oil. There was also no shortage of basic oil paint, the kind," he said damningly, "that you can buy in a Canadian Tire store for a couple of bucks."

In the same piece a certain Kelly Davidson, Professor Emeritus at the University of Regina, and authority on Mayan script, insisted it was time to revisit what he called "my Scandinavian hypotheses," a theory proving to his own satisfaction that the Mazinaw Rock drawings, the Curve Lake pictographs, along with the Hickson Mirabelli site, were all the work of artistically minded Vikings who instead of raping and pillaging spent their summers painting obscure figures with outstretched hands on the rocks of the Canadian Shield. "There has never been clear proof of Native authorship of these sites. I have seen identical ones in Sweden and I have no doubt that the Vikings left them here as trade markers and proof of willingness to engage in commerce with local people. Three horizontal lines could represent the passage of three moons, meaning we will be back in three nights to trade for copper, or furs, or whatever they wanted to trade. Why not the Vikings?" he asked.

A council chief from the Curve Lake band was interviewed and insisted that from what he knew "a clan system was spelled out on those rocks; wolves, loons, crows, bears, herons, power lines coming out from the head of stick figures, tell me what any of that meant to the Vikings? The skyscrapers of Manhattan were built by the high steel Mohawks of Akwesasne. No one is out saying that the Empire State Building was built by Mohawks. Or outer space people for that matter. Why no story there?"

Paul was left with flesh on his body, but very little of it. Three times the piece referred to him as a professor, which he wasn't, and an academic; "Professor Prescot is not the sort of man found outside on a Saturday morning playing road hockey with the neighbourhood kids," wrote Arthur, suggesting he was the sort of man who you *would* find out Saturday morning doing that. "You might try looking in at the Faculty Club where he will be comfortably seated, reading critical theory." The piece ended ominously:

"Calls left at Prescot's last-known residence, the Waverly Hotel in Toronto, were not returned. The Institute for the Preservation of Aboriginal Rock Art, established by Prescot with funds from a federal grant in 1984 does not have a listed telephone number, and beyond a post office box with a Kenora, Ontario address, no longer exists."

FOR THE NEXT TWO EVENINGS Linda lay on the sofa and watched the story play out on her screen, where it appeared with some insistence and was swollen by several Euro-supremacists, Carlos Castaneda groupies, nutbars, and Piltdown Man believers who waded in and advocated a spiralling network of conspiracies. Professor Seth Blumrich, of McGill, caked in makeup, restated his position that the pictographs of the east boreal region were painted by aliens from an uncharted planet in the Andromeda Galaxy. He was insistent on this; it had to be the Andromeda Galaxy, no other galaxy would do. A retired NASA scientist appeared on television and made it clear that ancestral aboriginals had the power of flight. How else could they have escaped from Atlantis, which he insisted had been built on the Lake Superior reef. The expert had derived his theory from what he explained was, "an extremely close reading" of the Prophesy of Ezekiel, who witnessed his first spacecraft in 592 BC. Richard Kimball, a scribbler with the Arizona *Daily Courier* had it from an impeccable and un-named source that the rock carvings on the Hopi Reservation near Mishongnovi, Arizona, depict "a definite connection between Indians and visitors from outer space." According to Mr. Kimball, of the two hundred flying saucers seen over Prescott, Arizona during the summer of 1972, at least half of them were piloted by Hopi airmen.

The segment ended with Paul Prescot, an expert on Canadian Aboriginal rock art, revealed as a man who could not distinguish a daub of prehistoric sturgeon oil from a three-dollar can of Canadian Tire oil paint.

25

THE RETURNING

FOR WEEKS THE WORKERS HAD banged away at the blackened shell of the church, hacking at it, tearing off the scabs of melted black tiles.

As they squatted up top on the scaffolding with their tool belts, she watched them, saw the tanned torsos and black grottos of hair showing in their armpits. When the sun was full up, they took their shirts off and she sat at her desk and looked through the window at them, waiting for them to fall, which they didn't. They moved without concern, like squirrels.

She forced herself to look away, down at the sheets in front of her. "*Do you have visions of veggie patch paradise with flower-filled borders, a sandbox for the kiddies and a gravel-lined dog run?*" In fact, she didn't have these visions. She didn't understand how such visions came to a woman. In a dream? Perhaps after three days of fasting in a menstrual tent a vision came to a woman of the purest of veggie patches, burning on the retina of her third eye. The purest of veggies, the most holy of gravel-lined dog runs. What a woman dreams of. She didn't know exactly what a dog run was. Like a mill race maybe.

The doorbell sounded twice against the silence of the house. She got up at once and walked downstairs to oblige it.

Paul stood before her, grinning. She had the feeling he'd been standing there all night. It did not surprise her that he rang the doorbell to his own house. "I'm ruined," he said cheerfully. "Dying of exposure. Can I come in?"

He'd left the house with two bags, but had returned with one. It was the first thing she noticed.

"You've managed to shed some of your baggage," she said.

He didn't laugh. Neither did she. Instead he swung a canvas sack from which he removed a dented gold-painted tin with a bottle of Abelour scotch inside. He clapped the container on a table. "Would you like some breakfast?"

"I've eaten, thank you."

He removed the bottle but didn't drink from it, instead he picked up the canister and examined it.

"When I was a boy, our house was afloat with these things," he said, and then he coughed.

WITHOUT SPEAKING MUCH, THEY RETURNED to the symbiosis of their marriage, to its habits and peculiarities, to its open secrets. There had always been something glacial about their love, she knew that, something unstoppable. It moved, but it moved invisibly. "I'm back," he had said to her, in a hollow, theatrical way. "Yes," she said. "Like the cat in the hat." She did not say it, but suspected he would leave a pink ring around the rim of the bathtub. They always did. Linda did not say whether she was back too. I have never gone away, she thought.

They lay in bed like two ships abreast. Paul exuded a heaviness that rose from him with each breath, pressing against the ceiling. How many families had filled this house, she wondered? Wives and husbands, trembling as they held each other? Do you forgive me? The question seemed to emerge from the pores of his body. She didn't want to hear it spoken. She heard it rattling in the minds of men. Forgive me, please. So many who had need of being forgiven. An entire world full of them. What sort of goddess was she to do that? Or woman? She imagined, somewhere in the black afternoon of the Labrador winter, among stunted trees, the ragged figures carrying the body of a young woman aloft. Forgive us all? It must be done now, before the end comes.

Paul was half awake. He lay beside her again, his wife. He had a past again. The rope of his memory, she held the other end, without her it was only him holding on to a half of it. He was distracted. There was a confession he wanted to make. Do you forgive me? He muttered these words into the dark. "Do you know what I need to be forgiven for?" For the people that I am? That which I am a part of? He could explain that to her, she would understand.

"Does anyone?" she said.

He lay beside her, wondering if he'd perhaps gone blind. Somewhere between the first people and the newcomers his eyes had failed him. He should sit up in bed and make a hardboiled statement about their love. He did, but the words did not sound like his words. "Just don't bring her back here," was all that she answered, half asleep. "Don't give me some wicked disease."

He felt the time pass strenuously from one moment to the next. "I love you," he breathed. He looked at his wife's face as she lay on the bed next to him, her face. He knew it better than anything.

"I love you," he said again. But she was asleep.

26

THE FACT CHECKERS

In Newfoundland, Demasduwit, one of the last of the Beothuks, was captured and died....Isabel Gunn disguised herself as a man and worked as a labourer for the Hudson's Bay Company until her secret could no longer be hidden.

DICTIONARY OF CANADIAN BIOGRAPHY, VOL. V. 1801–1820

IN THE MORNING SHE ROSE before him and went to her desk to ponder Vesuvius; the herbs, fennel, feverfew, hyssop — *very attractive to bees and butterflies and hummingbirds*. He came downstairs soon after and, without speaking, they resorted to the old rituals. She was responsible for the coffee, their drug of choice. It was not clear how that particular responsibility had fallen to her. "Hey white man," she often said. "Here's your coffee." Today she said nothing.

They hovered around the coffee pot in the kitchen, sucking on the narcotic bean, feeling the heat in their mouths and throats. When he was done, Paul left the house with a loose air of purpose and returned with an armful of newspapers including somehow even the *Thunder Bay Chronicle News*. He spread the papers on the kitchen table and read with a mounting chorus of hoots and chuckles. With a collapsible pair of camping scissors, he cut out stories that he taped into a large notebook. His Doomsday Book, he called it.

HE DRANK LIKE AN ATHLETE only to damp the thirst of his efforts but did not become drunken or sodden or maudlin. Three deep grooves showed between his eyebrows, popping into existence to accompany the new him. He had accepted his fall, he told her. He had accepted the loss of whatever reputation he had, his few books, several strident articles in obscure journals, rarely cited. He was scourged clean, fallen, free to be another man that lurked in the same aging body. He was dead of exposure. Like all of us, he said. The prospect of dying of exposure was in fact deeply intriguing to Paul. He had a great respect for men who died of exposure, exposure to the elements, exposure to what was inside you. It was all media exposure now and he couldn't imagine a less interesting way to go. There was a time when he was fond of quoting something he'd read about Captain Scott's demise on the Antarctic barrier ice, his body frozen solid in what the author had called, "an attitude of sleep." Not sleep, but an attitude of sleep. The distinction appealed to him. Only Brits were allowed to expire in an attitude of sleep, the rest of humanity just fell down and froze to death. Scott's last diary entry: "We are getting weaker. I do not think I can write more. For God's sake look after our people," was a favourite of his. She'd find a note stuck to the fridge; "Have gone for a quart of milk. I do not think I can write more. For God's sake look after our people."

With a glass of scotch at his elbow, Paul scissored articles from newspapers. The leftover sheet he made into a hat and put it on his head. Mad as a hatter, he said. In his notebook he compiled a great deal of confusion, four column inches on a family knifed to death by the daughter's boyfriend who was later picked up wandering on the shoulders of the highway in a trance and holding a carving knife. An elderly woman found decomposing in her bed. A man who bit a dog. A dog that got cloned. He was constructing a quilt to cover the times. He was sewing everything back together, he said.

She stood in the doorway, annoyed with him. Annoyed even with her own annoyance at him. She knew couples whose relationship depended on an ongoing and fervent annoyance with each other.

"Paul, what did you do to that woman to make her hate you so much? Were you too paternalistic, too caring? Did you tell her how to do everything? Show her the right way to hold her fork?"

"She ate with her fingers," he said, extracting several more column inches about a Korean family that had contracted H1N1, and whose house was burnt down by neighbours. He flattened it into his book. "It would seem that if you grind up the brains of cattle, throw in a few steroids and then feed that stew to other cattle, things go very wrong very quickly. On the other hand, you keep horseshoe bats in cages next to caged marmots, hedgehogs, and Chinese cobras at a food market ..." He knew this approach was not going to work. "Ramsay is her family name," he said quietly. "She is the offspring of an odious fellow named David Ramsay. That's what she believes. I don't think she is frankly. Have you heard that name? Ramsay, David. Not to be confused with David Ramsay, the American, who wrote a book about George Washington and was then shot dead by a madman."

She recalled something appearing from a sheet of creamy thin paper, words that seemed somehow to emerge from an afternoon when the blossoms of Herr Holderlich's pear tree fell on her shoulders. The *Dictionary of Canadian Biography* open on the backyard grass, a blue jay shrieking. Rale ... Ramezay ... Ramsay. There in the Rs, something had happened, she could almost remember it; a man had done something hateful. He wasn't the first one.

"He was an Indian killer. David Ramsay. He slaughtered them in their sleep, with a knife. Men, women, the children even, scalped them all. It's a declaration of war to do that. He knew that. Became a folk hero for doing it. You know the sort, the man who heroically rescues himself from drunken Natives, dispatches them to hell. That sort of thing. In truth, he was drunker than any of them. It was his booze as matter of fact. He was selling it. Quite a piece of work that fellow, the dark side of being Canadian really, and that's who she is, who she believes herself to be descended from. I don't think she is but so what? It happened quite close to here. The crimes that call to us from the past. It's because of him. Atonement. The last of the Beothuks, Mary March, Waunathoake, the crimes that call to us from the past. She calls it that." He slugged his drink to the bottom, placed it on the table, and turned to look at her. "I don't recall being any more odious to her than anyone else. You, for example." He tried to smile. "Perhaps she needed to crucify someone. We all need to crucify someone eventually. It was my turn. I was due, wasn't I?"

"And she painted the L.R. site on the Coldwell Peninsula? You couldn't tell that? I thought you were an expert?"

"Well," he started. "An expert, yes. Of course, she didn't paint it. You could spend your whole life looking for that site without ever coming close to finding it. Let alone faking the writing on it. That would be the easy part."

"She said she did."

"She was lying. Don't you see that? She was atoning for the crimes that haunt us from the past. Lying through her teeth. She was making a career for herself, God bless her. They all have to do that now."

"It was in the papers. On television."

"Yes."

"Those paintings were carbon dated. They found paint, real paint, like you buy in the hardware store."

"You can't carbon date rock paintings. You know that."

"Yes. But you can date other things. You can analyze them, you can determine what they are. Whether it's oil-based enamel from a hardware store. Or whether it's sturgeon oil. They did the analysis."

"Who did?"

"I don't know." She was irritated now. He was nitpicking. "Someone in the news. An expert. One of those experts that forever get dredged up."

"Like the ones they pull out of thin air."

"Is that what they do?"

"Apparently they do. Prendergast. Walter Prendergast? That man? With Beta Analytic Inc.? Right? Am I right?"

"I can't remember."

"Walter Prendergast, believe me. Lab technician with a D.SC. from the Université de Paris? Just happened to be kicking around the Algoma District in Ontario during blackfly season, running a lab out of a local college and waiting for a reporter to send him a hundred micrograms of carbon from a rock painting that is situated somewhere, and I mean somewhere on the north shore of Lake Superior. Superior for God's sake. It's the size of Portugal. Somewhere between Missing Horse Creek, and Dead Horse Creek? but on the coastal side, right? Is that how it worked? Somewhere east of Aguasabon Falls but slightly west of Chigamiwinigum? Is that it? She canoed forty-foot breakers and put in rather handily at latitude forty-nine degrees north and west of the prime meridian at latitude forty-seven? Closer to forty-six really. She just showed up there?"

Linda watched him with some uncertainty as if Paul were suddenly another person standing there in her husband's body. Three months ago he'd been invited to give a lecture at the Art Gallery of Ontario on the subject of historical Aboriginal rock art. The lecture had been cancelled.

"I don't know how it works," she said.

"Beta Analytic Inc., is based in Fort Lauderdale, Florida. Was based in Fort Lauderdale. They closed down shop three years ago. It doesn't exist anymore. That reporter made it up. Don't ask me why, and her, she believes she's related to that man, Ramsay. That's what I think, that's what I found out. That was my crime. I was snooping. I was an old man in a young woman's room. That's never right. I found some stuff, a folder. She's got everything, the genealogical charts from the archives, even transcripts from the Western Historical Society get-togethers. Those meetings were held in *nineteen-forty-four*. There's not a lot. She's got it all. It's in her head, a great big murder spree. It galls her. She's on fire with it. She wants to make amends."

There was a sustained silence out of which Linda suddenly said, "You must have found her so beautiful."

"No. Not really," Paul said quickly. But he was lying. There was the matter of her face. "Her face," he wanted to add. He couldn't stop himself. "It was her face," he said softly, staring into nowhere. "I think she reminded me of my mother."

He laughed ruefully.

27

SAVE YOURSELVES
MY LAMBS AND LOVELIES

FOR SEVERAL DAYS PAUL HAD the topographical maps on the table in front of him. He'd already assembled his camping gear with the same sort of fetishistic devotion with which her father had fixed his stamps into binders. He would visit his ailing mother, he said. Priscilla had taken a turn. When that was done, he was going back out on the land. The Port Coldwell site. His reasons were vague to her. Atonement or vindication. He had no interest in proving Loretta Ramsay a fraud. It was something different. "I am going there to save the world," he said. He looked at her without smiling.

"You do that." She sat at her desk proofing a galley page on Hosta plants, and the twelve species of the variegated weigela (*tough, versatile, and easy to grow*). The variegated weigela was also attractive to hummingbirds, but she had not seen a hummingbird in a very long time. No one had. "It's because they've deforested certain tropical islands," Paul had said. He named an island she'd never heard of. It was mid-July without hummingbirds. A close hot summer spent in the city. She couldn't recall the last time she'd spent the summer in the city. She looked up from the pages, the workmen were there, high up in the rigging of the church roof, shirts off, their skins long ago tanned almost charcoal, topped with yellow hard hats. She stood up and went downstairs where her husband was assembling his gear into two large packs.

Paul pressed against her in the hall before the door. He was remote and determined, like an actor in a war movie, she thought, before he goes under the lights to fake his death. She found the moment of their departure almost unbearable. At any moment she feared he would take some personal item; a ring, a chain from around his neck, and place it on her body. He wore no chain. Instead he wrapped his arms around her like hawsers holding a boat to the shore.

"Linda," he clung there. He was not good at this clinging, neither was she. "I want you to look after yourself."

"I do that," she answered coolly.

It was true. She knew how to do that. He knew that about her too, she was good at it. She followed him out the door to the van and slid the key into the ignition. The vehicle responded to her at once, the way it had so many times. It always felt like an animal to her, taking something from her hand, and visibly grateful for it. They made their way across town to the bus terminal without speaking, the wires and the buildings did all the talking. He stared out at the city like a child who was new to it all. Gawking at it. The buildings, the countless windows that reflected lives constantly in motion, the teeming wash of people moving in all directions on the streets; the bicycles and the food deliverers, the wheelchairs. The city drenched him in its life. It always had. He would always leave it, always come back to it.

Several times Paul reached out and laid his left hand on her thigh, but did not appear entirely convinced it belonged there and removed it. She was aware of the crush of Chinatown traffic pushing her to the station, the streetcars, the taxis, and delivery trucks crushing her forward like a vessel stuck in the pack ice.

"Terminal bus station, this is it," he said gloomily.

She parked on Chestnut Street and soon they stood together in the familiar grey hardness of the place, breathing the loneliness of the bus station with its diesel and blue fumes, the grit in the air, and the gamblers in depressing suit jackets that were creased for all time, clutching racing forms. The names of towns and villages fell from the speakers, *Ipsala, Wabigoon, White River, Sintaluta. Shining Tree, Parry Sound, Garden River. Manitoulin.* "Last call," said the woman's voice on the speakers. Last call she said, almost with relief.

For the first time she didn't envy his going out into those names. Suddenly she was appalled by any place that wasn't home. All of those ridiculous places that did not have her bed in it, her sofa, her books. She was sick of motion, impatient with the endless distance between things. They held each other next to the muddy hull of the bus. The luggage hatch slammed shut. Paul boarded. A few moments later, she watched the bus pull away.

Through a blaze of Chinese neon symbols and feeling numb to the city, she walked back to the van. The key was in the door when she felt a touch light as paper brushing against her right shoulder. Paul, she realized. Her heart jumped in her chest. She didn't say anything. She caught herself, startled by how much she wanted him back right now in this moment. It was Paul at her shoulder in all his ridiculousness, grinning, explaining to her the dream was over, she was awake now. He was not going anywhere, he had found what he was looking for. The world the two of them had come to know together would continue to drift with them inside of it. They had years of life yet, years to journey into the piney woods to camp and to lie together in the dark night beneath the shriek of the owl.

She turned and confronted a woman wrapped in a shower curtain. A faint beard clung to her chin and her teeth appeared to head in directions teeth were not meant to go. She smelled of bleach and something less familiar, the miasma of cat dander and moulding clothes. Her eyes were red-rimmed and circled in vermillion greasepaint. Across her shoulder she wore a tattered yellow sash that proclaimed her "Miss Universe." The woman stood in a random moment the way leaves assemble when the wind tosses them into piles.

"Good day lady, good day. That's right. It is you know. Truly it's a good day." She seemed to give Linda the opportunity to speak, but that was not her plan and she resumed in a rasp of pavement and cigarettes her tale of injustice. "I just been kicked out of three lousy churches lady, three of them. What? I ain't good enough for the house that God lives in? Jesus Christ. I'm as good as you, right?"

"Better," said Linda and began her escape into the van. But the woman restrained her by laying a large pasty arm on her shoulder. "You know what's happening, don't you? You get the picture. You know lady? That last little piggy? The one that went to market? That little piggy is going to blow. First he's going to suck, then this whole freaking shithouse is coming down. It's melting see? You know that. I know that. You see? The whole world is an ice cream sandwich that's melting. There's no stopping it." She handed over a folded sheet of paper and stared at Linda with a look that witches exchange when they meet beneath the bleeding neon signage. The knowing look of sisters. Linda took the piece of paper and pulled herself into the van, watching the shower curtain lady turn and flounce away, rustling a thousand plastic skirts, some of them made of green garbage bags, all of them compressed beneath the shower curtain.

When she reached home, she found an unwanted newspaper stuffed in the railing of the porch. She circled it warily as if an improvised explosive device had been left there. From long experience, she knew she'd find it packed with a thousand exclamations, indignations, and fevered opinions and that any one of them could put her into a coma. "The news is the only thing in the world that never changes," Paul had told her repeatedly and she'd come to agree with him.

She picked up the newspaper and took it into the kitchen where she dropped it on the table. There the note from Miss Universe fell out of her shirt and she stooped to snap it up from the floor, then unfolding and staring at the spread of text typed in a strange font that was intended to resemble handwriting. *My children*, it began,

Save yourselves my lambs and lovelies for the end is truly upon us. Shortly there shall come that day when cataclysms of the dogmatics and the dogmatism of the catatonics will bark and bay at your windows. An awful smelling liquid will rain down on the earth and contaminate your water and your brain. The icebergs shall melt away into nothing. Your buildings will fall, your banks shall choke with greed, your funds will be hedged, the hurricanes shall strike, your girls and women will be snatched from the highways and murdered, your young men shall die in the desert in their death orgies and your greed shall be transformed into virtue, the virus will live inside the virtue even as the songbirds drop from the sky and the waters rise. Prepare warm blankets and clothes. Pray pray pray that you are not killed in the white days of darkness . . .

She left the note on the table and walked through the house without aim or even what she considered sanity. She sensed that she was becoming one of those haunted figures from literature, Ophelia or Lady Macbeth, or the madwoman kept in the attic in that dreadful novel, or that other dreadful novel in which that other woman slashed herself or set herself on fire or threw herself beneath a train or waded into the Atlantic. The new woman always ended badly in the novels of the old boys. In novels it was always open season on women.

She went to the fridge and was stopped by a note taped to the fridge with duct tape. This seemed to her the most normal of things. Unable to find scotch tape or a fridge magnet, Paul had unsheathed his role of duct tape, and fixed his note to the fridge where it would remain stuck for all time.

Darling, the note started. But *darling* had been crossed out and improved on: *My dear darling it is the time of the Fifth Fire and there have come among us those who promise great joy and salvation. It is a false promise. The great struggle is coming now. The greatest struggle. I love you. Even beyond my attempts to tell you. For God's sake look after our people.*

28

TURTLE ISLAND

HE LEFT THE CITY AS the Wawa 7 fire burned from the Pukaskwa coast to the provincial interior. North of Parry Sound, the flames had reached the Trans-Canada, examined it for several minutes, and then leapt across the tarmac and entered the new forest. By day seven, the vast thunderheads of smoke had reached an altitude of 30,000 feet and altered the flight paths of aircraft. The smoke had been observed in London, England.

He slept uncomfortably and woke uncomfortably. He found himself squeezed next to a young man with a ring in his nose, a bolt in his tongue and several more pieces of hardware protruding from his ears. The face appeared to have been assembled in a hardware store for reasons that weren't clear; maybe a raised middle finger, he thought.

Paul closed his eyes. The miles rolled outside the bus; the rock, the miles, the moss and the rock, and more miles, and the rock, and then more rock and more miles. He was daydreaming. He fell asleep and when he woke he saw that he was in a rock-filled world with his facially armoured seatmate smiling at him.

"You were snoring," the youngster said cheerfully.

"Sorry."

"No problem. Look." He held up a book. "It's a book," and with some daring, added, for emphasis, "A novel, it's a novel. By Stephen King. He's really famous."

"Oh."

"Really famous."

"Is he Native?"

"Maybe, I don't know. He writes super scary shit. Not that I get it." The youngster dropped his voice into a deeply intimate whisper. "I don't know how to read. I'm illiterate, right? I can't read." He looked at Paul with wild eyes in which the stain of amphetamines was visible. "You keep a book out it makes people think you can read, right?"

"I guess," said Paul. Who were these kids, he wondered? Long-gone offspring of Kerouac and Kesey, little Benzedrine daddies fleeing across the Shield, armed with books they couldn't read. The boy could not read and for some reason this provoked a longing in him for his wife, with her books, and her devotion to them. Even his books.

He returned to himself and felt the engine vibrating the steel walls around him. The country flew sideways outside the window.

"What's in the box?" he said.

"The box?" responded the boy suspiciously.

Between his legs he squeezed a cardboard box tightly, protectively, fidgeting every few seconds with a stained dishtowel tossed over the top.

"The box. What's in it?"

"Oh." The youngster glanced uneasily behind them, through the crack between the two seats in front. "I'm not supposed to do this. It's against the regs. Look at this." He drew back the dishtowel and to Paul's amazement an ancient spherical shape rose slowly from the interior, the hairless head of a buried zombie, potted with cracks and markings. It resembled the bald earth itself, and he saw inscribed on its back the thirteen square patterns that mapped the full moons of the year.

"Splendid," said Paul, "My God."

Out came the phallic and reptilian head with the yellow stripes and the grey eyes. The creature gave off the mouldy odour of socks and moss, and craned its neck to ascertain that everything falling within range of its prehistoric eyes was as uninteresting as it had been when it last took a peek.

"It's a turtle."

"Yes, an eastern red ear. Its blood freezes solid in winter."

"No shit?"

"None whatsoever."

"It's sick." The boy held back the dishtowel so that Paul could see the creature. He looked closer; the great bearer of the earth was sick. A scum of white fuzz built up in the cracks of its back, like some turtle mange that had come to destroy the world.

"I'm taking him to British Columbia. He'll get better there." The boy stroked the shell with a deep and tender affection. "Won't you buddy? Sure you will." He looked at Paul again. "He's going to be all right."

"Sure he is," said Paul.

A sick turtle in the company of an illiterate boy with pierced eyebrows, crossing North America by bus. It'd be all right. Just fine. A better time was coming. Paul forced himself to sleep, or at least to close his eyes.

AT BLIND RIVER, HE GOT off the bus and hauled his gear into a Motor Inn where he suffered the inspection of a severe woman who took his money but otherwise remained unconvinced by him. He flopped on the bed and for the first time understood how hot it was, a broiling heat filled the small and painfully neat room, but he felt no inclination to fiddle with a thermostat or even look for one. He took a mickey of Bell's out of a rucksack and sucked on it. Frequently he heard the helicopters rattling overhead, back and forth, as they took their loads of retardant to drop on the Wawa 7. He wondered if this close sticky heat was caused by the fire, the eruption of fire on earth, a hell that had broken forth while his attention was elsewhere.

He lay on the mattress, scrolling his aimless way through a large television screen positioned at the foot of the bed; commercials for beer, no end of commercials; pickerel fishing on Lake Erie; the familiar footage from Paisley Head, Ontario, a severe reporter in a grey suit counting up the E.coli victims, eleven of them. Death was coming out of the water taps, she explained. He sucked on his mickey, and savoured the life-giving force of the scotch. At the same time, he prepared himself for an attack of dread, a raw sensation of waste and wrong choices, of remorse and infant-like loneliness that he knew was preparing to grab him. Paul smelled it in the room with him.

He had a sudden memory of Linda pulling the bed sheets up to her chin and laughing. For a terrible moment he thought they had stayed together in this very room, with this same grinning television in front of them, watching the drunken world stagger into its own detox, but it had to be somewhere else. He wasn't sure why it had to be somewhere else, except that he couldn't bear it if this was the place. It was another town, another bead on the blacktop that stretched outside the door. Spanish, maybe, or Massey, where they walked high up on the banks of the Aux Sables, by the cemetery.

Paul lay and sweated and drank and flipped through the television: *... increasingly fanned by winds from the west* ... the dreary, grey smoke on the screen flicked away, channel after channel of young people grinning and saying foolish things to each other, always grinning. He saw a graphic estimating the number of domestic stock in British Columbia infected with bovine spongiform encephalitis. The number did not mean anything to him. Feeding the minced brains of cows to other cows. Who was the genius that came up with that idea? He watched stricken cattle wobble across the screen.

He looked up idly to the ceiling fan, but the fan was not working. Paul understood that he was drunk. He had achieved a type of lift-off. The phone was in his hand, he was ready to phone her, to have the assurance of his wife's voice and her calmness speaking to him through the ridiculous wires, but he was ashamed for himself, and he put the machine down.

The rat appeared in the doorway and stopped. It was no ordinary rat, obviously. Paul saw that a dream catcher had been tattooed in red on the animal's side.

"You are not *Rattus norvegicus*," said Paul accusingly.

"No, I'm not, and neither are you. Why don't you phone your wife," said the rat. "You have ended up alone in an overpriced motel room watching television and failing to summon up the courage required to phone your wife. You inherited the moral arrogance of your race. You have attempted to chuck the dead world and build a new one. You've been mad and drunk all summer and now you're talking to a rat."

Paul groaned. It was true. He'd ridden a great road and now he was lying on an unknown bed with a mickey of Bell's scotch and a talking rat.

"For God's sake," he said, convinced momentarily that he had the right to say such words. With a feeling of intense gratitude, he passed out.

29

HAS THE FIRE PASSED?

*"In the time of the Sixth Fire, it will be evident that promise of the Fifth Fire
came in a false way. Those deceived by this promise will take their children
away from the teachings of the Elders. Grandsons and granddaughters will turn
against the Elders. In this way, the Elders will lose their reason for living...."*

FROM THE PROPHECY OF THE SEVEN FIRES

THE ELDERLY WOMAN LAY ON starched sheets in the Lake of the Woods
District Hospital beneath the branches of trees she couldn't see.
Her hand was being held. Her hand was wrapped in a man's hand,
but it was not her husband's. It did not belong to the man who'd
sat in that room where the vellum books covered the walls, and
the amber of the lamps was reflected in bottles of liquor. She
called out to him through the tall pines that waved above the
church at Pickle River, "Joshua, I have no feeling I can find beyond
those miles we travelled." There had been a great passion. But not
for him. Sometimes she saw it floating behind her eyes. A boy.
Theodore, he did not like to be called Ted. He preferred Theodore.
He wasn't a boy, of course, he was a young man with wide

shoulders. He lost a leg at Monte Cassino, then he died. There were letters she kept in a tin, funny letters and letters of love. The boy had loved her.

A voice was speaking to her, repetitive, droning, like the voices that blared on the intercom; *Doctor Kohut to emergency please Doctor Kohut emerg…* "Priscilla," the voice said, "Mother." It would be Paul then, the boy, her only child, her son standing there in the dark where she could not see him, where so many things existed now. He had grown into a man with troubled teeth and hands the texture of bark. She felt something pressing to her. She wondered if Paul was an old man now too, her son. Had that happened to everyone? Even him? It wasn't fair. Everyone, it had happened to everyone. That the life written by her body grew old, disappeared and became invisible — she had made a peace with that; the paper shrivelled, and became dust. That it should happen to her children, too, she thought. That was the atrocity.

She remembered there was a boy out there, her boy, who searched among the rocks and roots of the ironwood tree and wielded his fishing rod through the spring pickerel runs. He was always searching. Always wanting to know. The boy had made himself an honorary son of Ronnie Whiteloon. He was dead too then, Ronnie Whiteloon, that smiling man who arranged his children in order of size, largest to shortest, as they walked through town. Her boy Paul had played in houses tacked with newspaper, snuck into bathrooms where there were no toilets, only bathtubs filled with coal. The otters clattered over the woodpile. "Mother," he said, I want to change my name to Weaselhead. Why would you want to do that? Because I love that name. Why do you love that name? Because it makes sense. My name does not make sense. Prescot is a foreign name. It makes no sense to me. His father had slapped his face for it. Weaselhead.

Joshua, she said, stop it, and she understood this was the last word she would speak. Joshua, she whispered, has the fire passed? Is it roaring? Do the animals still run in fear from the forest? Does your very son fear you? Does the land fear you? Is it time that we must leave our homes and rivers and go from here, Joshua? Paul? The heat was unbearable, on her eyes and forehead. The sun would not forgive them.

"Stop it," she cried.

Paul felt the thin bones of his mother's hand, a bare flicker of blood within it. In that moment he became aware of the giggling of Muzak that fell from the speakers, had been falling since the beginning. It came to him like a symphony rising louder until it filled his ears and eclipsed her breathing. She spoke, uttered frail words, then tried again.

"Stop it," she said. He was sure that's what she said.

"Priscilla?" His lips were against her ear, close enough to feel her hair, its dryness. "Mother."

Beneath the fluorescent lights he heard the laughter of two nurses. One of them had a date. "He has his pilot's licence," she said. The other one responded to this with some awe. "Oh, a fly boy." But her colleague would have nothing to do with it. "It's never worked before. Why should it with this guy? So what he has a pilot's licence?" This was followed by an outbreak of laughter from both of them.

Paul closed his eyes.

30

EMBARKING

THE FOLLOWING DAY HE WENT to visit again, but she was not conscious. Paul left the hospital and walked the harbour on his way back into town, past the grand old Kenricia and into the Whistling Monkey for two quick therapeutic Johnny Walkers. Televisions hung from the walls above the bar and he watched stupidly the exploded streets and bleeding people in Bali, Madrid, London, the unreal cities in which shards of glass mingled with flesh and teeth. Between the laughter of stars and starlets, the bombs were located in the shoes, in bicycles and in baby carriages; missiles directed by satellites lurked in the Milky Way, the most sophisticated weaponry, exploding in villages that had no running water. Terrorists, they said. Like microbes, Paul thought. Everyone had suddenly become a terrorist. Even the gods.

"Another one," he said to a figure that appeared to exist in black and white, moving into the dark, emerging briefly with a small glass. Disappearing once again. "Another one." It was like prayer. There was nothing else to say.

The drinks lacked any therapeutic value at all, not counting the brief half-hallucination in which he saw his father swaying beside him, intoning in his baritone lines from the Hymnody of the Church Universal, "When the strife of sin is killed … When the foe within is stilled …" He consumed two more drinks, largely because his teeth had begun to hurt again, a pulsating pain that came out of a recessed pocket in the back lower gum. It should have been looked after, would in fact have been looked after had he not forgotten his appointment. He comforted himself with the knowledge that a vial of yellow pills was stashed in his pack somewhere.

Still tasting the wash of his last drink, he entered the Kenora bus terminal and went downstairs to relieve himself. In the bathroom a young man was attempting to have a bath in a sink. It was an old habit of Paul's, peeing in bus station bathrooms. Back upstairs a number of Native women sat in dispirited plastic chairs and waited uncomplainingly for a Grey Goose bus to haul them out to God's Lake Narrows or some similar place.

Twenty minutes later he was on the road, exhausted, his eyes shut as the highway pulled him southeast out of Kenora, the bus clinging to the grey asphalt. He opened his eyes long enough to read a billboard wheeling by on the roadside: *Are you vaccinated? It's not just a good idea. It's the law.* Another sickness on the earth. Paul tried to will himself to sleep, but managed only a dull state in which waking dreams wound their way through the wheels of the bus.

BY MORNING HE WAS AT Marathon among the leaning pickup trucks of the sports fishermen, the grey rocks and brilliant water. The white sprawl of the pulp mill crouched beneath the mountain, steaming and feral. Soon he spotted Joe Animal waiting for him, perhaps he'd been standing there all night, for days even. His black hair hung below the battered green baseball cap stained with sweat. *Red Man Chewing Tobacco*, it read.

"You look great," called Paul.

"Don't I."

Paul transferred his gear to the boat and they pulled away from Marathon harbour in a blue-painted Peterhead borrowed from the Pic Mobert reserve. Through some decades-long evolution that Paul was only vaguely aware of, the vessel had migrated south from the upper peninsulas of Nunavik where it had been engaged in the walrus hunt in the sixties. It sat low in the water, but the tall narrow cab toward the stern reached to the air, giving the boat a nervous dimension, as if waiting for a particular wave to topple it. There was a persistent rumour that Marilyn Monroe had been on this very boat, more than once. She and Clark Gable. A door made of mahogany took up half of the cabin wall. Paul was not confident the boat was entirely waterproof, but felt no urge to ask questions about it. He leaned against the door exhausted as the vessel thumped along the gleaming sandbars and gnarled spider-stumps of dead trees crowding the shore.

The vessel cleaved northwest through the sapphire water and followed the walls of rock to what was likely Point Isocar on a map and in the same latitude as the Kuma River which he knew expired into the Caspian though he had never been anywhere near that part of the world. What useless knowledge we are stuffed with, he thought. Me in particular. Michipicoten, the island, floated out of sight and out to sea. For a moment, the island crested the water like a ghost ship. Michipicoten. He had tread on it, and recalled vividly the collapsed fishing shanties there. Michipicoten. Some said a piece of it had sunk the *Edmund Fitzgerald*. A great sea creature lived there, kept guard over the copper. The copper could kill a man, had killed many. The island fell behind him. He inched his binoculars along the shoreline, scanning slowly, deliberately, the way a Cree guide had done in front of him on the Moose River, taking a quarter hour to complete his survey, moving the glasses imperceptibly, as slowly as the earth's rotation. Paul gave up quickly. The pitch of the boat, the spank of the water, and the shoreline magnified four hundred times by the lenses sickened him at once. He fought off an urge to spit over the side. The rock shore seemed to demand this gesture from him. Instead he wiped his hand across his lips. As he did, the gold of his wedding band flared in the sun.

The boat skirted the great bend beyond the mountains, then straight north in easy reach of the shore. He preferred it that way. In a moment the clouds eclipsed the sun. He wrapped his jacket against the cold, smelling an old watery danger. He returned the binoculars to his eyes and held them there despite the pitching of the vessel. Again, the magnification jolted him and made him nauseous. From his pocket, Paul retrieved a small plastic water bottle filled with Cointreau and drank from it. He was drinking Cointreau. This felt ominous. Only the dinosaurs drank Cointreau. Look what happened to them.

The door swung open and clapped against the side. Joe Animal, inside, leaned against the wheel.

"Mr. Animal."

Paul knew he would be grinning stupidly even though he could not see his face. He had perfected the art of grinning foolishly. The man wore a chequered woolen shirt with packs of emergency cigarettes cached in various pockets. "Joe Animal. You ever going change that name?"

"I'm thinking 'Fred.' 'Fred Animal.' You like that?"

"Fred is good."

"Fred is dead," said Joe.

Paul tipped the Cointreau into his mouth. Tastes rotten, he thought, though in fact he felt the sweetness flow into him like a river and at once felt the urge to embrace everyone, all of his friends, even those who had died. Especially those.

Somehow, in the face of an obliterating wind, Joe Animal had managed to light a cigarette.

"You want a drink?" yelled Paul. It did not feel right to be in a vessel captained by a man who was not drunk. Something un-Canadian about that. "You want a drink?"

"Maybe." Joe Animal appeared to be ruminating deeply on the subject. Long ago he had come to the conclusion a man could be sober, so long as he was careful about it. He could be sober as a judge, though in fact the only judge he had ever met had been blind drunk and drove his car into a ditch after trying to buy a bag of weed off Wendy Maracle during the Serpent River powwow. If he recalled it right, she wouldn't sell it to him. "It don't make me no wiser," he said.

"It's not Wiser's. I don't have Wiser's."

"Wiser's makes you stupid," said Joe.

"I have Cointreau."

Joe Animal looked at him. "No shit?"

"Be careful now. Cointreau is a product of monasticism. Without monasticism we wouldn't have Cointreau, or Benedictine or even Chartreuse. The drink I mean, not the colour. Interesting how all those sequestered and womanless monks spent half their lives in prayer and the other half making top-drawer booze."

Whether that was interesting or not did not show on the face of the other man. "If it wasn't for those monks the world would not be reeling across the universe looking for a toilet to be sick in."

"Yes it would," answered Joe.

Paul thought it was possible he was about to be sick as well. He looked across the water to steady himself and saw two loons shoot by in a perfectly flat trajectory, their dark wings whisking the air in a rhythmic one-two. His nausea proved brief, leaving him as he scrutinized the fowl and their impossible aerodynamics. From his reading in Kohl he tried an old Native trick that could supposedly stop a loon in flight and make it circle their canoes. "Orray," he cried. "Orray." The loons ignored his call and vanished like two black shells fired from a shotgun.

The man watched Paul Prescot trying to be like a Native person from one of his books and was filled again with a dubious feeling about where they were going. As far as he knew, those things on the rocks, they could be something you had your kids do to get them out of your hair, he'd told him that; you said Johnny, take this bowl of sturgeon oil and crushed ochre and go over there and don't bother me. But once, as a child, he'd shored deep into Quetico, on a cobble beach where the rock face showed the old drawings, and his aunt took him aside and said, "You don't go anywhere near those things, you listen."

"You should be careful, Paul. You should." He rolled his cigarette from one corner of his mouth to the other and managed to avoid any trace smoke from entering his eyes. He had not read the man's books, but he had nothing against books. He held books in esteem, the way he valued an oiled .303 Savage rifle. As a grown man, he'd read several books, all written by Louis L'Amour. He could quote from one: "I haven't been much of a wife to you have I Jim?" "No Lottie, you haven't." It couldn't get better than that. He'd tried a novel by Zane Grey and another about a man who had a job that involved breaking the necks of spies and saving beautiful women. He'd read some pages of a book by John Steinbeck because he liked the name. He thought he would change his name to Steinbeck. Steinbeck Animal. Or maybe Joe the Steinbeck Animal. It had a ring.

"Orray, Ooray. O-raaay." Outside the cabin, Paul was trying to talk to the animals again. Some people could do that. Some couldn't. His grandmother would not shut up when it came to talking to animals. Whitefish in particular. She lured them on to her line with a continuous chatter. For a moment, as the coastline came closer, he entertained a vision of himself entering the American Vista Casino at the Red Cliff Reserve in Wisconsin wearing his black, ironed shirt, though who would iron it now that Wendy Maracle had emptied her rifle into his truck was unclear. There were some women that shot up your truck and that was it, they weren't coming back. He could iron his own shirts.

PAUL HUDDLED OUTSIDE WITH HIS back against a board on deck, using the gunwales to keep the wind off him. A notebook pressed his knees. *Dear Linda*, he crossed it out. This was the hardest part. *My dear wife my my* ... He couldn't get it right. *My mother is about to pass now*, he wrote, *she admired you very much, did you know that? Did you know I just wanted to revive myself from the rituals of our marriage, of any marriage?* He could not write this. He saw his fingers spread on a sheet of paper. Have I let this love go away that we made together and fought for? Has this happened? Have I wrecked the house where we lived? *Dear Linda, I have no business telling you this, I barely feel myself here beneath the engine of the boat and this water. What a foolish thing. I would rather express myself with teeth on birch bark or fingers on a stone* ... There was nothing, he realized, nothing he could write that could tell what she meant to him. He wrote brokenly now, trying to inscribe himself on the pages of his notebook.

31

IN OTHER DEVELOPMENTS

"If they come carrying a weapon and if they seem to be suffering, beware.
Behind this face is greed. You shall recognize the face of death if
the rivers are poisoned and the fish are unfit to eat."

THE PROPHECY OF THE SEVEN FIRES

SHE STOOD IN FRONT OF the black door with a peek hole drilled in the middle. The door opened and Arthur Gratton stood in front of her before turning his back to indicate she was to enter. Inside the room, a television droned dimly and revealed grainy footage of a bog or a cracked riverbed laden with the rotted hulks of fishing boats. A woman's voice explained the Aral Sea had drained away and was gone. It wasn't coming back. "Officials estimate that thirty thousand fishermen have been left without a sea to fish in." She seemed utterly thrilled by the prospect.

Arthur turned from the screen. Behind his right ear a fist-sized pewter bust of Stalin stared sternly at her from a shelf.

"How's your husband?" It excited him to say this. He put his finger under her chin and turned her face to his. The Aral Sea gave way to a backwash of tinny music. "Play scratch and win. With your busy lifestyle you don't have time for a common headache." The words seem to materialize out of the air. He took her bottom lip between his knuckles and squeezed it hard enough for her to wince. "Darling," he murmured, "darling." She turned away, but he put his finger to her and lifted her chin. She was to look at him.

Her arms hung down uselessly.

You don't have time for a headache.

Suddenly he slapped her.

"There," he said.

He took her by the hair and tugged her into his chest, forcing her to look at the black eyes that drilled from his head.

More doctors recommend.

"Everything's fucked," he whispered. "Especially me. I'm especially fucked. He pressed his hips into her. "There," he said. "Open your eyes." He touched her on the side of the face. "Open your eyes." But she didn't. He slapped her gently this time.

Her face stung.

The television roared.

"Turn it off," she said.

He shook his head. "The soundtrack of history. Get used to it." He put his fingers to her face again.

She closed her eyes, but couldn't protect herself from it. "From Halifax now." The voice droned. A six-year-old boy in a Halifax schoolyard had kissed a girl. Police summoned. Zero tolerance they said. Why zero? she wondered. Couldn't we afford just a little bit of tolerance. One little bit of it. For the sake of the children. For the sake of love. Just one percent.

"In other developments."

Arthur had put his index finger into her mouth, his free hand was on her stomach, and was about to stomp across her body, like a beast over the savanna. He squeezed her between the legs, his foot between hers, spreading her limbs. He said a word, several words. She was to go to her knees. Get on your knees. "If you don't mind."

"People must open up their hearts …" The words circled from the television, a crying Native woman with the remnants of a black eye. A police officer had taken a photograph of a steak knife, put a caption on it. *Squaw killer.* Internal review pending. Linda watched her on the screen, the woman cried; "They desecrated my sister's body."

"Don't come," he ordered.

She had no intention of coming. She wouldn't come. She would only go. She would go to where Paul was. Clearly, he was writing to her at this moment with a headlamp on, burrowed in his sleeping bag, *Linda dearest the lights over Chapleau, the long evenings of our wedding journey, you cried beneath the aurora, I could not take my eyes off you.*

"Open your eyes."

She had no intention of doing anything like that. She was sick of seeing. "I can make you do whatever I want," Arthur said, but he did not sound certain of it. He didn't sound certain at all.

She realized Arthur was frightened. Beneath the fabric of his clothes; beneath its weave, he was frightened. Like everyone. All of those men who hid behind a cascade of opinion. He was one of them. He'd told so many lies. He'd written them, he forced them into people's language. What people, she wondered. He'd made liars out of all of us. He was turning people into lies, putting truth into a machine. He was one of them.

"You fucked up our stories," she said wildly. "You took them, you made copy out of them. Now there's no way to get them back. They're all locked up in there." She pointed to the television screens. He paid no attention.

"You need to do what I want you to do."

She sensed this was a lie too, his behaviour. He needed her in order to write his stories, for them to mean anything.

"What are you trying to prove?" Linda formed a wedge with her forearms, snapping outward and made room for herself to breathe. Arthur slumped against the wall and for a moment she thought he was about to cry, that he was crying already. She looked at him, collapsed, the crows shot out from the sockets of his eyes crying, *quo vadis, quo vadis.*

"Where are you going," he said suddenly. But she turned on him, and left.

LINDA CAME HOME IN A cab driven by a solemn man wearing a caftan. They sped swiftly around stalled streetcars and fallen bicycles. He glanced over his shoulder, occasionally, smiling at her. He brought the cab to a stop in front of the church.

The machine sulked away and, as it did, the blare of an ambulance filled the space under the trees. The sound funneled up between the houses, dopplering a weird semi-tone of hysteria that ended when the ambulance pulled up and braked on the sidewalk before the Holderlich's house. The door popped on the passenger side and at the same moment the front door of her neighbours' house flew open, and Mrs. Holderlich appeared wearing a housecoat, wailing.

"Help him, my husband," she cried. "Help the poor man." Her voice keened off the church. Two emergency workers rushed the house and the woman went in after them. Harriet, was that her name? Henrietta?. They had spoken in the aftermath of the burning church: "Where is your husband," she'd demanded with considerable suspicion.

The older woman went swiftly indoors into the house she had shared for fifty years with the man who lay in an awkward way at the bottom of the stairs, hardly breathing. In the darkness, neighbours appeared in doorways and front yards dressed in house-coats. Women who had survived Treblinka and were stout now, they stood gravely on front porches. The veteran cat, Rover, looked on from a distance approving of none of it as Mr. Holderlich was carried out on a stretcher with a yellow fleece blanket spread over top of him.

32

THE PREPARATIONS

The following spring he went on a hunting trip with his Indian friends
and later described the adventure, which included an encounter with an
alligator-like reptile: "there layd on one of the trees a snake wth foure feete,
her head very bigg, like a Turtle, the nose very small att the end."

RADISSON, CITED IN THE DICTIONARY OF CANADIAN BIOGRAPHY VOL. II

PAUL DROPPED THIGH HIGH INTO the water of Superior and felt the coldness stab his groin and shock even the base of his chin. "Aaah-ha," he cried out. He was aware of his oldness, that it had finally come and built a nest in him.

Joe Animal shouted from the boat. "I can't get no closer." The vessel pitched alarmingly between two outcrops of rock. The air hissed.

Paul swore again.

"It's fine once you get used to it, right?"

"It's fine once you get out of it," shouted Paul.

"Yeah, once you're out and you got a fire going and you're drinking and you're in bed. Then it's pretty good. At least it's not cold anymore."

"A week," said Paul, taking down the gear that was handed him. "One week exactly. Seven days. Not six, or eight. White man's week, right? Old-fashioned colonial-style racist week."

"You mean a week like?"

"One week."

"Seven days?"

"If I get weathered in, you call someone. You call the Coast Guard."

"No coast guard," shouted Joe. "They shut it down. Been shut down a year. They don't got the money anymore. Get weathered in, you're screwed. You got enough food?"

"Next Saturday, right here. Get the crazy guy out of Jackfish to come and get me if you can't do it."

"That guy's dead," said Joe Animal. "I'll be here next Saturday. You going up the trail, to those pits?"

"That's right."

"You stay out of those things."

"I will."

"You won't." Joe was not comfortable with Pukaskwa pits, or goodbyes either, and he turned his head into the wind dragging his boat around with him. The vessel followed like a willing dog, pitching sideways on the curling water.

AS HE CLAMBERED THE WHITE cobbles, Paul startled grasshoppers that popped madly into the air as if mounted on pogo sticks. They seemed to be deliberately luring him away from the nests of their beloved young ones, clattering against stones with the strange sound of *chucka chucka chucka*, their wings snapping and jerking them into the air, like helicopters, he thought, malfunctioning helicopters. A snake slid sideways on the rock.

He negotiated his way under a fallen tree that had tumbled

down from the timberline. The trunk was smooth as a tusk. The rock surface under his feet was deeply scratched by glaciers. He felt the familiar comfort of being on rock. He'd read Louis Agassiz's writings about rock; that hateful man who had turned his hatred into science. Paul, as a young man, had poured over his writings while sitting on rocks, the Precambrian pillow lava showing like the waterways of an ancient map. He had made love on rock, the girl was dead now, but this was not his fault. A car crash had taken her, years ago. He stood on the rock and watched the shield unfold before him to the north.

Soon he was leaping from boulder to boulder like some younger incarnation of himself, moving quickly, searching for a route between the stone terraces while the surging and sucking of the seas played out beneath him. Great heaves of green water entered the caverns, sloshed and broke like gunshots. The waves fragmented into pools scummy with algae and crisscrossed with spiders. A gull turned above his head in the white sky. For several minutes, Paul sat and faced the water, watching the waves flatten into a frantic turquoise agitation at a point far away. He tried to visualize the American shore a hundred miles southwest, to Copper Harbour, and the abandoned graves of Cornish miners. The miniature graves of their babies. Linda had wept when she saw them. His eyes shifted west to where the Keweenaw finger would be, the Apostle Islands, the cliffs where old stories said a scroll existed, buried under the roots of an ironwood tree.

A scatter of black birds left the branches and were wind-tossed back to where they started. "*Quo Vadis … Quo Vadis*," cried the crows. Where are you going? Where? Into what future? Paul followed a quartz vein into the forest and turned with it, throwing his arms up as he rammed through the bush. The shore was not navigable and he was close now, he sensed it from the fallen hush in the trees and from the growing silence in himself. The birds, the insects, had given in to stillness. A stream leaked from the woods, lapping softly.

He found the pits on the other side, on the creek shore, barely visible, two concentric terraces of rocks built into the ground, layered in regularity to form a hole, deep as his arm. The stones themselves seemed braided into a type of bird's nest and imbedded in the ancient shore of a diminished ocean. Each pit made a pocket large enough to curl up in and dream, or sleep, or die. Or to cook fish in. Five thousand years old. Three hundred years? He didn't know. He was not aware of anyone who did. Dream pits? Pits for the storing and curing of meat? Long ago, on a campus radio station, he'd debated the raving Seth Blumrich who insisted the structures were built by Andromeda Galaxy aliens. No, answered Paul, they were constructed by the hands of men or women, people, ancestors about whom we know almost nothing. They are beyond our capacity to understand. Or our right, he thought. Beyond our right to understand. Part of a story we do not understand. What about the records, Blumrich had insisted, why have we no record? What happened to those people? What spaceship were they on? What deadly microbes did they leave behind, that have come back now in these times? Mark my words. The paintings, Paul had always insisted. The paintings on the rock. They were the record, a living record. On Michipicoten, he had seen pit structures extending two thousand square feet, large enough for a clan of people to curl up together and dream. Large enough for a space vehicle to land, Blumrich had insisted.

Paul went to his knees beside the largest of the two pits. He unpacked swiftly, whistling to himself and poled the tent low to the ground next to it. Once, long ago, they had gathered here, people who weaved with stone, paddled stone canoes before disappearing into rock faces. I am practising the religion of life, he told himself as he pegged the tent. The life that death covets; blueberries and rock and water, women, and men, and stinging insects and tobacco; most of all tobacco, which heaven had none. Nothing in heaven tempted him. Nothing tempted him, not even tobacco. All heaven had going for it was dreary eternity. And whiteness, a thick whiteness, like shaving cream, he thought.

He heard the high *klee klee klee* of the osprey.

Hunger clutched him, but he wouldn't eat. His tooth bothered him a great deal, but he refused to think about it. His pills lay in a container somewhere in his knapsack. Pink ones in another container. He should have taken care of all of that before he left, he knew it. He was getting careless.

Paul went down shore to the rock cliff and angled himself in front of the paintings, on a low ledge that barely protruded from the face. They showed there like rust on the surface; fine clay impregnated with ferrous oxide congealed with sturgeon oil, the yellow ochre transforming into red oxide through heat. Some of it had lasted four hundred winters. Such paint could not be replicated. No one had that knowledge now. He stood in front of a grey vertical face displaying the letters, L and R, and next to it, the date, 1781. The face had once been overgrown by lichen, now withered away, revealing figures of a rabbit-eared man with both arms crooked. The three fingered man, the man with a bird's head, the man with antlers. The figures appeared to be waving at something, not him, something beyond him. *Pre-literate gropings toward the written word.* The attitude had not satisfied him. He did not consider them pre-literate gropings. He considered them a concentrated formal and literal expression of the end of time, a visual display of past and future, when the animal joined in sickness and greed and avian diseases and the diseases of monkeys and swine mingled with the people and great sicknesses came. It was written in stone, the antlers emerged from the head of man, a false prophet, or the true one, in a time without truth.

Paul touched the rock. He wanted to feel on his finger a language that was made of something other than words. Different language. No one had been here, he knew that. No one who was alive.

AT NIGHT HE BOILED RICE on a stove and allowed himself to eat only half of it. He would starve to a point. To stoke a hunger for dreaming. His tent was pitched, but he would take the night outside.

When the moon came up over the tree line on the mountain, he entered the pit and lay with his back against the sloping cobble walls. He felt the moisture, the stones were soaked with it, soaked with the night. Joe Animal wouldn't do this, he thought. No matter how sober he was. Paul reminded himself that he was not entering into a place that was forbidden to him. Everyone was native of the earth. Even him. The rock was his. He was native, finally, his body lay on stone, he had achieved that. Native of the earth, like stone. Ancient now, like stone. For a moment the cold sheer discomfort of the cobbles was unbearable to him.

He pulled the sleeping bag around him, wedged his eyes shut until finally and wretchedly he slept. Within two hours, he awoke hard. A root had snapped in the forest or in his mind. His tooth throbbed insanely. He had not dreamed yet, instead he lay awake, feeling that something was observing him.

33

DREAMWORK

Wheeler's informant told him that the old medicine man
searching for a cure for a sick woman said he received powerful medicines
from the men who lived in the rock.

GRACE RAJNOVICH, 1994

OF COURSE LINDA WAS DREAMING, she knew that, she had to be. What else was there for her to be doing? She was dreaming of a spot where she'd once camped with her husband, he was shirtless and sketching a snake petroform on the ground at the Manitoba border. A soft-drink machine glowed from the depths of the forest. She recognized it from numerous rainy nights camping on the Sleeping Giant, when Paul had given a talk. Later, through the mesh of the tent, she saw the machine by the visitor's centre, glowing blue between the trees. "Feed me," it said, "put coins into my mouth." She had been dreaming, then too. She had been dreaming even when she had her dream. Now she was at the water's edge. The sturgeon lolled there, such a slow gentle beast with its two soft mandibles. Its skin of leather. They'd bound books out of its skin, left its carcasses rotting in heaps on the shore. She slid into its toothless mouth, head first, the way she'd tobogganed as a girl, tugged into a warm belly as if a sledding down a snowy hill. Inside it smelled like the St. Lawrence Market on a Saturday morning when the rolls came out of the oven, and the meat was stacked and raw on a mat of wax paper. She remained in there, in the dark of the belly of the great fish. Softly at first, coming near, she heard it, the familiar snort and snuffle of a bear and she listened, unafraid, while it chewed a hole in the sturgeon's side. Sun entered in shafts, cycling through the widening wound; with some childish delight, she found herself being washed through it into the earth on the tides of the fish's guts, into the hubbub of a language that sounded from the trees, "Da-da-edewenh-hye, da-da-edewenh-hyedagh-satka-ghtoogh-seron-ee." Something bat-like swooped to her ear. The cold nose of a deer nuzzled against her palm. "Give my meat to your people," the creature instructed her. "Your rivers are distressed." Whose people, she thought. Her hand reached into a wooden barrel in the basement — Sunday then, baking day across the north — Linda plunged her arm deep into the isinglass for eggs; the frigid sturgeon goo that kept the eggs cold, isinglass. The word appealed to her. Isinglass. She would live there one day, in the Kingdom of Isinglass, where the men were long-limbed. She reached in without distaste, groping for eggs, but what she came up with was not an egg. Her hand emerged holding the severed head of a dog, the mouth bound shut with twine, its eyes white and brimming with mucus. She let the dog's head fall back into the barrel and saw without surprise, that her father was there beside her. Her father again. There had been a time she had wanted so much from him. She had no idea what. "The Chief of Gardens," she'd called him that for years. His back was turned, and the leather patches on his elbows in need of mending. "Look after your garden Linda, listen to me. Don't let your children kick the hell out of it."

Linda held up her hands to indicate she had no children hidden there. "I don't have any children, Dad. Sorry." She saw that her hands were covered in filth: the earth and the dirt of the earth. At least the humus was still willing to stain her skin. Her wedding band was lost however and she sensed with mounting relief that she was dreaming. There was nothing in her hand but a chestnut-sized nugget of mud that Linda tossed flippantly into the lake. As she did that she was stricken by the urgent need to pee and squatted in the blueberries watching the rivulet of her urine search the ground and snake through the grass and sand. Without looking up, Linda understood that she was being watched; Arthur, that foolish man, was hidden behind a tree watching all the girls pee. He held a powerful pair of binoculars, shifting from one side to another as he sought to get a better look at her cleft. "Linda Richardson," he cried. "I want to hump thee."

She understood that she was dreaming or was very close to it. "Of course, you do Arthur. You can get in line with the rest," she said coolly. But Arthur had no intention of waiting and leapt from behind a white pine wearing a loincloth that he ripped off. "That is really too much, Arthur. For God's sake." Linda laughed, but she had to admit that he possessed an impressive cock. No sooner had she conceded this point to herself than she saw that the poor man had no eyes and this saddened her. Another man with no eyes. How long could this go on? All that staring they did, at screens that never blinked. At words. Two pink craters showed there. "I warned you, Arthur. This happens when you constantly fool with that thing. You have gone blind, you silly man."

"I was faking it," he cried. "I was always faking it. From the start. I faked the four winds. I fabricated the four stations of the cross. I wrote Hitler's diaries. It was me." At that moment, Arthur was no longer there. He had been replaced by the elderly fellow standing next to her. She felt she knew the man, that she recognized him somehow, from somewhere. "Can you believe I slept with that guy," she said. "More than once. It was the only thing we knew how to do. Now look, I've lost my wedding ring." She turned and fully regarded the statuesque old man next to her, his reams of white hair, some of it emerging from his nostrils. She suspected it was a mistake to say this to him, but couldn't stop herself. "Wait a minute. I know you. You're Longfellow. Henry Wadsworth. Aren't you? You're the Gitchee Gummee guy!"

The old man examined her severely. "You foolish woman," he answered brusquely. "Look what's become of you. Do you have the faintest idea where you are?" With a trembling and knotted finger, he indicated the ground. "This earth which is held together by billions of years, now worn down by the feet of the runners of the confederacy of Iroquois. They ran even at night, guided by the constellations. Do you know what this place is?"

"Let me guess. Would it be the forest primeval?" Linda was pleased with this comeback. She didn't hold a postgraduate degree in English literature for nothing. "And you and I are just ships passing in the night, right?"

The old poet smiled in spite of himself and snapped open a locket, with the ease of gesture repeated many times. He turned it to her. A woman's face in miniature, hand-coloured, wrapped in folded grey hair.

"Your wife?"

"I tried to save her. Her gown, you see, I tried to save her with these hands. She burned. From the lamps. She died screaming. I failed to save her." He seemed to recover himself for a moment, and pointed at her. "What is it that you hear? Your husband, he's dead as well? Do you hear him? Are we here to grieve? You and I? To grieve together?"

"Of course not," cried Linda.

Even as she spoke, she saw a man lying face down on the forest floor, wounded in the thigh, "He's writing in a notebook right now. If you must know," she said archly. "He is out somewhere on the north shore of Lake Superior saving us with his dreams."

34

COLDWELL PENNINSULA

My friend told me it represented his dream of life and that he had this dream
on the St. Croix River when he was quite young. He fasted ten days for it.
"Canst thou impart to me all the circumstances of this dream," I asked him.
"No, but when I am in great danger and on the point of dying then I shall collect
all my family around me and reveal to them the entire history of my dream.
KITCHI-GAMI: LIFE AMONGST THE LAKE SUPERIOR OJIBWAY,
JOHANN GEORGE KOHL, 1860

AFTER SEVERAL DAYS, HE MADE his way to the shoreline and lapped
water in the manner of a bear, following it with three pieces of
dried papaya. His vision had sharpened, become more intense; a
silver phosphorescent glow sprang from all things. This pleased
him. His teeth hurt him very much however, and in defiance of
the pain he gargled the chilling water of Superior over the aching
region of his face.

He spent the day at the side of the pit with his shirt off, pressing
his skin to rock. His notes, assembled in a spiral-bound book, lay on
the ground. *The hairy-faced ones, the little ones of legend, they entered these rocks*
with offerings of tobacco and for this they were given the knowledge of rock medicine.

In the afternoon, a light rain nudged in from Superior and loosed a steaming vapour in the forest, damping the mosquitoes and flies. He retreated to his tent, and permitted himself to swallow a thousand milligrams of Novamoxin, hoping they would punch the pain away for a time. It annoyed him he couldn't find the blue pills. He had not searched everything yet, but he was sure he'd forgotten to pack them. They remained on the bedside table back home, beneath the chiming of the Greek church. It was a mistake and he was annoyed by it. Expeditions had been wiped out by small mistakes.

In the afternoon, he removed his watch and threw it into Lake Superior. On the day of wrath, he thought, every precious thing shall be useless and we shall chuck our precious silver into the street. The watch was gone, but a band of white skin remained on his wrist. He retreated from the water. The flies had come in their fury. He lay in his tent, trying to ignore the throbbing of his teeth. Indecipherable forest noises came through the nylon walls. A silver film bled across the rocks and trees, casting down finally a quarter moon. The waves sounded on the shore, the repeating thud of waves came to him like someone moaning.

He awoke poking at his jaw. He got out of the tent and scoured the rocks at the treeline for blueberries and found them in meagre clusters. He drank from the lake but had difficulty raising himself. His legs burned from the inside. They had been worn out with the love of walking. Walks of three or four days' duration had been nothing. Unbounded walks. His glorious legs, he felt the burning in them. It was a sign for him to sit down, but he stood and went to the wall of stone and to the paintings. The forms were expiring, leaving only figures of rust. The paint was medicine, and he touched it. The canoe, no larger than his fist, contained six warriors, stick men, stick everything. The artist had no interest in form, not like the Kalahari, or the Lascaux artists. Everything content, a short-hand of urgency, of a time fast coming.

Two letters, ʟ and ʀ, crossed into four of the drawings. Ornate letters with grand serifs that spoke of a pork-eater who knew his own initials. Paul put his fingers to the stone. The face of it lunged to him. He wanted in it, to join the rock, in beyond the surface. "I'm in," he murmured, looking up at the great wall of stone. He was crouched in a place of power, and conjured two dark-haired lovers with their fingers dipped in ochre and animal oil, the hematite mined at the old pits at Wawa, painting on a four-billion-year-old face, picking insects from each other's hair. *Mishe Mucqau* loves *Ohbahbahmwawa-geezhhaqoquay*. For all eternity. For fifty bucks.

My mother will be dead, he thought and then spoke, strangely into the air, "I loved my mother, I love you." He cast about for the presence of others, dreamers who had been here before, holders of otter bags. Men and women who loved their mothers.

He heard a fox bark. The rooting for grubs and snails, the unfathomable orchestrations of the forest began, the cacophony of twitching insects and groaning branches. When he woke, the sun was up but invisible behind the black rock of the peninsula, flooding the day in green. Paul felt his teeth on fire. He began to write in a notebook, *signs fading from the rocks. Too much scrutiny. Scrutiny washed them away. Thought. Words, Language. What are these things now? The door's closed on the rocks. Don't know them, the songs. Or the dance.*

The entire day, he ate nothing. The infection in his mouth cooled. At twilight he went into the tent and did not dream. Every part of his body ached. Hours before dawn he was out of his tent, his tent a cold sagging membrane now drenched with dew. It would rain, he could smell the rain coming in. He began a chant to the roots and the shrubs he had gathered. "I am the roots and the shrubs and the ferns and the bracken and the tidal pools. I am the songs." He could sometimes not keep his father's baritone from sounding behind the thick fog of years gone.

Paul leaned back and found the cold rock with his flesh, scratching his neck on the moss, soft as the nuzzling of a cat. A patch of rock tripe broke away and fell to the ground. He held it between his fingers, *tripe de roche*; vulva-shaped wings of grey and black. If I go mad with starvation, I will eat this, he thought, like the Jesuits. He inhaled the cold, fecund stuff. The terrible song of insects seared across the rock, along with the rattle of grasshoppers. Their orchestrations seemed to swarm behind his eyelids. He felt he was being watched now, and soon he saw a deer twenty paces off in the shadows. In one effortless gesture the animal flexed its neck and body, leaped a fallen beech tree, and was gone into the forest. It seemed afraid of something.

The disappearance of the deer frightened him. He roused from his position, exiting the woods to sit upright on a rock, facing Superior. Paul felt the nausea of hunger and the readiness to accomplish great things. He saw himself at labour, a greasy body hauling baskets of hematite from the pits outside of Wawa, transporting them on the paths to the rock cliffs at Agawa, to heat in pans, to make the paint.

He reached down and collected a handful of cobbles.

"Mamaquishawok," he recited and hurled the stones at the sun, delighted as they transformed into butterflies, weaving, driven in every direction. There were children about, everywhere, and they squealed "mamaquishawok." The colours fluttered and weaved through the sky in front of them. There, he thought, I have given butterflies to children. What more could a child want? The stones fell to the ground. He'd given butterflies to the children. He'd give them song too, but song had already been gifted them by the birds. The birds, God bless them for giving their songs to us. For teaching us to sing, from which came speech. "Thank you for giving us butterflies, Mr. Prescot." They were so very welcome, all the children of the earth. The stones fell to the ground and he heard the insane sound of cicadas sawing in the forest. His hunger transformed into an insistent clutch at his belly directing him to the water, as if to eat it. He shut his eyes and felt that a headless form was about to erupt from behind him, but nothing happened, only the shuddering fear from an old prophecy; *if you do not move you will be destroyed.*

He moved from the water and struggled over the rock back into the forest to the Pukaskwa pit. Before its cobbled recessions he went to his knees as he had done as a child, addressing God, calling forth the names of those who needed protecting. Who did not need that? What name could not be called out? Hunger coursed through him. He was ready now to topple into time. He lay himself carefully in the pit and felt the twilight fall on top of him. It was not entirely uncomfortable, the cobbles knuckling the bones of his body, his eyelids crushed tight. The world first, then the end of it. Linda's chest pressed against his back, he felt her breasts and her forearm on his hip, but realized he'd only made the first shallow pools of sleep. Linda. He wasn't sure if he'd spoken her name out loud. Her name. She was unzipping some sort of leather folder, they were on a train, he was writing in his notebook, writing the words that had struck him like a hammer, appearing in front of his eyes on paper: *It is increasingly clear to me that the impact of Indigenous values and attitudes has shaped us more than we will ever comprehend. More than I will comprehend.*

The night entered at last, dropping with the meteors that flamed from far Cassiopeia.

35

WAKING UP

This savage woman was assured that if she were strong in her Faith,
the Devil could do her no harm, especially if she no longer believed in her dreams.
"I hate my dream even in my sleep," said this poor creature.

THE JESUIT RELATIONS, 1640

"LINDA? IS THERE COFFEE?"

The words were spoken by her husband, but sounded haunting in the rock caverns on the shore where they had always sounded, where they had originated in time immemorial.

"Linda? Is there coffee?"

She turned to the elderly man, the poet of renown with the bristling nostril hair, the seer, the pontificator, but he was no longer beside her. Not surprised by this, the inconstancy of men no longer surprised her, she found herself impulsively rubbing the white circle of pale flesh that showed around her finger. Her wedding band had slipped into a barrel of trembling isinglass, she remembered now. She was dreaming, she thought, with relief. The relief gushed through her. If she dreamt, it meant that those bothersome men sitting on that fallen cedar, circled in sunlight, the one in particular, marked by a noteworthy ugliness, it meant they were not real, were not anything to her. One of them she knew, had seen before, she knew him in some capacity, whether he was real or not. His tattooed body conveyed a dangerous kind of attractiveness, the very kind that she'd forsaken in her life, if only recently, today even, or tomorrow. His skin was charred black in places and veined with a complex network of tattoos, and his head, she noticed with great annoyance, was a seething tangle of snakes, green snakes. His hair was entirely made up of vipers, snapping like whips at the air around him, gulping at the flies. For some reason this annoyed her too, she had no faith in snakes. She approached him boldly, even insolently.

"You got a head full of snakes, mister. Are you trying to tell me something?"

The man made no response, but to remove the pipe from his mouth. Then, in a terrible sickening moment, his head detached from his shoulders and lunged at her, crazily, like some sort of toy she remembered from her childhood. His head, the snakes, his stricken face came at her from a distance, a balloon shape, spiralling wildly, until its very eyes were up close, peering into her own eyes, hungrily trying to enter through them. It was always like this, she thought. It was through the face they came at you. Linda felt herself rise up from herself, unfolding her body as if from a prayer position. Her hand held the electric hair dryer Paul had given her. She had not used it in some time; the last time, she believed, had been to defrost the freezer, now it was in her hand, like some charm that would see her through the most impossible of situations. She knew even without bothering to check that her initials L.R. would be monogrammed ornately on the leather case that lay on the ground. She whipped the device to the level of her eyes and clicked the trigger. "Made in China," she said. "Say goodbye to unsightly and unwanted curls, mister." The snakes hissed and flapped hideously in the blowing heat, their skins fell in smoking shards to the ground and withered into ash. The man's muscled torso wobbled and she stood back in fear, aware that something was trying to expel itself from inside him. Something terrible. At once his body erupted soundlessly with a bloody rain of flesh, and fragments, and then it was over, a puff of red vapour, dark bits, and the smoke of a life that had ended violently. The birdsong returned, tentative at first, from the forest around them.

The other man, the silent one, stood now and came to her in measured steps, the shells trembled on his body. "If you want me to be your husband you will have to put him inside of you."

Linda was somewhat appalled by his audacity. "I already have a husband," she said, aware immediately of the inadequacy of anything she could say.

"Both of us," he said. "Both of us must go in you." He indicated the blotted and blood-soaked bits of his companion already seeping into the earth. "Both of us must go inside you."

SHE WOKE TO THE WHOOPING cry of a cardinal, high and repetitive like some infernal machine, entering her room with the sunlight and the comforting noise of the city. She loved this sound. She loved the way it crawled into bed with her. A choir of birds, a racket of squirrels that chittered at the air, a child laughing. Many children laughing. Many bells ringing.

She opened her eyes to the stucco ceiling and the hum of distant diesel trains northbound through the corridor of the metropolis, sounding whistles into the hiss of the expressway. Above everything soared the laughter and crudities of the workmen. Linda got up from bed and saw them descending from the scaffold dressed in head scarves, waving spears, their triumphant bare and sun-blackened arms raised in victory. The church was done, suddenly it was finished, the dome, built in bronze, shone in the sun. On a sudden impulse the men turned and like mad drummers began pounding their hammers against a wooden board that leaned against the wall.

36

QUO VADIS

The boys are warned, so as soon as a nightmare or a bad dream oppresses them, to give up the affair at once, come down from the tree, and return home ...

JOHANN GEORG KOHL, 1855

HE WOKE TO FURIOUS CROWS that broke through the morning and carried off any remnant of his sleep. The black shapes above him shifted in the trees where the moss hung from the branches, and roared at him as they twitched from one tree to another. To endure the contempt of crows was necessary now. Paul propped himself with his elbows against the cobbles of the pit, but found it more difficult than before. Touching his jaw, he felt his fingers sink deep into the swelling. It was remarkable he'd slept at all. He took long breaths and fumbled with a notebook that was damp and spongy. Probably the pen didn't work. This was a good thing. More pens shouldn't work. Especially his. Slowly the nerves in his legs activated in a peculiar re-awakening until he felt strong enough to lift up and carry himself out of the pit and a short way through the bush.

When he made it there Paul discovered his campsite in ruins, the tent smeared and collapsed as if a balloonist had crashed on this very spot. The nylon food bag lay shredded like tissue on the forest floor thirty yards away, wide open. An animal had ripped his pack from the trees. Grains of rice lay on the ground. A lone red bean, shreds of plastic, wax paper, and the vial of pills, empty since yesterday. Paul located his remaining notebook. Its top margins had been chewed. The raccoons had come. He was unpleasantly hungry now, dizzy-hungry, and he stopped for a moment to recover, leaning against a tree where he clutched his notebook and coughed.

He remained there for some time, several hours maybe, but not a day. It couldn't have been a day. Yet when he moved it appeared the sun had rolled across the sky like some great stone. At points, the insects swarmed him in intense waves. Several of them screamed in his face. Immense blue dragonflies droned in front of his eyes. A fly landed on his lip. Stupid fly. How could it possibly know where his lips had been? Did it imagine it was immune from the germs that bred on his lips? On the lips of man? Paul forced himself to chuckle.

The sun moved swiftly behind the trees and the clouds came on like dark draperies that were turbulent at the bottom. He drank water from a wineskin and when he opened his eyes it was dark, either with weather or the night, and he knew the Milky Way would not be seen this night. It wouldn't course across the universe carrying the souls of every single person who had lived and died. Paul shivered. He realized he'd been dreaming. His smallness was suddenly unbearable and he was thrown back with fear onto the strange moving objects of his boyhood dreams, the freight trains and a terrifying snail that appeared to crawl forever up immense curtains when his eyes were shut tight and his father was in a mocking rage in another room. Paul was ready to enter sleep. In the speck of darkness, he heard a train shuddering down the tracks, unsure whether he was awake or not.

When his eyes cracked open, he heard the crows shouting at him, in Latin it seemed. He waited for the wash of dreams to flood him. Linda, in jeans and a sweater stood in front of him. "You have been mad and drunk all summer," she said sternly. Tears surfaced on his eyes and he heard the rains pattering first on the dense canopy, then rattling harder, dripping through it until the moisture fell on the sponge and the rock of the forest. The dream ebbed from him and he clung to what he could; Linda warming her hair with the portable hair dryer, the one he'd given her.

He realized he couldn't get up. Something seemed to be lying on top of him like a fallen tree. Tears fell from the sky. He couldn't get up. He needed to get up and tell her the truth, but there were no words, simple or not, there were only things and memory; the endless bushwhacks through tight woods, ragged ferns scratching them, the Assiniboine River, in a canoe ducking beneath fallen logs to avoid decapitation as an eagle shot over top, its shadow passing across her face. For a strange moment, he'd thought the eagle had flown directly into her face and emerged from the other side.

Paul tried to make his way back toward the pit and the cobbled stones that waited there. Nausea twisted him. Halfway, he stopped and attempted to vomit. Nothing came of it, except a few drops of bile that burned on his lips. He staggered forward and cooled his mouth on the cold white cobbles and when he drew away a line of saliva joined him from lip to stone. He made it to the pit and folded himself into it. Removing the red Swiss Army knife from the pocket of his trousers he pried the blade open with his fingernail. "Here," Her long neck loomed in front of him. "It's for you," she said.

The blade shone as Paul pressed it to the fabric of his right pant leg and opened a seam, probing further now pushing beneath the skin through the fat. He would invoke his skin as the Récollets did, whipping themselves with briar, and torturing their own flesh for the visions that resulted. Paul saw the blood race down his legs and wondered how Enno Littmann would have handled this, that grandiose cataloguer of Ethiopic manuscripts, most of them purchased for the price of a few rifle cartridges. Littmann would do it differently. Littmann would be in a library, sunk into plush upholstery, learning to read and write Coptic Egyptian in less than three weeks while the swish of gaslight illuminated his own personal fifteenth-century copy of the *Apocalypse of St. Paul*.

His eyes were shut. He felt the sweat break on his forehead. The gaslight flowed down his legs. The blade found its way beneath his skin and slid down and he did not scream. For the first time in two days, the pain from his teeth left him. Then he screamed. The sound was not unpleasant to him and did not even appear to be his, or to be from him in any way. A wafer of his flesh came free. It looked like a piece of Arctic char. A pulp of his skin the size of a nickel rested in his hand, and he convulsed, as if jabbed with a cattle prod. Paul cried out and began to shake. After the spasms passed, he put the wafer of flesh to his lips, tasting salt, and lard, pork fat, and the grease of man. His saliva was bloody when he spat it out. "Linda," he spoke her name deliberately. He needed to get up. It was imperative that he get up and go to her.

Paul tore a patch of moss from the rock and pressed it to his thigh. What had he done? What good was it to be mutilated and have no visions? He removed a kerchief from his pocket and wrapped the moss to his wound. Exhaling, he tried to get up but his shins wobbled and he went down again, knees clashing on the stones. They have taken my marrow, he thought, they have taken it and eaten it. The endless hiss of Superior cleansed itself against a rock. It was not daylight any longer, he saw. It was starlight, or moonlight bright enough to read by, but the shining of the white meridian hurt his eyes and a steady pain pulsed from his legs. How had that happened? It occurred to him that all the quartz veins of the planet were burning blood.

Paul yanked another handful of moss from above the pit and pressed it to the kerchief. This is an odd way for a man to die, he thought and yet, it was precisely the way he does, foolish, frightened, without understanding. He was astonished by that, as if it was something he should have known a long time ago. It was dark now, finally, either from night or the swift enclosure of extreme weather. He could not remember it being so dark. No animal had appeared to him; the crow only, cowled black and rasping in trees. He needed to get up. He heard the shushing of the spirit ocean. It was whispering to him. He stood in the halls of his high school, a child with bad skin, a reader of too many books, alone, listening to the silver whisper of girls, sounding to him like surf against the shore of a lake.

Paul tried to get up, but his bones would not allow it. He thought he might just roll over and try to find some way to break through and embrace his wife, to make love to her, to crawl to her on her knees, like a proper husband, but he encountered an old discomfort and feared neither of them would reach their passion. They had held that for others and got nowhere for it. He felt the tightness of her belly, clenched and waiting for release. Linda Richardson. He realized with some alarm that he was crying.

He needed to get up. He needed to crawl back down the path out of the forest and onto the cobbles for Joe to meet him. The idea pleased him; Joe coming down that trail whistling a tune and smoking American Spirit tobacco. Soon, tomorrow. The next day. Joe Animal. He wondered if the man existed. His leg had become grimed with blood. Paul tried to stand and failed. Sweat rolled on his face. A fox barked. He wanted to tell his wife about the love he had for her, enough for both of them and for the entire bloody world. Even his own. He knew that. It had written them and rolled them in the same bedsheets, nights of shooting stars and sheets of lightning when they rode the Ontario Northland, brilliant on wine, in a train clattering on shadowed rocks under the moon. He had to tell her that. It was the only thing he could tell her. The dereliction of this duty bothered him unbearably.

Dark came and the aching of his mouth merged with his mutilation. He felt his thigh and told himself he was not bleeding very much. He felt foolish and chastened. From somewhere nearby he heard panting, his own he realized, and water, he thought. A hissing from the surf, the metallic sound of Superior grinding on the sand and rock. Life had started out there, not his life perhaps, but life; it began in the foam that washed off Lake Superior. It was raining again, falling water dripped through the canopy of foliage, pattering, the most beautiful sound on the earth, but what he heard was not the rain. It was different.

PAUL BECAME AWARE OF THE source of it standing motionless between the trees quite close to him all this time, a tall thing. Standing there watching him. The flesh on it was without any form of skin that he recognized, red and black, and crisscrossed with veins or tattoos and red lines. Two curved, slender antlers spiralling toward the top, rose from the head. He saw the white foam of Lake Superior clinging to the shoulders and thighs and then it began to move. It advanced smoothly into the trees, luminescent even, loping, with one hand outstretched toward him. The long penis swung like an eel that was hardly attached to its loins. Suddenly the thing stopped and turned its head from east to west before staring directly at Paul, registering only then the sort of creature that he was. Slick-skinned like a salamander, the form came at him through the woods, almost curiously, beckoning to him with long fingers and uttering a low moan that Paul understood at the end was the sound of his own voice sobbing in the trees.

37

AT HOME

SHE STAYED ON IN THE rented house by herself. She woke and slept. There was nothing else she needed to do. Nothing was in front of her. She paddled through a place she thought of as Catatonia, a wilderness tourist resort without tourists, only birds with enormous wings, like pelicans. There she flat-lined into a dreamless landscape indistinguishable from the horizon or from the interior of her shut eyes. The highway, she thought, the vast Canadian road that had kept her young and in constant motion, that endless river of macadam. She attempted to sleep at all times, to remain there in a state of absolute sleep.

When she couldn't convince her body to sleep, she lay on the sofa and watched television. She stared at the agitated ghost-dance of burning pixels taking place in front of her. On the little screen she witnessed something she'd seen before, more than once, the disappearance of a lover. Arthur Gratton. There had been a day when she enjoyed the taste of that name on her tongue. "Arthur Gratton." His name was voiced repeatedly, his picture shown, not a flattering likeness. It surprised Linda to learn there existed an unflattering picture of the man. By the end of the week he did not exist. Arthur Gratton had been caught out and exposed. Quotes attributed to various people turned out to be completely fabricated. People who'd led to the ruin of other people turned out to be not people at all. Crucial statements had been lifted from websites desperately constructed by Arthur himself, staying up desperately all night to piece them together. "Frequent acts of journalistic fraud," is how it was put. "Extremely frequent." In all, 137 verified acts of journalistic fraud. They were read out like a death count and for three nights the numbers climbed. An award-winning, two-part feature on a methamphetamine addict who sold herself for drugs and food for her equally-addicted daughter is what caused Arthur to evaporate. *Jenny is a seven-year-old third generation methamphetamine addict, a precocious little girl with sandy hair.* The sentence had been held up as the gold standard of investigative journalism and had earned Arthur a Michener-Deacon Fellowship.

Only there was no addiction, no mother, not even any sandy hair. Fabricated from start to finish like a dream everyone thought they should have had. Arthur was let go. Resigned, they said, citing personal reasons. A puffy-faced and contrite senior editor put himself in front of the camera; "If we can't trust the accuracy of our stories, we are finished as a society." "Whose stories?" she thought angrily. "Whose stories, mister? Whose society? Who we, white man?" She watched from the sofa. A pixelated face made sympathetic remarks about the effect of a competitive work environment on men under stress. A decaying apple had been uncovered. That's all. The barrel was sound. On consecutive nights she watched this story and when it was over Arthur Gratton had been put to bed, plucked from the barrel and tossed away. Dead of exposure. Gone.

Linda thought that very soon she would get up from the sofa

and phone him, not because she wanted to speak to him. She didn't want to do that, she didn't understand why people wanted to speak anymore, but to listen to his phone ringing without answer, each sound growing fainter until it went nowhere.

She was not asleep when her own phone sounded and she let it ring repeatedly to prove its faithfulness to her. It was Paul, she knew it. He was calling her from heaven, from the Milky Way, he wanted to know if the coffee was on. He was there, among the souls of everyone who had died, and he missed her. I miss you, he said. I miss you unbearably. Linda lifted the device and heard the desperate strained silence of a man who couldn't speak anymore, or cry, or sing. She knew, from the silence itself, she knew.

"Arthur?"

Nothing came back to her. The loneliness burned with a hiss. "Arthur, it's all right." She wanted to tell him that what he'd done was all right. You made a story out of a living man, you led men to take their own lives, you took our stories and fed them into your machines. They paid you to do that. There are no more stories, we've sold them all. Turned them into a spectacle for the telling. You made a way of life out of it. We can't get them out of the machine anymore. She understood that if she spoke she would sound exactly like her husband. Our songs have been taken from us. They've turned our stories into silicon. "Sing for me," she whispered. "Can you sing? Can you sing the song that your mother taught you? Who mothered you and what is the name of your mother's mother's mother? What are her dreams?"

The silence burned on the line, it came out of the sky and filled the room. She heard the sound of a man shuffling in a lonely apartment. She waited for the word "darling" to break out and to bridge it. Darling followed by an obscenity. Darling. Darling. Let me count the ways in which I must have thee immediately.

"Paul," She tried crazily, "Paul?" She didn't know what she was saying. She wanted to speak to him, only to him, about mornings when the sun broke in on them, and they lay there wrapped together on the bed, this bed.

But no one was there. The line had broken and was dead. She put back the telephone and pressed her face into the pillow.

38

IN TEARS LET US SMOKE TOGETHER

*Now, now this day, now I come to your door where you are mourning
in great darkness, prostrate with grief. For this reason we have come here
to mourn with you. I will enter your door and come before the ashes and
mourn with you there. Yea, therefore, in tears, let us smoke together.*

THE IROQUOIS BOOK OF RITES, CIRCA 1400

TRANSLATED BY HORATIO HALE

SHE SLEPT FOR ELEVEN HOURS and in the morning went downstairs
to the kitchen where she drank three cups of coffee and ate four
eggs. When she was finished, she entered the living room and
removed a half-full Scotch bottle from a gold-painted tin canister.
She considered drinking from it, venomously, with the same bot-
tomless thirst that had destroyed her mother.

Linda placed the bottle on the table without drinking from
it. Instead, she took down the shining steel canister containing
Paul's ashes from above the fridge, unfastened the two clasps that
were shaped like playing-card spades and poured the grit into the
empty tin. Because she felt no urge for a drink in the slightest, she
poured one and threw it down. Cheers, she said aloud and felt stupid

for saying it. Stupid for drinking it.

The moment she put the glass down a bird smacked the window pane. She heard the dull thwock of bird on glass and saw the foggy smudge left on the window. She went to the window and looked down and found the bird on the bush tops, a small starling with its neck angled aggressively to the side. The situation demanded something from her, but she didn't know what, and willed herself against doing anything.

As she made this decision, the doorbell sounded twice and she saw herself cross the room with the same arched disapproval that Rover used when he exited the house the night before. The bell rang once more, insistently.

She opened the door and confronted a fat and grinning set of lips on a brown face scored with two vertical grooves. A bolt of salt-and-pepper hair, tied at the back, was jammed beneath a stained green tractor cap with the words *Red Man Chewing Tobacco* on the front.

"Joe," said the lips, opening to reveal a set of large teeth in some need of repair.

"I've been expecting you." She didn't know why she said this. In some dream he'd stood there. She was not expecting anything. Not him.

"Joe Animal. I was upriver fishing, that's why we couldn't come down to the funeral you know?"

"Yes. There was no funeral. He didn't want one."

The man nodded. "I found him. Paul, I found him in the pit, there."

"Yes." Linda looked at him skeptically. "I was under the impression Paul died in the arms of a younger woman."

"Yeah sure." The man grinned somewhat warily and at that point a boy came up to him from beside the bushes. Nine years old, she thought, at the most. What did she know about children, or their ages? He looked brazenly at her as if to determine what manner of life she was. Both his eyes were glazed by a scattering of milkish cataracts similar to those she'd seen in the eyes of several Husky dogs. His eyelashes were jet black and thick.

"This is Joe."

"Joe," said the boy. "Joe too. Like him."

"Nope," said the man quickly, "Joe One. Not like me."

"Joe one and two," said the boy.

"Come in," she said.

They came into the house and she saw the man wore a jacket of blue denim ornately, even traditionally embroidered with fantastic colours that took the figure of a nude woman displaying herself on a chair. He took the jacket off and beneath it a T-shirt read, *No One Knows I'm Elvis*.

Joe, the little Joe, left his jacket on. She stared at him, the velvet skin, the eyelashes that appeared to be an inch long. She thought he had the beauty of every child. Linda felt she'd seen him before, years ago, leaping into the brown green water of the Grand River.

"You're that guy's old lady, aren't you?" the boy said.

She nodded. "His old lady, yes. He's dead," she added purposefully.

"Yeah, dead as a door knob right?"

Linda snorted a type of laughter.

"Enough." Joe Animal scanned nervously around the room and seemed relieved to spot the black box of a television in the corner. "Maybe you should watch some television for a few minutes."

"You got cable?" said the boy. "Or satellite? At Tyendinaga we got satellite."

The man raised his palm to the child as if to smack him. "Will you shut up about Tyendinaga. At Pays Platt we got an old lady with no teeth. Give her a dollar and she'll turn into a bear and play harmonica for you."

"Satellite's better than that."

"For a blind kid he sure likes his TV, eh?"

"I'm not blind," protested the boy, hotly. "You're blind."

"No, it's just I can't see so good." Both of them spoke this at the same time and both broke into a gasping laughter. It was something they had clearly done before. Indigenous vaudeville, Linda thought. Wonderful. The boy became suddenly and stonily serious.

"That's where they dream, you know, on the television."

"Who," she said, "who dreams?"

"The ones that aren't born yet. I don't know. The ones that have trouble being born. Mostly them. If you can't sing, that's what you do. You go inside television and dream." He stood examining a spot off her left shoulder, two black rings shone from the whiteness of his eyes. She was aware that Joe Animal was looking intently at her.

"Maybe you should watch TV," said the man. You got one of those clickers?"

"Remotes. They're called remotes," said the boy scornfully.

"We do it the old way here," Linda stood up distractedly. "The way the cave men did it." She was about to do it for him but the boy crossed the room carefully and went to the TV and slid his hands along the surface of it, exploring the glass with his fingers. "Is this how you turn it on?"

The screen flowered into colour, followed by images and sound.

"Kid's a pain in the ass." The man spoke loud enough to make sure the boy heard. Quickly the dull noise of the machine rose into the room and Joe Animal undertook a series of gestures that saw him at last remove a green pack of cigarettes from one of many pockets.

"I found him."

"Yes, I know that."

"I found him in one of those pits. You know what they are?"

"I know what they're called. No one knows what they are."

"He was like —" He was about to make an imitation of Paul Prescot in death but thought better of it.

"In an attitude of sleep?"

Joe shook his head. "No, he wasn't sleeping."

"It was something he liked to say."

"I told him not to. Those dream pits, you don't want to go anywhere near those damn things. Who knows what the hell they are? We used to picnic on Michipicoten and they were all over the place. You don't go near them. I never did. No one did."

"He did."

The man nodded at her and silence came into the room, drifting, touching everything.

"He was a dreamer," she said.

"Yeah, well. Somebody was." A cigarette lighter appeared in his palm and he made a swift pass at his face and somehow the cigarette ignited. "You don't mind if I smoke do you? I had this cousin, eh, he could make women fall in love with him just by blowing smoke in their faces. Light up a rollie, blow a little smoke, and bingo. They're all over him. It had to be the right stuff, you had to pick it, you had to know when to pick it." He looked in her direction and sent a tight shaft of cigarette smoke at her.

"You need an ashtray," she said, sounding, she thought, like someone's mother. She went into the kitchen and came back with a pickle jar lid and placed it on the low table in front of him. It occurred to her that she didn't like pickles, that Paul bought the jar a very long time ago and that he didn't like pickles either.

The television spewed inane choruses and the boy sat entranced, giggling, rocking forward on his knees.

"Do you want a drink?"

"Yes," the man answered immediately, even, it seemed to her, before she'd finished asking the question.

She went to the mantle and took down Paul's Scotch, pouring two drinks straight up.

"Cheers."

"It don't make you any wiser." Joe Animal raised his glass and responded with a satisfied post-swallow grunt. "This come out of there? He pointed to the dented tin. "Paul's scotch. The Aberlour?"

"Yes, I put his ashes in there."

"Paul would've liked that. He does like it. He likes it right now." The man laughed. "Don't you Paul?"

"Yes," she said. The thought pleased her, but she had no way to believe.

They sat for a moment waiting for where the drink would take them. "My husband was going to save the world." She stared into the amber of her glass.

The room thickened with the screams of television; someone was getting tortured or having an orgasm or had won a car.

"Sure," said the man. "Someone had to." Then he spoke softly to her. "That lady, that painter lady. I heard about that. She didn't paint those rocks I bet. She just copied all that stuff out of Paul's books that's all she did. That's what I think." Joe Animal stared with some alarm into the bottom of his glass, as if one of his eyeballs had fallen in. "And that reporter guy was a plain old liar. He didn't know the truth. He thought he could make it up."

"She signed it," answered Linda. "Her initials were on it. The legs that walk by themselves." She swallowed another mouthful of whisky.

"Sure, well they belong to someone, someone else maybe. You, I bet. Linda Richardson, that's you right? I know that. It was you. Why not? You're a person, right? Everyone's a person. Even Mr. Nobody. Even God is a person." He grinned at her, his face had lapsed into an easy and ready drunkenness, but the rest of his body was sober and even alert. "Believe me, someone dreamt them there a long time ago. Hey Joe," he said, but the boy did not seem to hear him. "Joe, whose initials are those, on that rock there?"

"What rock," the boy shot back, not looking away from the screen.

"At Coldwell. The Coldwell site."

"Hers," he said, not looking. "Lillian."

"My name's not Lillian."

"The kid knows things. He's pain in the ass."

"My name is not Lillian."

She saw that a cigarette was folded in the pickle jar lid and that he had another one going. She reached over and took one from his pack. "I haven't smoked in twelve years."

"Well sure, if you got 'em, smoke 'em, right?" He inhaled happily. "You know why the gods are always screwing us around?"

"Yes, I do. It's because in heaven, they don't have any tobacco and we do."

"Because in heaven, they don't have tobacco," he said, "and we do."

"I knew that," she said. She thought she might be shouting. Why did men never listen to her? Linda once again entered the ancient ritual of tobacco, feeling herself float upward with a sinew of smoke. In her first dizzy exhalation she saw Joe Animal looking at her carefully.

"She had to say those things, you know. She had to tell those lies." He gulped at the air, fish-like. "That's what I think. She had to tell those lies, and that newspaper guy, he had to tell those lies too. That was their job."

"What do you mean?"

"To get Paul away from you, get him out of your bed, I guess. It had to happen. You're not going to have any dreams with Paul snoring like that. I camped with the guy, remember. He snored worse than me. Sometimes a person's dreams are important." Joe Animal squirmed on the sofa, reaching for another smoke or another drink or both together.

"I don't know what you're talking about."

"Me neither. I don't know, I mean, someone's got to dream right? It's got to be someone. You, me. He was big about that. It's the visions, see. He thought that."

They sat across from each other not speaking. The television emitted a jubilant song about improved bleach molecules.

"He was into the prophecy stuff. Visions and everything. Maybe he thought that girl was, you know, a false prophet. It's all screwed up. I had this cousin once, he's dead now, swore he could cripple a man by blowing smoke at him. He says hocus-pocus, only he says it in an old language, and the next thing you know the marrow in that guy's bones has gone all soft and he can't even stand up."

"This guy was your cousin?"

The man nodded.

"And he could destroy the marrow in a man's bones?"

The man shrugged.

"Did he kill Paul?"

The man shook his head.

"You have a lot of cousins."

"Yeah. I do. Don't you?"

She said nothing.

"Sometimes a man and woman, they got to get away from each other for a while, right? That's what happened."

"He's dead," she said stonily. "He died of exposure and blood poisoning from an infected tooth. There was no marrow in his leg bones. That's not the same as getting away from each other for a while."

"So he got in the path of some wicked medicine, I guess. Some of those guys are serious, I mean, a dog comes into their room the next thing you know that's them in the dog. They can be in the rock and then be men again. Or in the bear and then out. I heard of it happening, I have. My father's seen it. He told me."

She watched her hand reach out for another glass of Paul's liquor.

"He thought he had to go out there and have some big dream or something, didn't he? A vision. He didn't dream nothing I bet." He sucked on the drink, making sure that every gram of it made it onto his tongue. "I bet Paul didn't dream a thing. If anybody, it was you, why not? Maybe it was you. It wasn't me. Maybe it was me, and I just forgot." He assembled himself into an uncomfortable posture with his body. "Probably it was you."

"Me?" she said.

"I don't know," he trailed off miserably, as if it was her fault. "I fix small engines. Two stroke, four stroke engines. I like playing blackjack at the casino. That's what I like. What do you like?"

Linda thought she was about to cry. She felt her eyes burning with salt.

The television had gone silent and the boy was now standing on the carpet. "We need to get going," he said. "We need to go."

"Why?" Linda was unable to stop herself, to pretend she didn't want them there, both of them with their semi-mute easiness. She wanted them there desperately. "Where are you going?" She was not prepared yet to take on the bullying company of herself. Not yet. She wanted them in her house with her.

"West," said Joe Animal as if he had stated the most specific of destinations. "West. To Wisconsin."

"Yep," the boy chimed. "That's where the food grows on water."

"Rice. He means wild rice." Joe Animal flexed the muscles of his upper body. "He can gather up all the rice he wants to. That's him. He can poke around in those caves looking for stuff. Rice. Really. I don't eat the stuff, never have. I knew a guy choked to death on a grain of rice at Garden River. I stay away from it. I go to the casino. The Red Rock Casino near Bayfield, up lucky highway thirteen through the Reservation." He drained his drink and erupted proudly. "It's winning time. My time. Our time, all of us. It's time to be winners," he repeated, with less confidence. He looked at her and the boy and then around the room as if he meant to include even the wallpaper in his generosity. "It's time to be winners," he said again, more softly.

The boy nodded. She saw that his eyes were closed and that his face beamed.

"Everything is good now," said the boy. "Look."

Her own eyes had shut for a moment, and when she opened them the boy was standing next to her, nudging her.

"Look." In his hand he held a small bird, black, flecked with white. It was the starling that had slammed against her window and fallen into the hostas with its neck broken.

"It's dead," she said.

The child squeezed softly with his finger and the eye of the bird, the size and colour of a peppercorn, opened instantly, vivid and alert, indignant even, eager to see everything all over again. The tiny throat heaved and the bird righted itself in the boy's palm, but showed no inclination to take flight.

"It's not dead. It's alive."

Joe Animal frowned. "Stop bothering the damn birds. He's always doing that." His drink was empty and his jean jacket was folded across his arm.

The boy tugged open the front of his T-shirt and folded the bird beneath it, against the warmth of his belly.

"Okay pal?" The man moved heavily toward the door like a sheepdog separating his herd. The boy searched the room with a last wide, slow sweep of his head. He seemed satisfied with what he saw.

"Goodbye, lady. I like you. I like your face. You have big dreams I bet. Do you remember them?"

"Never," she said at once.

"Yeah … dreams. That's how I knew." He seemed unsure what to say next. "To come here, I mean. To have sorrow. Sometimes you just need to move, right? Or everyone gets sick."

Linda put out her hand and felt stupid doing it. She wanted to hug him, to desperately hug him.

The boy hesitated and shook her hand limply, even whimsically, giving her a northern handshake without any pressure at all, a handshake soft as lake foam, one that made it clear he'd not come back to this place again. He was merely passing by and she would never meet him again. He'd be back in God's Lake Narrows where he belonged and he would never be seen by her. He looked at her strangely. "I'm not blind," he whispered, grinning.

"No," she said. "You're not. Me neither."

Joe Animal nodded at her, and they both turned and edged out the door.

39

THE COMMENDING

AT A RUTTED INTERSECTION, THE Westfalia left the lane of its own volition and veered onto a dusty trucker's stop where it crushed the gravel and shuddered to a halt. She had landed, but the earth still reeled in the space in her eyes and the molecules of her body. She had landed in a place of gasoline and woodpiles, worms, cold beer, overnight and seasonal campsites; a lone Johnny On the Spot loomed. She was here finally at a roadside diner that sold Jiffy Pop and bottled water for when the lakes and rivers ran with poison.

Out of nowhere, a dog appeared, advancing fiercely across the pavement. Within inches of her it melted in adoration and glossy eyes and proceeded to wield its dry and cracked muzzle obscenely between her thighs. I have done all this before, Linda thought. It was not déjà vu, it was only the repetition of physical things on hot tarmac beneath the same sky with the same droning of trucks on the highway. I've met this dog before; have pushed open the screen door that yields inward with the creak of summer cottages and the grumble of a tin bell mounted on the doorframe. She heard again music from a radio that couldn't be seen and light from a television that wasn't to be heard, a black and white screen with a horizontal line of interference drifting down the face of it, blinking on what looked to be a curling match but could have been anything.

The woman who owned and ran the Neys Diner stood in front of her, small and silver in colour, with silver hair as well. Two burgers hissed indignantly on the grill.

"Howdy-do?" the woman offered.

Linda saw the sign announcing a sale on Deet, and yesterday's cinnamon buns. It had been there last year, she was sure of it. The same sign, same cinnamon buns. Same sale. Trout lures the size of her hand hung on the wall next to bottle openers and fierce tinned hams. Decks of playing cards wrapped in cellophane. They had met this way before, more than once, she and this older woman.

Is your husband with you? She was about to say this, surely, but stopped herself. For all its vastness the north was a small place where people knew of each other. She'd heard something, she remembered, she knew better than to ask. Her own husband was out back smashing at a heap of wood with an axe, where husbands should be.

She knows he's dead, Linda thought, or has left me for someone younger or his drinking polished him off. You could count on it being one of that holy trinity. The two did not know each other's name, but shared a knowledge of the grandiosity, the ridiculousness and, even the usefulness of men. Men they had followed, for their own reasons, beyond the oaks and the maples into the pines, into black spruce and the borealis. This made them complicit.

"You were here last year."

"Yes, and the year before." After a moment Linda added, "and the year before that too." The woman nodded and rotated her attention from grill to TV and back again.

She left the truck stop with a loaf of bread and a litre of water and was outside on the gravel. The old Westfalia took the key and responded at once, leaping across the surface of the Trans-Canada and down the sloping side road, across the double rail line where track signals shone votive red, on through bush to the campgrounds at Neys.

At the park gate she was processed by a young dark-haired woman tanned with health, a dark-eyed beauty. She saw a brilliant future rested on her skin, and tried to summon up some envy for the girl but couldn't. Instead she received a piece of paper with a red number scrawled on it. Her reservation in the woods.

"Enjoy yourself. And by the way, you have to boil the water."

"Yes," Linda said, and unable to stop herself added, "for rivers shall run with poison and the fish shall become unfit to eat."

"Pardon me?"

"Nothing."

"Give it five minutes," resumed the girl. "It's an advisory from the medical officer, she wants it boiled."

"Everything needs to be boiled." God, she thought. Did I say that? Am I becoming one of those?

She restarted the van and rolled past the gatehouse. On the first bend, she was forced to brake for a wolf that padded wearily across the road, its tongue out and lolling. Linda was shocked to see how thin the animal was, a pale, dehydrated tongue hanging loose and long. A cub scurried behind fearlessly. In their hunger neither of them paid her any mind at all. She accelerated and suddenly Lake Superior showed between the trees appearing like a jewel that had just arrived there, shimmering with an intense white glitter. A low approving groan came from Paul, it always did at this spot. "For Christ's sake ... For Christ's sake, Paul," she said out loud.

WRITTEN IN STONE | 243

Linda backed the vehicle into the campsite and prepared to execute the old drill, this time alone. She hurled the roped tarps to the packed ground and at once the chipmunks advanced on her like the most obsequious envoys, furious for food. As she set up the old Kelty tent she inhaled its smell of must and bodies, Paul, herself and a hundred thousand miles. The smell of Minaki and Wiikwemikoong, of wood smoke and Rainy River, and the Assabaska, with the wind sleeting off the lake and the great bucks leaping like hares over the bald trunks of fallen trees. She smelled mosquito coil and north wind. Her life, she thought. This is what my life has smelled like. It smelled like Paul.

The last peg had been pounded neck deep when a truck pulled up to her site, a white and green provincial park vehicle with a bear cage in the back. The park superintendent wore a brown uniform and leaned his torso out the window.

"You need any help there?"

She felt the salacious confidence of his voice, and his eyes going up and down her like a paint roller. Wanted to know if she needed help. Of course she did.

"No. Thank you."

"There was a bear in the camps up top. Big bugger. Took a porterhouse steak and a pound of butter from some jerk's cooler. Guy left his cooler out. Really." He shook his head and looked at her, letting her know he ranked her ahead of such people; city folk who brought forth bears with their unwashed fry pans and city ways.

"You be careful," he instructed her. The man drove off and Linda sat on a picnic table, numb in her body, feeding soy nuts to her chipmunk. She knew from experience that chipmunks were not partial to soy nuts and ate them only out of loyalty to the nut family. It was one of the compromises made in their frantic lives. Years ago, she'd watched a chipmunk chew the face off a dragonfly and scour out its brains with the intensity of a child licking ice cream. It had felt wrong to her, obscene, the blank pleasure it took. She entertained no illusions about chipmunks.

Soon the first of the trains boomed against the mountains, the screech of its wheels piercing the woods, uncurling across the sooty stanchions over the river, echoing off the mountainside until it rang all about her. Watery plates of sound settled in the trees and up the river valley. The earth trembled beneath the weight of it. When the train was gone, she lay down and slept outside the tent lying in the blueberry mantle dreaming of a strong, unfettered man with a rattle in his hand and who danced with a woman whose laughter seemed to emerge from her very pregnant belly.

When Linda's eyes opened, she saw a blue kingfisher sweep the shoreline, and then directly before her the waxy green leaves of the blueberries came into focus and she craned her neck to chomp the tiny blue balls, leaves, twigs and all, raking the matter off the stems with her teeth. The way Paul had eaten, she thought, at the end. From the treetops the crows made their distinct cry of *Quo Vadis*, cawing at the sun and at her. "*Quo Vadis*," they cried. What is your direction? Who is your partner? she thought.

EATING BREAD AND FRUIT FROM a nylon bag, she waited until the sun cooled in the trees. A bank of dragon-shaped fog broke from behind the cliffs and advanced on the lake, as if on its belly. Turning from the blank mass of it, Linda went to the van and removed the tin canister from the passenger seat. Then she was back on the beach, the cool white sand extending in both directions, broken only by the driftwood, like so many skeletons randomly emerging from it.

She walked the crashing shore until she reached a concealed stream trickling from the mountains, cleaving the beach in its run to the lake. Linda went into it pausing, knowing from experience how cold it would be, exhaling as the creek water cut her ankles, then her calves and the water closed her throat and rang old fillings in her teeth. When she reached the other side, she pivoted, gasping, toward the forest, into a black opening into the bush and started in on an animal trail that was dark and murmurous with birds and insects.

In minutes she was through the dense bush and back on the rocks where she hopped the pools, recklessly, until she stood at the heaving Superior shore. The waters slid upon the rocks like the opening and shutting of a great eyelid. Removing the dented tin of Aberlour's from under her arm, she faced the lake and tried unsuccessfully to pry it open with her fingernails. It was harder than she'd thought it would be, the business of finishing with Paul, the theatrics of commending his ashes to the water. She could barely get the lid off the tin.

At last, she fixed her thumbs beneath the rim and popped the lid. She heard at once a breath, her own breath, a loud terrible sigh, and in her exhalation she felt Paul flashing upward to the western sky, leaving behind the tin and the grey ashes of himself. He was leaving her, leaving her lungs. "Paul," she tried. The wind lifted a skiff of his remains and took them, whipping them to the side of her, scrambling them across the stones.

Holding to the tin with both hands, she rocked it vigorously until the ashes fell, pocking the surface of the great water in front of her, dissolving in milky streamers that lingered before sinking swift as gravel and leaving a dusty stain that broke up on the surface. The tin was empty, there was no more heft to it, only a few particles of Paul's dust wedged into the corners. Suddenly the grains that flecked the rocks around her skittered in the wind and chased one another across the stones. For an unbearable moment a pinch of grit blew into her eyes. Paul was in her eyes and beneath her fingernails. She'd inhaled some of him, she was still inhaling him, his thigh, she thought wildly, his powerful thigh entering into her lungs. The last traces of her husband dissolved in the moisture of her throat, breaking up there like salt.

"Paul," she spoke. "I am not starving. Not in that way. My heart is good. My heart is not weak. I refuse to boil my water. I have taken off my mask. Please, for God's sake, look after our people."

She tossed the canister into the water and saw it angle downward, flashing, before throwing the lid in after it.

ACKNOWLEDGEMENTS

My great appreciation also to the people at Cormorant Books, and to Marc Côté in particular, for his enduring and passionate commitment to this novel.

We acknowledge the sacred land on which Cormorant Books operates. It has been a site of human activity for 15,000 years. This land is the territory of the Huron-Wendat and Petun First Nations, the Seneca, and most recently, the Mississaugas of the Credit River. The territory was the subject of the Dish With One Spoon Wampum Belt Covenant, an agreement between the Iroquois Confederacy and Confederacy of the Ojibway and allied nations to peaceably share and steward the resources around the Great Lakes. Today, the meeting place of Toronto is still home to many Indigenous people from across Turtle Island. We are grateful to have the opportunity to work in the community, on this territory.